The Fifth Trumpet
FIRE IN THE BLOOD
An Angus McPherson Mystery

The Fifth Trumpet: Fire in the Blood, a novel by
Mark W. Stoub www.bloodunderthealtar.com

Published by Bald Angel Books,
www.baldangelbooks.com

First Edition, October 2017

Copyright © 2017 Mark Stoub

Author Services by Pedernales Publishing, LLC.
www.pedernalespublishing.com

Library of Congress Control Number: 2017951950

ISBN-13:   978-0-9835736-3-0   Paperback edition
            978-0-9835736-4-7   Hardcover edition
            978-0-9835736-5-4   Digital edition

Printed in the United States of America

"Set me as a seal upon your heart, as a seal upon your arm; for love as strong as death, passion fierce as the grave. Its flashes are flashes of fire, a raging flame."

Song of Solomon 8:6

The Fifth Trumpet

FIRE IN THE BLOOD

An Angus McPherson Mystery

a novel by

Mark W. Stoub

12·18·21

To my Mother the Rev. Barbara E. Kleyweg;
my muse, my mentor and my friend

To Nancy

You never know
what's coming around the
next corner!

Enjoy

Mark Wood

Acknowledgments

I would like to thank my wife, Janie, my sister, Betty Stoub, Betty Ladner, Louann Sledge, Mary Jane Kirkham, and Lori Hilscher for helping my novel make sense. I would like to thank Martin Coffee for forcing me to add things which made the whole so much better. And a special thanks to Jose Ramirez and Barbara Rainess at Pedernales Publishing for making this book a reality.

CHAPTER ONE: Burning Desire

The dragon in the blaze devoured flesh and bone, but more than that, it sucked the very life out of her in an instant. Although unnoticed most of her life, in death, she would become infamous in the small town of Shoestring, Texas. The blaze would shed light on far more than a simple house fire; it would also expose something unexpected, sinister, and twisted. As the house's roof fell in upon itself, flames soared skyward and its explosive collapse could be heard from miles away.

Police Chief Hector Chavez had just finished his breakfast and poured a second cup of coffee when he thought he heard something in the distance. The scanner immediately squawked news of the fire, putting an end to the predawn quiet. He gulped one last mouthful of hot coffee, kissed his wife, and rushed out the back door. The words *fully engulfed* and *resident unaccounted for* made him cringe and whisper a string of expletives as he started his car and roared out of the driveway.

The scene of the fire sickened him. His sixth sense went into overdrive and he was on full alert. Something told him to hang around. He sat in his patrol car and watched as the fire department rushed to subdue the blaze.

Once the beast was under control, Hector climbed out

of his car. Fire Chief Ralph Crenshaw turned as Hector approached the house. The two men had known each other since junior high, but only as mere acquaintances.

Ralph was a short man with red hair and a barrel chest. After purposely staring at the rising sun for an unusual amount of time, he huffed, "You do know that we won't know anything for several hours. It's too hot." Refusing to meet Hector's gaze, forever trying to make Hector seem smaller than he was, Ralph made no effort to conceal his disdain.

"Anybody inside? Any idea?"

"Like I said—"

Smiling slightly despite the cold reception, Hector replied, "Yeah, I know. It's too hot. You won't know for hours."

"I'll give you a call when we find something."

"I think I'll hang around." Hector knew Ralph would try to one-up him and refuse to cooperate.

Ever polite on the surface, Ralph's attitude roiled Hector. Ralph had some small town county clerk's predilection for hoarding information and being utterly uncooperative—often doing more harm than good. The man had power issues and resented authority as much as he demanded others respect his.

Something was wrong with all of it. The intensity of the fire, for one, the fact that little evidence would remain. It was not a furnace fire or a chimney blaze. The house had been remodeled—it had to have smoke detectors. Lois Myers was the town oddball, but even so, Hector was certain the fire was deliberate. She was known for keeping unusual hours with strange company. The townspeople told stories for years about odd lights and noises, but most of it was chalked up to gossip. With that thought, he got out his cell phone and looked up Angus' number. As soon as he could back up his suspicions, he'd get Angus' opinion.

MY WIFE SAW the Realtor's paperwork and the For Sale signs in the garage before I had time to tell her I'd listed the house. I meant to tell her last night, and then over coffee this morning, but I had honestly forgotten until she came storming back into the kitchen from the garage. Her eyes were ablaze and I knew what I was in for.

"*Angus!* I am not moving! You listed the house, didn't you? Without even talking to me? You can't sell it without me. And my answer is no."

"You don't listen, Angelica. I don't have any other choice and we've been having this same argument for a year."

"I don't listen? I don't listen!" She was so angry she nearly levitated off the floor as she hissed the words at me.

I grabbed a yogurt out of the fridge to give myself a minute to think. "We have to sell the house, that's final, and it is no easier—"

"No!" She shook her head. Her long brunette hair became a cascade of motion. "You are the one who isn't listening. I can't move!" I watched her plow her hand through her hair in exasperation.

"Christmas is coming, and that's the best time to sell a house." I knew I couldn't win this argument, but I didn't want to go down without a fight.

"It is not." She turned her back on me. "No one wants to go house hunting during the holidays."

"What better gift to give yourselves than a wonderful home to live in for the rest of your life."

The knife the silence cut into me left a mark. The ache for her response was real.

She turned, straightened herself, smoothing the front of her white dress. "My point exactly. What better reason *not* to sell this house. I am done with this conversation and if you try and sell this house, I am done with you!"

Some say, "Silence is golden." Now I felt totally impoverished as her anger escalated into a burst of tears. I knew it was anger and she had no intention of backing down. Even so, I hated to see her cry and took her in my arms. No matter how bitterly we disagreed, to me her hair smelled of sunshine and her scent struck the very fiber of my soul. Her tears always broke my heart.

Pulling away, still glaring at me, as she swiped at her tears she spewed, "Sometimes I hate you."

I stood watching her as she slammed the door behind her on her way to work.

The phone rang and I jumped. Ever since the events in Shoestring more than a year ago, I had developed a little tick where the phone was concerned. It always seemed to bring bad news. This time it was mixed, from Hector Chavez, the police chief of Shoestring.

"I haven't heard from you in some time," I said. "How are you doing?"

"Busy and about to get busier." Hector told me about the fire and the human remains they found in the house. "We know who owned the house. We might get an ID on the victim from dental records, but that's about it. It's going to take some time."

"But why call me?"

"It has to do with the homeowner." There was a pause.

"The fire looks to be arson and the homeowner was possibly involved in some shady stuff."

"Well—"

"I need your help. I'd like you to see the house before they remove all the evidence. It's important."

"I'll be there in an hour."

I ALWAYS find myself in transition. At present, I am Angus McPherson, a Presbyterian minister who cares for the souls of south central Texas. I am what they call a General Presbyter.

I headed upstairs to change. As I looked in the mirror, I saw the same man staring back at me that's been there for the last sixty-three years—tall, with black, stringy hair, graying at the temples. What troubled me sometimes was to look into those bleary, blue eyes. On the face of things, I had every reason to be happy. But to look at my eyes, the evidence just wasn't there.

I was in decent shape, although I needed to lay off the pancakes. It's a curious American custom. In Scotland, the country of my birth, we made pancakes only to get rid of flour going bad, and ate them during Lent. Here, they're served all the time.

I put on a new pair of jeans and a flannel shirt because, even though this is south central Texas, it can still get cold in early October. Not like my native Scotland. As much as I've found a home here, I am very much aware that I am a foreigner and that Texans, as a rule, "don't take kindly" to foreigners.

IN THE TWO and a half hours it took to make sure the smoldering fire was out and would not rekindle, a crowd had begun to gather. Hector took control of the crowd, keeping them a safe distance away. He also studied that crowd because he knew that arsonists often returned to witness their handiwork.

He took note of each of the people and vehicles there. A man in a Houston Astros cap and blue jacket wearing sunglasses on a cloudy day was the first to attract his attention. He observed him watch the firefighters in action as they searched for any fire that might be lingering. Hector also noticed the man's hand was bandaged, fairly recently by the look of it.

"What happened there?" Hector asked.

"None of your damned business. What's it to you?" replied the man, jerking his hand away and wincing.

"I'm sorry, I didn't introduce myself. My name is Hector Chavez, the chief of police here in Shoestring. I'd like to take a look at your hand." Hector stared at him sternly.

"Sorry. I didn't realize you were a cop." The man sheepishly gave Hector his hand. Hector unwrapped the dirty, sloppy bandage and saw a hand that was a deep red with pale white striations.

"You need to get that looked at by a doctor."

"Yessir, I will."

"How did that happen?"

"Got too close to the grill; burned instantly. I just did a dumb thing—not paying attention I guess." The man smiled weakly, showing two missing teeth.

Hector took his name, Doug Able, as well as his address and phone number and continued to monitor the crowd.

BY THE TIME I arrived, the house was reduced to a smoldering and blackened shell of its former self. The acrid smell assaulted my senses; the smoke-filled air felt heavy and made it difficult to breathe.

I met Hector outside the front door, which had been knocked in and was collapsed to one side. "CFI is already here," he said.

"What?"

"Certified Fire Investigator, Miles Stone, from Austin. On fires, the first thing to check is for arson. I'll introduce you later; he's quite a fellow. Right now, I want to show you something we've already found. It's why I asked you to come."

I was very aware of my surroundings. As bad as the home's exterior looked, it paled in comparison to the interior. Stepping inside was like entering an unlit cave. The utter blackness was overwhelming. Light coming through the windows was absorbed by the shroud of the burned-out interior. The floor was covered in a few inches of putrid water and debris from the fire. But what worried me most were the beams sticking out with nothing holding them up.

Hector motioned for me to follow him up the badly burned staircase. Now we were *on top* of those beams that had nothing to hold them up! It was amazingly reassuring, however, following beside Hector, who seemed to know what he was doing.

We went into a room to the right of the stairs which might once have been a bedroom. The roof was gone, exposing this present darkness to the light of day. Clouds passed by above, seemingly unconcerned about the destruction visited upon this lone, despairing house.

HECTOR KNELT DOWN carefully in the far corner of the room, looking at something and motioning for me to join him. When I knelt next to him, I saw a gold Celtic cross, tarnished by ash and soot, along with what appeared to be the remains of a charred clay sun with some writing on it I couldn't make out.

Miles gave us permission to gather all the evidence in bags and bring them with us. Miles then stopped by the side of the burned-out bed.

"The fire started here," said Miles.

"In the bedroom?" I asked.

"Yes."

"How do you know for sure?" asked Hector.

"Because of the residue and the smell of gasoline near the door and window. So not only was there an accelerant, but the fire had multiple points of origin. Therefore it had to be arson." His nose turned up slightly as he spoke. "It's all too simple for words. Even you could have figured this out," he said, looking over his glasses at Hector.

As we made our way carefully downstairs, seeing all this destruction and the ashes carried away on the breath of the breeze, I thought, *how fragile life is*. I pictured Angelica and the boys, and thanked God for them.

Finally, Hector said, "I'm sorry to get you out here for nothing, but I thought you might be able to help us understand what we have here."

"No, no," I said, "I'm glad to come out and look at this. This isn't a wasted trip. I'm curious about the cross." Then I thought *thousands have been curious about the cross for centuries*.

LATER THAT SAME afternoon, I drove through the tree-lined lane, up to the library. The building itself was unremarkable—black opaque glass and white steel girders. The grounds were overgrown and the white paint was peeling. It looked tired and run down, and was therefore quite a surprise, because the rest of the town looked vastly different. It was not how I had remembered it the last time I drove these streets with Angie, when we had stayed at a very sweet bed and breakfast that turned out to be the home of a killer.

I introduced myself to the lady at the front desk. Short, with curly black hair, she was in her late sixties. I told her I wanted to do some research on the computer and she showed me where to sign in.

Having been raised in Scotland, I knew about the tug of war between the Catholics and Presbyterians about most things, and in particular about who claims rights to the Celtic cross. But of course, its history goes back much further than all that. I knew the cross had links to Druid history and might have gotten its start as a navigation device on the North Sea.

This particular cross was different. Most Celtic crosses have flowing designs that can mean any number of things. But this cross had a distinct story to tell.

According to my research this was a replica of the eighth-century St. Martin's cross from the east face of Iona, Scotland. It featured the sun with serpent "bosses," an architectural term for raised relief. They surround the sun and the Virgin Mary and Child. Far from being a wasted trip, my imagination was caught up in the wonder of it all.

As I drove home into the waning sun, the serpents on the cross writhed around in my mind, wrapping me in their mystery and wonder. They were symbols of wisdom and secrecy as well as evil, as depicted in the Garden of Eden. Their relation to the Sun and, in particular, to the Virgin and Child were also worth pondering, considering what the CFI said about this fire having been deliberately set.

What disturbed me now was ascertaining what the dead woman was trying to tell us with this particular cross clutched in her dying hands. The cross, along with the clay sun, held questions and I hoped answers of their own. I knew I would need to stay close to Shoestring and to Chief Chavez for the foreseeable future, at least until these questions were resolved.

What troubled me more was the idea that that land of my birth could once again play into what I was trying to do now. The snakes not only wrapped themselves around my mind, but now squeezed my throat. The image of my Dad on his deathbed, unable to speak, trying to make up for the years of abuse and the swill of alcohol flashed to my mind, clouding my sight. I decided to pull over to compose myself before continuing my trip home and my uncertain future there.

CHAPTER TWO: What He Didn't Do

MAVIS BELMONT WAS tall and elegant, with equine features. Her stride more like a gait than a walk, her long blond mane trailed in waves behind her as she went. The sea of humanity within Nashville International Airport teemed around her without intent or speculation. Just another cog, Mavis was one more ant working her way up the hill, bringing food for the queen.

Mavis knew her aunt needed her. They hadn't spoken in months, but they were close. Ever since the death of her father, Mavis had reached out to what family she had left, a lifeline on the sea of trouble that was currently her life.

She contacted the airlines at the last minute and took a taxi from her home in Antioch. She now rushed to make the plane. She hadn't heard from her aunt; she had just sensed trouble the same way you smell rain in the air before it blesses the earth with sustenance. On the surface, it appeared as if she were acting on a whim. But such an assumption was wrong. It was a premonition, something she felt in her bones that made her ill, unable to work, unable to concentrate on anything besides finding out what had happened to her aunt.

AFTER SAYING goodbye to Angus, Hector went back inside the skeletal remains of the house. While he didn't believe in such nonsense, he wondered what it felt like to be in a haunted house. His curiosity was about to be satisfied. Surely now this house was haunted after everything that had happened here today. Who would want to kill a nice old lady like this?

He couldn't help but think of his own mother in San Antonio. These things always affected him personally. The thought that the old woman was the victim of some madman made him angry, and anger always seemed to get the better of him.

Hector took one step forward, not looking where he was going. The scorched boards gave way and he crashed through the floor up to his waist. His fall was stopped by a floor beam. The pain in his groin far outstripped the pain his legs felt. He screamed for someone to help him. Luckily, the firefighters and paramedics were just finishing up and came running when they heard him. As they worked on him, his anger blossomed like a mushroom cloud. *How could I have been so stupid?* He thought. *This investigation is just getting started, and now this. It's as if someone doesn't want me to find out who did this.* His earlier thoughts about the place being haunted made him laugh. Those around him looked at him, but said nothing.

Hector contacted his desk sergeant, Max Brown, and asked him to find his deputy, Sean Spencer, so he could start canvassing the neighbors for anyone who might have witnessed anything. Sean had been with him for almost two years. Everyone in the office called him "Psych," because he had the same name as the fake psychic on the TV show. In the meantime, he'd get a head start finding witnesses.

After insisting he was all right, Hector hobbled through the blistered wood and soaked grass, smoke still billowing from within the maelstrom. As he made his way to knock on the front door of the next house, a person from the crowd gathered outside came toward him.

He was of average height but very overweight, with tired eyes and a disheveled look, as if he hadn't slept for some time.

"Can I help you?" he said warily.

Hector introduced himself; the man did not respond.

"Who are you?" asked Hector patiently.

"I'm Joshua. People call me Josh. Josh Manning. Can I help you?" he insisted.

"I'm just wondering if you may have seen anything last night or this morning that might help our investigation."

"So this wasn't an accident?"

"We don't know that for sure yet." He decided to err on the side of caution for now.

"I first heard the fire before I saw it."

"When was that?"

"About 7:00 this morning. I went over to see if anyone was in the house. By the time I got to the house, it was engulfed in flames and I didn't get too far. Since then, I've been watering my house to make sure we weren't next. Say, was that Lois they took out of the house?"

"We think so, but we need to be sure."

"That's too bad. She was the best neighbor I've had since I've lived here."

"How long has that been?"

"Lois has been my neighbor for ten years. I was here a couple years before she moved in. She kept to herself mostly. She drove an old Lexus and I joked with her that

I'd like that car when she died because she only drove it to church and to the grocery store. She told me she filled up her tank once a month!"

"Some joke."

"You'd have to know her to know it was. Say, listen, I had nothing to do with this—I didn't kill her!" Josh's features changed, becoming hard as iron, flashing fire from his eyes.

"No one said you did, but why did you say that?"

"Isn't that what you're thinking?"

"Not 'til you said that." Hector took a step back. He could tell that Josh had calmed down, and so he continued. "Do you know if she had any family to speak of?"

"Lois moved here from Chicago because her niece was going to come live closer to her kids, but then changed her mind and ended up staying in Nashville. Lois came here after her husband died, about ten years ago, like I said. Good neighbor too. Funny in her own way."

"Did she tell you the niece's name, or the name of the niece's kids?"

"No on both counts. Sorry."

"You said she only went to church and to the store. Do you know which church?"

"I think she was a Catholic because she told me they were having a fish fry and did me and the Mrs. want to come. She never said which one. And no, I never asked her where she went shopping."

"Do you know anyone who might have wanted her dead?"

WHEN I RETURNED home, I found Angelica rubbing down Dixie, a gray mare we purchased from a lonely old man in town whose children were grown and gone. He practically gave her to us. The sun began to sink behind the house, a fiery orange ball against a regal sky.

"It's kind of late for you to be out here," I said, embracing her. She smelled of hay, water, and chalk dust.

"It was a long day. As you remember it didn't start out too well." She looked at me with a frown for a long moment. I was about to apologize, but she kept going. "The kids were a mess and I didn't handle it very well. And to boot, Gabe was observing me." Gabriel Sanchez, her boss, made a better teacher than administrator. But he was a nice man; Angie liked him and looked past his weakness to his heart for the kids.

"Nonsense!" I smiled. "I'm sure you were excellent. I had quite the day myself. Hector called me out to deal with an investigation he is conducting into a possible arson that resulted in a fatality."

She paused, finished up rubbing down Dixie and emptied the bucket.

"What did you find out—anything?" She retrieved a pitchfork from the rack and proceeded to feed the animals, like we did each evening of our lives. It's routine like this that sets the world right, spinning on its axis like it's supposed to; it's these moments that make all the rest worth going through. It's as though the apology passed between us without being spoken, the best kind of apology possible.

"I met the CFI, a strange but very efficient man. He labeled it homicide. The victim looks to be the homeowner, an old woman." I too grabbed a pitchfork and spread the hay around.

"Who would burn an old lady to death in her sleep?"

"Well, let's not rule out the church, for one. They have

rid the world of so much 'evil' over the years, I'm sure they haven't forgotten how," I said, making quote marks in the air.

"That's not *entirely* fair. They thought they were doing the right thing."

"And who's to say whoever did this didn't think the same thing."

"What made you think of the church's sordid history?"

"It's what we found with the old lady." I put down the pitchfork and sat on a bale of hay as Angie put fresh water in the trough. "They found a distinctive Celtic cross, with a clay sun marked with some writing on it that we can't make out."

"What about the cross?"

"It's a replica of a cross at St. Martin's in Iona—"

"In Scotland?!" Her face lit up like a Christmas tree.

"Aye, very good, Lass. You get a gold star."

"You don't think I'd be married to you without knowing a thing or two, do you?" She paused as she shut off the water, wiped her hands dry, and took my arm as we walked back to the house, beneath the only star visible in the darkening sky. "Anyway, it sounds like a road trip to me." Her eyes sparkled with warm affection and just a little mischief.

"We'll see, maybe." I told her about the cross—the bossed snakes, the sun, and the virgin with child. I left out the rumors Hector told me regarding the old woman's involvement in the occult. Then she asked the question that had haunted me ever since I first saw that sad, devastated, old house.

"What does it mean?"

"I have no idea," I said as we went inside to get some sustenance and what sleep we could.

MAVIS GOT HER bags and rented a car. Thankfully, her flight proved uneventful. She did not care for all the decisions one had to make when traveling. Just to do the simplest things like decide where to sleep and whether to eat now or later, decisions you take for granted in your settled environment, became paramount when traveling. *Maybe that's why it's supposed to be so broadening,* Mavis smiled at the thought. *I'm here on a whim, and I'm thinking about broadening experiences!*

She found the first motel that looked halfway decent. She made it a rule never to eat at a place with a sign that read "*Eat here,*" or to sleep at a place that advertised rates below thirty dollars. Her mother always told her, "*You get what you pay for.*" Those two decisions out of the way, she made another—any arrangements to get to Shoestring and to find out what's going on with her Aunt Lois could wait until morning.

THE PAIN WAS getting worse. The paramedics had recommended that Hector go home and rest until he was fully recovered from the accident, but with another killer loose in Shoestring, he didn't feel much like resting. An anxiety borne of responsibility, he gladly handled it as best he could, chronic nuisance that it was.

He hobbled to the next house, on the other side of the burned-out hulk that had once been Lois' house. It now looked like the end of the world had come to this block of Shoestring, Texas. He rang the doorbell and a petite woman in her mid-fifties with short red hair answered the door. Hector introduced himself and asked if she had seen or heard anything unusual in the last day or two.

She said her name was JoAnne—she spelled it out for him, answering in the thickest Texas accent, puffing on her cigarette, "I don't reckon I heard nothin'. But I saw her talkin' to some city official the other day. And they weren't exchangin' recipes, I can tell you that. He was pretty sore at her and Lois was her old stubborn self."

"Could you hear any of what they were saying?"

"No, no, I can't rightly recall. I think, though, he said 'Bill,' or 'a bill.'"

"That's fine," said Hector, making a note in his notebook, and noticing that the ash on JoAnne's cigarette was getting longer and longer.

"Had you ever seen him before? Would you recognize him if you saw him again?"

"Oh, sure, I'd recognize him. He's some suit at City Hall. He was involved in the murder last time at the church."

"You mean the killing of Pastor Peter Anderson?"

"Yep, that's the one."

"Do you think you saw the City Manager, Tom Branch?"

"Yeah, I reckon. That's the one I seen. That's the one, all right."

I ARRIVED AT the office about 7:30. It was going to be another long day and I needed to get as much done as I could. Shoestring was going to be a big distraction, just like last time. I sensed God's leading me to take the pastoral job there, but now, with another murder, it didn't seem right to disrupt the family and the Presbytery—at least until after all this business got settled. Besides, Angelica had other ideas about moving. I couldn't just pick up and move us all to show her who wore the pants in the family. This was going to be a long process, and now did not seem the right time to begin, especially since I saw the "For Sale" signs and the realtor agreements thrown in the trash.

Francesca, my assistant of ten years, met me at my desk with a cup of coffee.

"Did you hear about what happened in Shoestring?" I took a sip of the coffee. I don't know what she does, but she makes the best cup of coffee on the planet.

"You mean something else happened?"

"Aye, a woman was burned in her home."

"That's horrible! Do they suspect foul play?"

"They do indeed. I've been called in to consult."

"You didn't say yes, did you? You know the Presbytery hasn't recovered from the last time you played armchair detective. I won't allow it, and the Council won't either. You know that!"

"What they don't know won't hurt them. I have been called in to assist in this case, and as it does not involve a Presbyterian, it won't be as all-consuming as the first time. I can—*we* can handle it."

"Don't you drag me into your deception."

"It's not a deception. I'm merely doing my civic duty. You want me to do that, don't you?"

"When you put it that way, I suppose it makes sense. So what's the connection to you?"

"The woman had a unique Celtic cross on her, and Hector wanted a professional opinion. It seems there's always a connection to religion."

"Seems to be so," she said, shaking her head.

"I left you a message from Frank," she continued. He was our associate for congregational care. "It seems we've got a rookie in trouble in Cuero."

"In my old church? Who's there now? Sam—?"

"Sam Horn?"

"Right; what's up with Sam?"

"It seems it's not what he did. It's what he didn't do."

CHAPTER THREE: Rough Winter

MAVIS DROVE THE FORTY minutes to Shoestring in silence. She usually could not stand the quiet, especially driving alone. But this morning, she needed to get herself focused on what she was doing.

The soft frost on the grass and trees reminded her more of Nashville than of Texas. The gray sky hung low on the horizon, blanketing the land not with warmth, but a gloomy chill. *It's going to be a rough winter,* she thought.

She made it to Shoestring in good time. Her next decision was the worst decision of her life. She was there to see her aunt, but knew she could not face her on an empty stomach. She'd had no breakfast before her trip to Shoestring and decided to head to her favorite restaurant, the *Golden Fork,* for some of their famous biscuits and gravy. She had remembered going there as a child with her dad on Saturday, just the two of them. *It's been twenty years since he's been gone,* she thought. *How I do miss him.*

The diner was practically empty. A woman in her late fifties with an open face and inquisitive eyes came up to her with a menu in one hand and a pot of coffee in the other. "My name is Ruthie. Would you like some coffee?" she asked, smiling at Mavis. Mavis agreed and studied the menu quickly.

"I'm here for your world-famous biscuits and gravy—don't tell my doctor." Ruthie laughed, then stopped and stared into Mavis' hazel eyes.

"I'm sorry, Darlin', but you look vaguely familiar. Do I know you?"

"I was just thinking the same thing about you," answered Mavis, staring intently at Ruthie.

"Are you from here?" Ruthie put her hand on her hip.

"Well, I was years ago. I'm Mavis Belmont. My dad, David, taught history at the high school for about ten years, but that was quite some time ago."

"Of course you are! I thought I recognized you. David-David Davenport; you and your dad came in here almost every Saturday and ordered the same thing every time, biscuits and gravy. How have you been?"

"I've been fine. I'm just here to check on my Auntie."

"Who would that be then?"

"Lois Myers. She lives on the edge of town."

Ruthie's expression clouded over; her face went pale. Mavis noticed and was shocked by the transformation. "What's wrong? Is my aunt all right? Did something happen?"

Ruthie sat down in the booth opposite Mavis. "Oh, Darlin'!" Tears formed in the corner of Ruthie's eyes. "You don't know, do you?"

"Know what?" Mavis insisted.

"There was a huge fire in her house yesterday, and she was in it. I'm so sorry." She reached for Mavis' hand and squeezed it tightly.

Mavis' expression did not change. "I had expected something like this. I had a premonition that something was wrong. That's why I came."

"If you go see Hector at the police station, he can tell you more about what happened." Mavis stared out at the gray day, not sure what emotion to feel, too numb to feel much of anything.

"I'll put your order in. It'll be on the house."

Mavis had suddenly lost her appetite, but did not know what else to do. Smiling weakly, she nodded her head.

HECTOR HATED THIS part of the job. Looking at dead bodies at the scene was one thing, but looking at them on a cold slab in the morgue was practically more than he could stand. He knew the Medical Examiner, Philip Bliss, would treat the body with as much respect as possible in such circumstances, but still, Hector wished he could skip this part. When he got to the basement of the police station, he found Philip had another visitor. The Certified Fire Investigator, Miles Stone, was also there bending over the body. Hector could tell that Philip was not pleased.

As Hector approached them, Philip looked relieved to see him. "Chief, I've got a few surprises for you."

"I hope they're good ones. You know how I hate the other kind."

"Well, I'll let you be the judge of that."

Miles stepped between Hector and Philip, looking over his glasses, down his long nose. "It appears there is loose skin under her fingernails."

"How can that be?" Hector was stunned. "The lady was burned beyond recognition."

"She had her hands underneath her, and that saved them from much of the burning." Philip regained the floor and his footing. "We also analyzed the contents of her stomach, and found what killed her—"

"I knew that yesterday at the scene." Miles broke in. "In fact, she had been dead several hours before the fire."

"How could you tell?" Hector inquired.

"A couple things didn't add up. She should have been awakened by the smoke alarms in the house. Obviously she wasn't. Also, based on the fact the fire originated in her bedroom, she would not have succumbed to smoke inhalation before the fire got to her. And that certainly would have woken her up. Had she been awakened by the fire, we would have found her by the door or window trying to escape the blaze—not lying in bed."

"She was poisoned?" asked Hector.

Philip took the upper hand again. "Indeed she was. We won't know for a couple of days, but my guess is it was rat poison."

"Somebody must have really wanted her dead," Hector opined. "The fire was just an attempt to cover up the murder."

AFTER I TALKED to Sam and set up a time for us to meet and discuss his situation, I decided to call Hector and tell him what I had found. As I dialed the number, I happened to look down at my white shirt and noticed a spot. I quickly put my coffee down, and almost missed the desk, as coffee spilled on the budget I was working on. I stood and yelled "Bullocks!"

Franny shouted, "What happened!" Over the phone, I heard the distant voice of Hector saying, "Hello? Hello?"

I told Franny I was fine and turned my attention to

Hector. I told him what happened and we both had a good laugh.

"I thought you might like to know what I found," I said as my breathing returned to normal. "The cross is a replica of the one in the Ionian community of Scotland. I know that cross had specific meaning for the people in that community, but I also believe that either Lois or the killer was sending us a message."

"Could you do a profile of either scenario and email it to me?"

"Better yet, why don't I come sometime next week and we can talk about it in person."

"Sounds good."

As I hung up the phone, I thought that whether or not I would be pastor of the church there in Shoestring, at least I was now a part of its police department.

MAVIS WANTED TO curl up into a little ball. The only connection to her past was gone. Her life was spinning out of control and she couldn't stop it. Although officially an orphan when her mom left and her dad died, this somehow felt worse.

She ate her breakfast but she had lost her taste for it, leaving most of it on her plate. She decided to drive by Aunt Lois' house. That too was a mistake. When she rounded the corner on Sycamore Street she saw what was left of the house. She stopped the car several houses down from the wreckage of her aunt's life. It was a black hole into which her entire life was now lost. Mavis' mind reeled with shock. She didn't feel the sadness one experienced at the death of a loved one. She felt guilt. She couldn't explain it, but it was unmistakable and real. There was no escape. Seeing police cars there made her uneasy and she wanted to run. Maybe it was her guilty conscience or just the thought of authority figures. She didn't care; she only wanted relief from what she was feeling, and relief meant getting out of there.

Lois was her father's sister whom he had loved dearly. Maybe it was because of his connection to her that Mavis also developed a deep bond with her.

She knew there was something more to it than that; her dad leaned on Lois after his wife left him. He often was on the phone with her. One time, Mavis had badly needed to talk to her dad about some misguided business venture her husband had foolishly gotten them into. She tried to call her dad, but the line was busy for what seemed like hours. Later he told her that he had been talking to Lois all that time. Mavis was still angry about that, and Lois was dead.

I MADE IT to Shoestring a little after one. I had called ahead and knew Hector would be in his office. It was the ubiquitous blond brick of south central Texas, an altogether unattractive blight on this unique and fascinating land. It so contrasted to the late Victorian buildings that encircled the square downtown that made it stick out like an ugly stepsister amongst beauty queens. When it was built, they had tried to look so modern and "with it," but what they got was 50's bland and boring.

I greeted Hector in his office, remembering the number of times since we've met that we have attempted to add to the trophy bass that adorned his wall behind his desk. Until I had started fishing with Hector, I hadn't fished except twice with my dad when I was a kid. Ever since I came to this country, I had wrestled with the notion that my father hated me—the thought depressed me and filled me with dread. He very much wanted a son, but I'm pretty sure he hadn't wanted the son he got. We were like oil and water, and since his death I have tried to make salad dressing out of that. Maybe I have added a little vinegar to the mix. The only time we saw eye to eye was when we went fishing, and like I said, that happened twice in my life.

Hector sat behind the standard-issue metal desk and I sat in a hard armchair opposite him. Hector rifled through some papers on his desk, and I grew more uncomfortable by the minute. I wanted to reach over and start organizing his papers for him, but knew that would be impolite. Angelica calls me obsessive: I would say I'm careful. He finally found what he was looking for and I let out an audible sigh of relief, so audible that Hector looked up at me with a quizzical expression. He pulled the paper out with a flourish.

"Ah, ha!" he shouted, waving it in the air. "You may think I'm unorganized, when in fact I know exactly where everything is." I waved a dismissive hand with a smirk. "I actually have a couple of things to add to our case. The profile on this guy is growing. The tox screen came back confirming what Phil said: it was rat poison."

I was about to be sick when I heard that. I believe in the 'total depravity of man'; I believe there is nothing good in us without God, and yet it sickens me when I hear what we are capable of doing to one another. I am shocked that no matter what one feels for someone else, there is always an alternative to violence; always another choice to make without harming one of God's beloved creations.

"So that means the killer knew her, and that knowledge narrows the field tremendously," I said.

"I'm not sure that's an assumption that holds up."

"My guess is, she wouldn't take poison voluntarily, and the only way she would is if she were tricked into it. It was put in some coffee or in her corn flakes. And she's not going to let some stranger into her kitchen to do that."

"I bet you a fish dinner at our house that the poison could have come from someone who wasn't intimate with her, but had only just met her—someone like an encyclopedia salesman or maybe a service person."

"But what about motive?" I asked as I rose slightly out of my chair, extending my hand to his. I watched the light create a shadow beside us as we grasped hands, smiling.

"You're on," I said.

"There's something else." Hector's smile faded as if a shade had been pulled over his face. "The lab in Austin figured out what was written on the clay sun we found with the body. I thought this too was particularly up your alley."

He handed over the clay sun and I took it. Before I had it in my hands, I saw it. A profound shock registered on my face. Hector pulled the item and gave me a moment to compose myself.

The writing on the clay sun read:

"And the second angel sounded the trumpet, and a great mountain, burning with fire, was cast into the sea. And a third part of the sea became blood." – Rev. 8:8

All the memories of the first confrontation with evil upon the sleepy streets of Shoestring came flooding back to me. Only this time, Revelation was being used as a warning or a clue and not as a means of support and encouragement for a grieving people. My shock and surprise were more about the realization that I would have to be called on again to sacrifice something dear to me in order to see justice done. And quite frankly, I was not sure I was up to the task.

I wanted to ask him about the skin found under Lois' fingernails, but the phone rang on Hector's desk. It was Max, the desk sergeant who had been kidnapped in my first sojourn in Shoestring.

"I'll be right there," said Hector, standing up. "I'd like you to come too, Angus. I think we've got the first break in the case. A woman says she is Lois' niece."

MY CURIOSITY aroused, I followed Hector to the front of the station. The woman before me was a tall, statuesque blond with long, toned legs. She had an aristocratic bearing about her, although her clothes said strictly middle class. This country likes to think of itself as classless, but people's judgment and assumptions about others label them just as surely as any title in my homeland would do.

The woman said her name was Mavis Belmont. She wanted to know what happened to her aunt. Hector invited me to stay for the interview. I accepted, and Mavis said she didn't mind my presence.

Most of the information was introductory: she grew up in Shoestring, but had not been here in years; her dad, David Davenport, taught history at the high school and had since died; Mavis was very close to her aunt.

Then Hector shocked me. "What were you doing here a week ago?"

Mavis's eyes got as big as silver dollars, and her head jerked back. "How...?"

"I run a small-town police department, but I assure you, ma'am, I'm no hick. It was basic police work: check out all the relatives; interview the neighbors; check on travel arrangements. You came here last week, stayed only the weekend, and then left again. You tried to keep it as quiet as you could, but it's very easy to call the airlines to find out where you've been, and where you're headed, especially with the Internet.

Mavis' face changed to a rose-colored complexion. This frail, birdlike creature became extremely agitated, almost belligerent, blowing up like a puffer fish.

"What were you doing here last weekend?" Hector repeated. I began to feel very uncomfortable, wondering if I should be there, as though I were hearing something I had no right to hear.

Mavis stood up, and the chair reared back like a bucking bronco, on its hind legs, almost tipping over. "I don't have to sit here and be intimidated by you—"

"So, you're intimated by the truth, Mavis. All you have to do is tell the truth and then you can go home. I promise. What were you doing here last weekend? It's a simple question."

Mavis looked down, beads of sweat forming at her temples. She sat down again, the air gone out of her. She was a limp balloon, spent of all her energy.

"I was here, just checking on her." Her shoulders slumped and her lips quivered; she sat back down.

"But you hadn't been here for years. All of a sudden you show up and the same week she's dead. Kind of suspicious, wouldn't you say?"

Mavis didn't look at Hector, so he looked at me with a raised eyebrow, and I nodded. I could never be a policeman. I'm intrigued by the puzzle, invigorated by the chase, but this was just too much. I began to feel for Mavis, and actually started to feel like she did—depressed and deflated.

Hector stood up and the interview apparently was over. "Mavis, I'd like to take a swab inside your cheek to test for your DNA, if you don't mind?"

"Of course I mind!" shouted Mavis. This time, the chair fell over as she stood up. She was now nose to nose with Hector. Then she turned away and almost whispered, "I want my lawyer."

"Is that your husband in Nashville?"

Mavis nodded.

"Could you speak up, for the record?"

"Yes, yes. He's my lawyer."

"You are aware, aren't you, that we can hold you in a cell until he gets here. That could take a day or two. I hear the food at the jail isn't as bad as what they have at the county lock-up, and you're welcome to stay here until he comes."

"Well, no, I don't want that!" Mavis looked at me with pleading eyes.

She was holding on to the edge of the cliff with all her strength, and I threw her a lifeline. "Why don't you call your husband and tell him the situation." I looked at Hector. "He'll be on his way, then Hector can take your DNA sample, and they'll get the results by the time your husband arrives."

I looked from one to the other, and they both nodded. I said a silent prayer of thanks as we all emerged into the light of day.

THE NEXT day, Hector, along with his deputy, Sean "Psych" Spencer, paid Mavis a visit at her hotel room. Mavis came to the door in a blue terrycloth bathrobe with curlers in her 'dishwater' blond hair.

"Mavis Belmont," announced Hector, stiff as a shirt too heavily starched, "I am arresting you for the murder of Lois Myers..."

CHAPTER FOUR: *DIES IRAE*

HECTOR INFORMED ME of the funeral mass being held for Lois and asked if I wanted to attend. It was Friday, my day off, so I said I would. The Old Colonel's Bed and Breakfast was closed, with a for sale sign outside. As I drove by, I recalled the mayhem the proprietors had meted out on Shoestring in my first encounter with this enigmatic town. I found other lodging and called Angie.

"I'm staying over for the funeral, Lass. I hope you don't mind."

"Well, yes, I mind!" Angelica hadn't fully gotten over our last argument. It always took her a while to shift gears.

"I'll be home tomorrow and we can go riding then." We had planned to take our horses out for some exercise. With the boys mostly grown and gone, the horses were very rarely ridden. I was thinking of selling them, but that was also a conversation I did not want to have with Angie, as she treated them like her children. That conversation would have to wait for another time.

"I'm afraid I must, Love."

"If you must, you must." There was a pause. Her word not spoken hung in the air in anticipation. "But please, take care of yourself. And if...when...we go to Scotland..."

She was ever more ready to travel than I was, and I loved her for it.

"…I want to see where you were born."

"Aye, Lass, of course."

I FOUND A Best Western and settled in. I would not be properly dressed for a funeral, but I thought Lois would not mind.

I went to the Golden Fork for breakfast, and there, holding court, was Ruthie—the queen of Shoestring. She reminded me of my Mom, big and open, short but luminescent. I could see many a man following her beacon to a safe harbor, and a holy rest.

Despite the pandemonium resulting from Pastor Pete's murder a couple of years ago and as close as we had gotten, I never learned Ruthie's last name. First names tell who you are and last names tell where you're from. At least that's what my Mom always said. So I asked her.

"Cartwright," she said. She even spelled it for me because everyone leaves out the "w". "I'm Gladys Ruth Cartwright."

"So you went with your middle name?"

"I couldn't stand Gladys. I left home when I was 16 and never looked back."

I could tell that she and I were cut from the same cloth and that I would be back to bask in her glow.

"Yeah, Mom said we were just like *Bonanza* on TV. Our family had all the drama without all the money. Our people came from England. We made carts for a living, but we were stubborn and didn't see the use of switching from horses to cars and nothing has worked since."

I put my order in and as Ruthie went to deliver it, a tall man in his sixties walked into the cafe, dressed in coveralls with the name *Ben* stitched over his heart. When Ruthie turned her head, it was as if the world had stopped and her whole countenance changed. I remember hearing Hector say that the two of them were very much in love. Today, I didn't need anyone to tell me; I had all the evidence I needed to come to that conclusion on my own.

I ate my breakfast in peace, watching Ruthie and Ben interact like a couple of lovesick teenagers, testing boundaries, making connections, and Ben backing away with a deer-in-the-headlights kind of look.

I went to the counter to pay my bill, confronted by meringue soldiers lined up, ready for duty.

"It's such a shame about Lois," I said, as Ruthie rang up my bill.

"The dead woman? Yeah, it really is. I've heard Hector arrested her niece already."

"He did? But..." My jaw loosened its grip on my gums and flew open.

"Yeah, her name is Mavis somebody, from Nashville."

I paid my bill and stepped into the cool, crisp morning. The rollercoaster Texas weather allowed for morning temperatures in the forties and afternoons heating up into the eighties. It played havoc with my sinuses—one of the little sacrifices one makes for living in paradise.

HECTOR WAS taking Mavis to the police station, but on the way ran a stop sign and crashed into an oncoming car. These things happen all the time, and maybe even with rookie cops, but not to the Chief of Police. No one was hurt, except Hector's pride and maybe his job status. When he was on Highway Patrol, there were serious consequences for someone who wrecked a squad car. Having been Chief for a little more than two years, he had no idea what he might face. He and Psych were seeing to the driver of the other car, a young mother on the way to daycare to pick up her child. She was all right, if a little shaken.

Then Hector remembered what they were trying to do when life interrupted. He cast a glance at the wrecked squad car. The back door was open, and Mavis was gone.

THE CATHOLIC Church was a modern structure, a broad and welcoming space - pleasingly contemporary with a hint of tradition. One feature especially pleased me; they used light to mimic the flying buttress of Notre Dame Cathedral in Paris. The grounds, too, were carefully planned and cared for, indicating that a lot of money was present and available to this church.

I drove into the parking lot and had my pick of convenient spaces. It seemed few in the community even knew that Lois was alive, and now she was dead. *How quickly we pass from memory*, I mused as I made my way to the front of the church.

Hector hadn't arrived yet, and that surprised me because the funeral was about to begin. I went into the large space and took a program from a tall man with a broad face, and sat as near the back as I could.

Whenever I come into a Catholic sanctuary, I'm always struck by how ornate it is. I think I understand why my ancestors fought about it. Now I see how beautiful it is; I see the artistry in it. During the Reformation, the zealots tore down everything they could get to as far as their ladders would reach. Now my prayer is "Thank God for short ladders."

The service was formal but flowing. After the eulogy, delivered with sensitivity and eloquence by Father Paul, something happened that came as a total surprise.

MAVIS RAN harder than she ever had. Her only thought was escape. She had to get away in order to prove her innocence. She crashed through bushes, scraping her skin which caused her to bleed. She stumbled into trash cans, bruising her knees, and struggled over fences with great difficulty. She was in unfamiliar surroundings and the environment now took on a sinister tone. The bushes mocked her, the trees pointed at her in derision, and the trash cans got in her way on purpose in order to frustrate her attempt at freedom. The handcuffs dug into her wrists and she started to bleed. All she wanted to do was to see about her dear Aunt Lois, and now she was a wanted criminal accused of her aunt's murder. She couldn't help but think, *How did this happen?*

She was not an athletic woman, but the stakes were high. She rested behind some bushes alongside a red brick house. She knew she couldn't stay there long, but she also knew that if she continued at the same pace, she would be all used up and the chase would be over.

She needed to get rid of the handcuffs, but that would involve a locksmith, which would ultimately involve the law. *Maybe I could find a saw of some kind*, she thought. Better to add the charge of being a thief than to risk getting caught. Mavis really didn't like where this was headed, but knew she had no choice.

HECTOR WAS amazingly calm in the face of such a disaster. He had made a mistake; well, actually two, but who's counting. He knew he was a good cop and would get out of this mess, find the woman, and make good on the squad car. He had grown up in a family with three sisters and one of the things that taught him was patience. He took a deep breath and tried to sort out the accident as he waited for the tow truck to arrive.

Psych returned to the squad car and reported that the other driver was fine. Hector asked Psych to write him a ticket for failure to obey a traffic control signal. Hector gave his insurance information to the woman, and waited with her.

"This has never happened to me," the woman said, looking up into Hector's brown, blood-shot eyes. "Being hit by a policeman, I mean, and have it be his fault."

"It's my first time, too, and I guess it goes to show you, nobody's perfect."

Max, the desk sergeant, came to check out the accident and to see what more he could do.

"I want you to find that woman." Hector's gaze bore holes in Max and Psych as they listened to him.

AS A BOY I had been to my share of Catholic funerals. We lived in the town of Dumfries in the southwest corner of Scotland, the Borderlands. My father worked in a mining town a train's ride away. In the mines, accidents were a common enough occurrence to keep the local priest pretty busy, and the undertakers wealthy. In those days, pre-Vatican II, they used a funeral liturgy called *Dies Irae,* which is Latin for "Days of Wrath." The hymn began,

Days of Wrath! O day of mourning!
See fulfilled the prophet's warning
Heaven and earth in ashes burning.

For some reason, people love to be told how bad they are. But some churches gave up preaching "hellfire and brimstone" and instead aimed for proclaiming the grace of God. The trouble is that what you say about grace and how you show it are often very different things. Frequently, the wrath does not disappear, but just slips beneath the surface. So here it was again. I felt bad for the family who not only had to grieve, but to confront their guilt as well. It's true that grief and guilt fit together like a hand in a glove, but this was just so unpastoral, so uncaring. I wanted to have a talk with this priest.

MAVIS' LEG twitched with painful cramps. She remained frozen in that spot, paralyzed by indecision. Every option she considered yielded the same result. If she ran, she surely would eventually be caught. If she turned herself in, she might face additional charges for fleeing and escape. She began to miss her husband. He was a lawyer, after all. He was supposed to know about these things. She did not want to call him because he would not be pleased with her present predicament. Besides, he was coming to Shoestring and would soon enough find out his wife was not only suspected of murder, but currently a fugitive.

A squad car slowly came down the street, passing the alley where she now crouched, causing her to panic. All she had done was come back to try to work out her relationship with her sole surviving relative. She was now wanted for murder; she had never even had a parking ticket!

Her phone rang. It startled Mavis so badly that she lost her balance and fell over.

"Mavis?" a male voice began.

"Oh, Martin, I'm so glad to hear your voice. Where are you? I have so much to tell you."

"I'm at the Shoestring police department. Half the county is out looking for you. Where in the hell are you?"

"YOU'VE MADE this town the laughing stock of the county! Why I don't fire your ass is beyond me!" seethed Tom Branch, the city manager, his finger one inch from Hector's nose.

"You can't fire me! I was appointed by the mayor and city council to do this job, and I intend to do it until they say otherwise." Hector had no intention of backing down.

"Yeah, well, I can take that squad car out of your pay, and I'm looking into charges of neglect for losing that woman. I might not be able to fire your ass, but I can sure as shit have you suspended."

"You go right ahead, Tom. I'm just as angry about this mess as you are. In fact, nobody is as angry as I am. But if you want to catch the person who murdered that poor woman and torched her house, you need me. We'll find her killer, but you have to let me do my job."

"Why don't you take the rest of the day off? We'll see what insurance will allow for a new squad car, and your deputies can locate the suspect."

"I've got some loose ends to tie up, but okay, I'll take

what's left of the day." Hector looked at his watch. "I can catch my son's football game if I hurry."

"You do that," Tom said, not smiling. "Now get out of my office."

Hector reached for the door, opened it, and then turned back. "Say, Tom, can you give me a ride?"

I DIDN'T recognize him after the service without his vestments. In the church he looked like a regal, almost godlike figure. Now he was just a little man in black.

"Father Paul, my name is Angus...Angus McPherson," I said, extending my hand.

"I know who you are," he replied with a broad smile as well as a certain glow about him. He took my hand and shook it firmly. "Hector talks about you all the time. You've made quite an impression on him. I think you're the reason he's come back to church, and I thank you for that."

"Well, I think it's more to do with him and God than me, but thanks nonetheless."

"That was some nasty business that happened at your church. How's that going?"

"Well, they've hired a woman interim." *Why did I emphasize* woman *pastor?* "She specializes in calming troubled waters."

"You mean they can make such people?"

We both laughed.

"We all have our gifts, Father."

"Please, call me Paul." An awkward pause filled the immense space of the vestibule.

"Fa – Paul," I stammered, "I wanted to talk to you about Lois."

"Angus, I'd love to, but as you know I must run. They're waiting for me to do the graveside service." He started moving toward the door where another man in a dark suit was waving him on. "You can come with me, if you like."

"No, that's okay," I said, already regretting that decision. "I need to get home."

AS SOON as I got in my Jeep, I remembered I had promised Sam I would meet him in Cuero to discuss his situation with him. *Why hadn't he called me?* I wondered. Then I remembered I had turned off my phone during the funeral. I looked for a message, and sure enough, there was one from Sam. Going against the law and conventional wisdom regarding safety, I played back the message as I drove. "Angus, this is Sam. Did I get the day wrong or something? Sorry I missed you. Please call." I could feel my face flush with embarrassment. I pulled over to call him back. Naturally, he was not there. I left a message and vowed I would make it up to him somehow. The Hindus call it *Karma*; the universe is out of balance until you correct a mistake so that it turns out right. In the final analysis, whatever happens, it's in God's hands.

The phone rang, and I almost jumped. It was Angelica. The silence on the other end was not quiet and still, but full of noise and despair.

"Hello, *mi Corazon*," I said expectantly.

"Michael... He came to Shoestring to visit you..." Angelica stammered.

"What's happened to him, Love?"

"Oh, Angus, he's in a coma."

CHAPTER FIVE: THE MARK OF CAIN

"BREATHE, ANGIE, Love. What happened?"

"That's just it, they don't know. Jessica was with him. She said he woke up and seemed fine. By the afternoon, he was unconscious and began having seizures. She called 911 and then called me. They're running all the tests they can think of to figure out what happened. As of now, they just don't know. Oh, Angus, he's my baby." Angelica began to sob.

"He's a McPherson, Love. He'll pull through, I just know it."

"You...really...think...so?" Angelica hiccoughed softly between sobs.

"Of course I do," I reassured her, even though I knew no such thing. My PhD was in psychology. My mind turned to mush trying to comfort the woman I loved.

"Where did they take him?"

"They life-flighted him to Seton Southwest. I'm on my way there now. How long will it be before you get here?"

"I'll be there in about an hour. Please be careful, Love."

"I will. Please hurry!"

"I will." She hung up.

I put my phone on the center console of the Jeep. The engine purred expectantly, but I couldn't move. In my mind's eye I was swimming in molasses, frustrated by my lack of progress. A rage swept over me in a tidal wave of emotion. I had to get to my son's side as quickly as possible; if I could fly, it would not be fast enough, but I remained unable to move.

The avalanche of experiences from the last week came crashing down upon me, and I could hardly breathe. Reviewing them occupied my mind as I slowly gained my composure and put the Jeep in gear, easing my way onto the two-lane road. A car whizzed by me even as I swore I had checked behind me and saw no on-coming traffic. I gripped the steering wheel with enough force to choke the life out of it, while taking several deep breaths.

My one thought was getting to my son. This case, the fiery death of Lois Meyer, the arrest of Mavis, the Celtic cross with ties to Scotland, all of it dissolved into a fog of distant memory until I could see the apple of my eye, the solace of my soul, the hope of my tomorrow. I thought of my dad; a cold, hard, drunken black-from-coal-dust man, beating my sainted mother or one of us kids. I vowed I would not be like that, and thankfully I wasn't.

More than once I had wished my dad dead. I'd even thought about how I would do it. But fortunately his own life of dissipation accomplished this for me. I had to find a way out of the pool of dark emotions engulfing me. In large part, those sentiments drew me to God, to the church, and ultimately to ministry. So now I thank my dad—despite his cruelty—for driving me toward this life I love.

Thus, I too wrestled with the "Mark of Cain." At the University of Texas, I met a Rabbi and asked him to lead a Seder meal for us while I was Pastor at Cuero. A Seder is a Christian version of the Passover meal, the meal

Jesus shared with his disciples before he was killed. It was at that supper that he instituted his own meal, giving all his disciples His body and blood so that we could be one in him.

The Rabbi told us that there was an old story about the "Mark of Cain." He shocked us all by saying it was the belly button. His point was that we all share the same murderous rage, the same dark traits, the same shame, and the same laziness. That insight definitely helped me now as I thought about my son lying in a hospital bed. But the murderous rage only spurred me on to be by his side, even though I knew there was little I could do except pray and be present for Angelica.

I had forgotten about Mavis and her fugitive status, or Hector and the burden of finding yet another killer waiting furtively to feed his inner "Cain." With all my energy and focus, I sped toward my son's bedside.

MAVIS SAT slump-shouldered in her cell, her husband beside her.

"What in God's name were you thinking?" scowled the little man.

Mavis shrugged, not looking at him. The very sight of him had disgusted her for years. Frankly, he made her sick, but he was her choice and, occasionally, he did provide her with more than the bare necessities.

"Where was your head? What were you thinking?" Martin's blood-shot eyes became narrow slits. "You really think you could have gotten away? You were arrested on suspicion of murder. How does this stunt help your cause?" He threw up his arms in exasperation.

"You know," Mavis took her time standing up, "they say a lawyer who defends himself has a fool for a client."

"Yeah, that's an old joke." Martin dismissed her with a wave of his hand.

"I'm beginning to think that when a lawyer defends his wife, she has a fool for a lawyer and a husband."

"Only if she doesn't listen to him."

"Well, maybe I should get a different lawyer."

"Nonsense!" An icy silence settled between them.

"Okay," Martin said, hoping to repair the breach. "Please sit down and tell me exactly what happened."

HECTOR APPROACHED Mavis' cell as she and her husband were finishing their conversation.

"Martin, you said you were home on a case while Mavis came here to look after her aunt," Hector remarked.

"That's right."

"Had you ever met Lois before?"

"Sure," Martin stopped and turned toward Hector. "She came to visit us a couple of times. Even fixed her French toast once."

"Touching," said Hector with a smirk.

"Look, you have nothing to hold my wife on. There's no evidence linking her to Lois' death. The two trips she made within a week don't prove anything but her devotion to what family she has left."

"That may be true, but there was the escape at—"

"She came back of her own volition." Martin grabbed the bars and leaned into Hector's face, glowering.

"We'll let a judge decide her fate. In the meantime, Counselor, you are free to go."

Hector opened the cell door. With confusion spread across his face, Martin turned to Mavis and for the first time embraced her with a passion that surprised even him. After they kissed, Mavis looked at him in wide-eyed amazement.

"Don't worry, Darling, I'll get you out of here." He turned to Hector as the cell door closed on Mavis.

"How soon can she go before the judge?"

"Monday."

Martin grabbed Mavis' hands through the bars. "That's just a couple of days, Mavie. I've got something to do and I'll be right back. Is there anything I can get you?"

"How about a metal file?" Mavis laughed; Hector did not.

I COULD not sit still. Walking back and forth on the green carpet of the waiting room helped calm my troubled mind. *What could this be? Have they caught it in time? How could I have prevented this from happening in the first place?* I caught Angie's worried look out of the corner of my eye. I sat down next to her and we embraced in a wordless search for solace. Precious little was available for either of us.

Visiting hours arrived, and we rushed to Michael's bedside. A big man, my son looked like a child in that bed, with sweaty hair slicked back, and tubes dangling all over the place. His face was swollen like he'd been in a fight.

"Michael," I whispered, "can you hear me, son?" A flood of emotion washed over me. I wished God would allow me to take my son's place. However, wishing would not make it so. All I could do was stand helplessly by as my son fought for his life. Angie wiped away a tear as she attempted to speak. Michael did not stir.

A young woman with short, blond hair and a white coat came into the room through the sliding glass door.

"I'm Doctor Swann," she whispered.

Perfect! I thought.

"Michael is stable. He's heavily sedated because of the seizures he has been having," she said.

"Will he be all right?" asked Angie.

"If you could please follow me, we can talk in the waiting room."

"Of course," I said.

Once outside the room, Dr. Swann's voice returned to a normal volume. "We've put Michael in a drug-induced coma," she explained, but I wasn't listening. My head was swimming with thoughts of Michael, the mess at Shoestring, and trying to do God's will—whatever that was. Dr. Swann smelled of peaches and ammonia, the perfect irony for a hospital. "We did this to protect his brain and stop the seizures."

"You've done a lot of tests, doctor. What have you found out?"

"The good news is that we know it's not the heart, lungs or liver—not a stroke nor cancer."

"That's good news," Angie said, trying to convince herself.

"So what else is there?" I asked, my frustration rising like the tide.

"Well, there's a whole host of things it could be," replied Dr. Swann, putting her hand on my shoulder and looking into my eyes. "We'll know more after a few more tests."

"When will that be?" asked Angie.

"After a few days. We'll do three more tests today and

have the results tomorrow. We can then analyze what they mean and pray we get some answers."

"Now you're in my bailiwick." I smiled.

"Oh, we find ourselves praying all the time, Reverend."

"I don't know if that's a good thing or a bad thing. Either you know what you're doing and are just looking for confirmation, or you don't know anything and are hoping for a miracle."

"Just like the rest of us, I suspect." Dr. Swann smiled for the first time, and so did I—Angie remained unamused. The doctor broke the awkward silence. "We're going to continue the induced coma while we figure out what's going on. The best thing you can do right now is go home and get some rest. I'll call you when we know more."

Doctor Swann left and I hugged Angie. We decided to take the doctor's advice and go home. Arm in arm, we slowly walked through the green halls of the hospital.

This shade of green unsettled me. I teetered between anger and depression—I couldn't decide which. It wasn't just the color, of course, but I needed a fresh focus. Angie was on the verge of tears and I held her more closely to me. As I looked up from Angie's anguished face, I saw Father Paul coming up the hall.

"Father Paul, what are you doing here?" I stammered.

"I am here visiting a parishioner. Is everything alright?"

"Unfortunately not. It's our son, Michael. He lost consciousness and began having seizures earlier today and they brought him here. They are running tests, but they don't know what it is yet," I said, trying my best to keep my composure.

"I'm so sorry," he said. "How are you holding up?" he asked Angie, putting his hand on her shoulder.

"I'm fine, Father," Angie replied, lowering her gaze.

"Please, call me Paul."

"Where are my manners? Angie, this is Father Paul from Shoestring. He conducted Lois' funeral."

"Oh, yes," she said. "Very tragic business."

"Indeed. Do they have any suspects?" he asked.

"Well, yes, they do," I said. "But the investigation is just starting. They won't know much at this point." I wanted to tell him about Mavis, but decided to keep that to myself for the time being.

"The sooner they can wrap that business up, the better. Shoestring has suffered enough." Paul stuck out his hand for me to shake. "I'd best go look in on my parishioner."

"Is it serious?"

"No, just a routine gall bladder procedure. But the way he carries on, you'd think it was open heart surgery. He'll be fine physically; it's his attitude that's killing everyone around him."

"I've run into a few of those in my time," I replied. "The church seems to attract them like flies to dead fish."

"Life's a mystery, isn't it?" added Paul. Angie nodded. "I'm truly sorry for your suffering. I'll pray that your son recovers fully."

"We would very much appreciate that," I said, smiling at Angie and Paul as we shook hands.

"Well, must dash. Next time you're in Shoestring, you must give me a call," said Paul as he walked backwards down the hall before turning and hurrying away.

"I'll be sure to do that," I answered before he disappeared from sight.

CHAPTER SIX: Day in Court

S HE REFUSED to shower or brush her hair. Mavis was going downhill in a hurry, and there was no one there to stop her. She declined to eat and could not sleep. Being a fairly new facility, the jail was neat and tidy. Being stuck there with no way out made the terror of the place unspeakable.

The judge would decide Mavis' fate today. The idea that she could get out on bail was, well, not likely, it being murder. Martin figured she would not get a court date until a month from now. He had clients back in Nashville with court dates of their own who needed him, and they were paying customers. He did not know what to do.

He decided to talk to Hector about who might be able to represent Mavis while he was away. Later he talked to Mavis about his predicament and his proposed solution. She was not happy, nor did she seem to care.

Hector offered no help. Martin knew that Hector thought Mavis was guilty, and that was the end of it. The only evidence was circumstantial and no court would convict her without an eyewitness. Martin prayed, for the first time in his life, that they would not find a witness and that Mavis would forgive him for leaving to take care of clients who could put bread on the table. Besides, he did not have a license to practice law in Texas and getting one would take too long. He needed help, but as was his habit, he refused to ask and did not know where to look.

As he was leaving the jail, he heard an alarm. It was different from the many buzzings and bells that announced each successive activity. This was urgent, insistent, unrelenting, a cry for help within an institution that, by its very nature was itself a plea for help, a scream within a society of deaf mutes.

Martin saw men and women running toward the source of the alarm. He asked the guards at the last door what all the commotion was about. Because he was still within the jail proper, he was allowed to see for himself.

What Martin saw shocked and sickened him. Fire billowed from a cell. Smoke and noise, water and screaming; confusion and chaos erupted within the bowels of that wounded place. In the confusion, Martin lost his bearings, unaware of where he was. He normally had an uncanny sense of direction, which made his present feelings all the more unsettling. He coughed until he was almost out of breath, the smoke billowing into every crevice. Searching for the wall, he sought to steady himself. He found a small pocket of air as the hall began to clear because the fire department had responded so quickly, and acted with such efficiency. As he started to breathe, to come back to himself, he began to recognize familiar surroundings. It finally dawned on him that he had been here just minutes before. The cell belonged to Mavis.

He started to breathe heavily again, not for lack of air, but from sheer panic. With dread, he recognized the impossibility of surviving such a blaze. The screams he heard now came not from far away—they were his own.

HECTOR HEARD about the situation at the jail and rushed over. After the fire was extinguished and Mavis' body taken to the morgue, the black hole of the cell and realization of a life cut short blended perfectly with the somber atmosphere of the jail itself. Hector fought to regain his composure as he came upon Miles Stone, already there sifting through the debris. He wore blue plastic gloves and a mask. The heat still palpable, Miles seemed not to notice.

"Aren't you afraid you'll get burned working with this stuff so soon?" Hector approached him with his own gloves and mask in place. Firefighters were still working in the confined space, so it made movement difficult.

"I've been burned so many times," he replied, looking up with a part of the bed frame in his hands, "that it's second nature to me now. It comes with the territory." His expression was flat, his affect even. "Besides, these minutes after a fire are crucial to find its origins, and maybe even who set it off. That's what I love about my work—the challenge of finding out where and how the fire started. For instance, I know already that the fire started on the ceiling, probably from the light fixture. I'll have to get above the ceiling to confirm, but I've seen this once before. It's quite ingenious and would take some doing, but my hat's off to whoever did this."

"Yeah, and my prime suspect is dead. How could this happen?"

Miles said nothing and went about sifting through the rubble.

In the confusion of the moment, no one saw Martin, nor paid any attention to him. Appalled and upset by what he saw, he could not comprehend that such a thing could happen. All he wanted to do was run; he was not sure why, only that it was something he had to do. So he ran.

"YOU CAME all this way just to see Michael," I said, as Hector and I chose our food from the hospital cafeteria line.

"What are friends for?" asked Hector, smiling. "Besides, I wanted to tell you about this new lure I found. They just jump in the boat. It's almost too easy."

We paid for our food and sat down to eat. "Also," Hector broke a long silence, "I wanted to talk about the case, now that Mavis is gone."

"I heard about that," I said, through a mouthful of food. "That's awful. Two women, dying in fires. It's hard to imagine a worse death."

There was an awkward silence, as we tried to find our equilibrium in this strange place, at such a strained time. Then Hector said that the DNA from under Lois' fingernails came back, and was not a match to Mavis'.

I scratched my head, and Hector kept going.

"What has me baffled is who would go to such lengths to silence the niece of an old woman who lives in a small town in the middle of nowhere?" Between bites, Hector took off his cowboy hat and placed it on the table next to him.

"Someone who wanted them both dead," I replied, shrugging my shoulders.

"So you think they're connected?" asked Hector. "Obviously, or at least I can certainly see why you would assume that. But how and why are they connected? That's chewing the tough grass."

Hector was an orderly eater. He would eat one thing before moving on to the next, and he always waited to take a drink from his water until he had eaten all his food.

We reviewed the evidence: we talked about the Celtic cross with the "bossed" snakes and the Adam and Eve figures. Hector reasoned that it must be a warning used by the killer to let us know that the woman had been involved in some kind of illicit activity.

"Or it could have something to do with creation," I suggested.

Hector's eyebrows rose in unison. "As in family ties?" Hector asked for clarification.

I nodded, smiling, as Hector drank his water.

"I'm really stumped about the rat poison. No one takes that stuff willingly. She had to be forced."

"Or introduced to it slowly, over time, in such small doses she never noticed – until it was too late."

"That assumes the killer knew her pretty intimately."

"Yes, it does," I said nodding. "The only problem, now that Mavis is dead, is there's no one to prove any of this. If she did it, there was an end to it. Now we know with some certainty that she didn't do it, so we're back to square one." I made a big square in the air with my fork full of mashed potatoes.

"Not necessarily," corrected Hector. "She could still be on the hook for Lois' murder, and then someone silenced her to keep her quiet about something else."

"But what possible motive could that 'someone' have?" I said, leaning into Hector.

He sat back, shrugged and said, "That's what I'd hoped you'd help me with."

"What really has me stumped is the clay sun we found with Lois," said Hector leaning in again. "What does that have to do with anything?"

"The thing that leaps to mind is the occult. But Lois doesn't strike me as the kind that would go in for that, being a good Catholic and all."

"I've heard of stranger things."

"Yeah, sure; no doubt." I scratched my head, not because I had an itch; it was a reflex. "Let's not forget the scripture. What was it—Rev. 8:8?"

"The second angel blew his trumpet, and something like a great mountain, burning with fire, was thrown into the sea."

"I'm impressed," I said, quietly clapping for Hector's accomplishment. "From memory, no less."

"It's always helpful to have the facts at hand. Besides, every self-respecting Catholic gets a healthy dose of Revelation growing up."

"That's funny, because that's the only book Calvin didn't write a commentary on."

"Wise man...wise man." Hector seemed lost to me for a moment. "But what does it mean?"

"All hell is about to break loose, and it's going to get worse."

"But why did she have it with her? Did she wake up long enough to see the house on fire, and she took the time to grab the items? But because of the rat poison, she was dead before the fire started. That doesn't make any sense. Unless the things she knew were too much for her, and she just took the fire as a convenient excuse to end it early, but not without giving us a clue, no matter how obscure."

"That *does* make sense. So we're looking for someone who is angry and obsessed with fire. But who would want to kill a woman who, according to neighbors, was helpful and pretty much stayed to herself?"

The question hung in the air as Hector's gaze turned toward a group of doctors coming into the cafeteria. I followed his gaze as Dr. Swann, carrying a tray of food, led the group while talking with some colleagues all dressed in white with stethoscopes around their necks.

I stood abruptly, and made my apologies to Hector. We made plans to meet later for some fishing and catching up with each other's families. Hector also said something about talking with Lois' friends about the rat poison.

I approached Dr. Swann's table, a swirl of emotion churning inside me. I sat down next to the young, vibrant woman whose expression sobered the minute she saw me.

"Reverend McPherson, I was going to call you right after lunch," she said, shaking my hand. "We think we know what's going on with your son. We're pretty sure he's got the West Nile Virus."

"He's been bitten by a mosquito?" I said, as I felt my jaw drop.

"He's got a form of encephalitis, which is an inflammation of the brain."

"Will he be all right, Doctor?" I asked, wiping sweat from my brow.

"We'll administer a variety of antiviral medicines to see which one works. Unfortunately, there is no known treatment for West Nile. However, we want to prevent your son from developing any other illnesses, such as pneumonia. The virus will have to run its course. If he doesn't bounce back in two or three days, we'll reassess the treatment options. Given his age and overall health, we are optimistic that he'll be fine. In fact, we can start bringing him out of the coma so he can help direct us to the right medicine that'll work for him."

"That all sounds good, but I wish you were more definitive about which course to take." I could feel the creases growing in my forehead.

"I do too," the Doctor replied, standing with her lunch tray in hand. "But that's why they call it the 'healing arts.' With all the medical advances we've made, there's still a lot of trial and error going on."

I stood as well, worried that maybe I had overstepped my bounds. Doctors need some time to relax too. "I'm okay with the 'trial' part; it's the 'error' thing that concerns me."

"Just concentrate on the fact that he will get well, and leave the rest to us."

HECTOR WAS worried again. The evidence in the death of Lois Myers pointed to Mavis Belmont, her niece, and she even served herself up on a silver platter and was arrested. Everything was neat and tidy—just the way he liked it. Any time the end of a case came so easy, Hector never trusted it. He knew the other shoe had not dropped; it was only a matter of time. As he thought more about it, the "ifs" started to mount up.

He knew all this would come to an end "if" he could find Mavis' killer. That depended on "if" he could run down Mavis' husband, Martin. Hector didn't think Martin killed his wife, but surely he would know something that might help them find her killer, "if" he would cooperate. Martin was a lawyer, and in Hector's experience lawyers were a pretty cagey, tight-lipped bunch. He might be able to shed some light on Mavis' movements before she was arrested, but that would be a huge "if."

Mavis' death should be easy to solve. In a closed system like the jail, it's just a matter of time before all the impossible things were eliminated in order to find what was possible. However, Hector had no idea just how little time he actually had. He also refused to rule out the possibility that the perp had help from the outside. Prison walls become remarkably porous when someone wants something from the outside. He had his deputies interviewing inmates and staff at the jail. Knowing the levels of depravity present within prison walls, Hector reconsidered just how "easy" finding Mavis' killer would be. He determined to take it one step at a time, overlooking nothing and arriving at the correct conclusion.

The CFI found the origin of the fire, which was in the ventilation ducts above Mavis' cell. That definitely made this an inside job, the work of someone more highly placed than the newest inmate.

THE FOG cleared from my mind. Michael would be okay. I breathed a long-awaited sigh of relief. I called Angie and tried to be as optimistic as possible without being overly sure of the outcome. She greeted the news with an awkward silence. I had to say her name to reassure myself she was still on the line. A minute later, after I put her more at ease with this wonderful news, she fairly leaped through the phone with joy. We both could relax a little now that our "baby" seemed to be on the mend. Neither of us knew the danger that lay ahead for Michael and for us.

I decided to change the subject, and bring Angie some more good news I had discovered about the current case.

"I did some research online about Druids," I said. "It's all very interesting. Around the time of the building of Stonehenge in England, a tribe in what is now Scotland was wiped out. It's all very mysterious. No one knows the exact cause, but one theory stood out over the others. At least it's so fantastic that I remembered it most."

"What was it?"

"An entomologist by the name of Thomas Blackburn, who lived in the 1800s, had the idea that the Druids in this particular place in Scotland were wiped out when all the insects died."

"I don't understand. How would he know what caused their extinction?"

"Blackburn discovered that there was a great insect die-off in that region and a few years later, all the Druids were gone."

"So he connected the insect disappearance with the extinction of the Druids in Scotland?" she asked. "Kind of like the coming of the ice age wiping out many species of plant and animal life."

"Kind of, I suppose."

"That's beyond belief. It stretches every imaginative bone in my body," Angie replied in disbelief.

"I'm just telling you what I found. Apparently, Jonas Salk some years later concurred with Blackburn. Not about the Druids, but about insects. Apparently, they're essential for our survival. He said that if insects were to become extinct, then the human race would follow a few years later. But if you take the human race out of the equation, the world would flourish for centuries."

"That makes perfect sense. Was Salk a Presbyterian?"

I laughed. "I have no idea."

"Darling, I'll have to ponder this information for a while. It sounds so bizarre. Does Blackburn have any idea what killed the insects?"

"About that time, the Druids set a lot of the forests on fire to clean up the land for a housing settlement. His theory was that it was the combination of the smoke and the type of wood they burned that wiped out the insects."

"Actually, that makes a lot of sense," she said.

"It does?" I answered, surprised she grasped this wild theory so calmly.

HECTOR'S HEAD hurt. His prime suspect was incinerated in his jail, and her husband had gone missing. He went to his desk drawer and pulled out some aspirin, took a fist full, and choked them down without water. He couldn't be bothered to find a glass. He could just hear his wife saying he was crazy for throwing his hat in the ring to become Shoestring's police chief. The phone rang, startling him out of his dejected state. It was Psych, his deputy.

"Chief, I found something really interesting about somebody right under our own roof."

"Who is it?"

"The City Manager, Tom Branch."

"Well, what about him?"

"I think you'll want to see this for yourself."

"Where are you?"

"City Hall."

"I'll be right there."

"HECTOR, WHAT'S the matter?" Tom Branch furrowed his brow as he looked at his friend.

"I found something out about you that has me very concerned. I have a report here that says you like to play with fire."

"What do you mean?" Tom's gaze started to wander from Hector. He glanced out the window. It had been chilly, but the sun shone brightly outside. If you were unaware of the actual temperature, you would be in for a surprise when you walked out into it.

"When you were a kid in Tyler, it says here you started a fire in your dad's church, using an old inner tube."

"You're not going to equate that with—they never proved that!" Tom's perspiring forehead glistened in the afternoon light.

"You mean they didn't look too hard when no one was hurt and no major damage done?"

"Well, how in the hell did you get that information?" No matter how stressed Tom got, his south Texas drawl had the comforting cadence of a soft spring breeze playing over salt grass.

"It seems the pastor at the time said something about you being the one who reported it, and you were upset with your mom dating a woman."

"So now you think I love fire so much that I just can't stay away?" Tom's composure returned to him like a set of keys misplaced, then found exactly where you put them when they were lost.

"Well, that's one theory. People do get addicted to the most destructive things." Hector played Tom to an inside straight, and was about to call his bluff.

Hector leaned into Tom, so that he could see his nose hair. "What were you doing on Monday morning around 7:00?"

"I was taking a shower, probably, getting ready for work."

"Tom, you and I go way back. We played together as kids. You're all right, for a Democrat." Hector smiled. "We checked with Helen, your wife. She said you never showed up Sunday night. Said you had some kind of convention to go to in Austin. She told us you didn't come home until Monday night. So do you want to tell us what you were really doing? Otherwise, you look real good for the murder."

Hector's cell phone rang; fishing the damn thing out of his pocket before the phone stopped ringing always annoyed him to no end. This time he made it; it was his desk sergeant, Max Brown. He had just received word from the FBI that Martin Belmont, Mavis' husband, was spotted in the Nashville airport. Max also told him the FBI invited the Chief to Nashville to be in on questioning Martin about his disappearance from the jail the day Mavis died.

Hector did not respond for what seemed to Tom to be several minutes.

"Hector, is something wrong?" asked Tom. In spite of the trouble he currently seemed to be in, Tom was concerned about his friend.

Hector snapped out of his reverie. "Thanks, Tom, I'm fine." To Max he said, "Thank the FBI for the invitation, and tell them I'm on my way."

Hector instructed Psych to escort Tom down to the station.

CHAPTER SEVEN: Swift Justice

CUERO IS one of those small towns that define the Old West. The main street is basic, without being solely utilitarian, yet possessing no consideration for charm or aesthetics. The closest thing to a nice place to eat was, of course, a Mexican restaurant that had seen better days.

The church was an A-frame structure with buildings on either side constructed of the ubiquitous blond brick so prevalent in central Texas, a design that definitely looked better on paper than it did in real life.

My body sat in Sam Horn's office talking to a young minister in trouble for the first time. The rest of me remained with Angie in Michael's hospital room. The small office appeared even smaller due to the clutter of books and papers piled in every corner. This being Sam's first church out of seminary, I assumed he wished to communicate the image of an intellectual but scattered shepherd of the flock—probably not the image he should have wanted to portray.

Sam's eyes darted around the room, looking for anywhere to escape; his foot twitched with every beat of his heart. His chances for happiness seemed to be dying with the waning light of a spent day.

"They just blindsided me, Angus," Sam stated, his

eyes lowered in contemplation bordering on a prayer for a miracle to save the situation. "The first two years were pretty good, then the denomination goes and allows gays to be ordained and all hell breaks loose around here."

"Was it 'all hell' or just one or two people?" I asked with a smile. "Did you explain to them that whoever they ordain is up to God and to them? They aren't being ordered to ordain gays."

"Yes, I told them, but these two—one's a funeral director and the other's a bank manager—say that we shouldn't be a part of any denomination that allows something that goes against scripture."

"I can't say as I blame them."

"What?" Sam did a double-take. "What do you mean?"

"Remember that Groucho Marx quote: 'I don't care to belong to any group that would have me as a member?'"

Again, Sam began to breathe a little easier. I remembered once more why God called me to this particular work.

I leaned into his face so we were eye to eye. "One of the first things to go in times like these is a sense of humor," I remarked. "You can't butt heads with these people. You'll always lose. But if you 'hold it lightly,' whatever 'it' is, they may take their cue from you and do the same."

Sam's eyes grew red around the rims.

"I'm beginning to feel a little like Elijah or Jeremiah. I'm undergoing a baptism by fire, as if God is trying to purify me or something," he said.

My mind had wandered, thinking about Michael and how hard everything had been on Angie. But the words "baptism by fire" snatched me from my own personal fog.

"Huh, what?" I stammered.

"Baptism by fire. I've really been through it, and I think I will come out the other end a better minister and, I hope, a better person."

"Yes, yes, I understand. I'm sorry."

My mind reeled. "Baptism by fire!" Of course, why didn't I see it before? Lois' burning was an act of purification. She sinned in some way and was made to pay. Or her death served as a message to someone else close—Mavis maybe—so that Lois had to pay for sins Mavis had committed.

I was getting way ahead of myself. There was nothing theological about this murder. It was simply a case of Lois knowing too much and having to be eliminated in order for their plan-whatever that was—to go forward.

But fire seemed to be the key. It wasn't just arson for arson's sake—fire actually meant something to whoever was doing this. If I could find out what it meant, I'd be halfway to knowing who did it.

I finally saw Sam as if for the first time. His look of concern was disconcerting.

"I'm sorry, Sam, it was just something you said, 'baptism by fire.' I think it has something to do with the death in Shoestring."

"How so?" And in that instant, I saw all the worry about his present predicament and his future prospects vanish from Sam's face. It was as if he had shed all his worry like a snake sheds her skin, and I knew, sooner or later, he would be fine.

I told him about Lois' burning, the Celtic cross, and the scripture from Rev. 8:8. I also told him about Mavis being burned to death in her cell.

"You know, it's funny about that 'baptism by fire' quote," I said. "It came from John the Baptist about Jesus and had something to do with Christ's passion for God and for people—"

"And turned into a description of a young man's introduction to battle," Sam interrupted.

I smiled with pride. "That's right! It starts out as a description of a passionate life and ends up as a hope for surviving death on a battlefield—very strange."

"In some ways, they're the same, aren't they?"

"It's because the story of Christ's death was called 'The Passion' that equates a passion for life with facing death." I thought about a piece of scripture my mother always recited about my dad's drinking. It was Proverbs. *Can a man take fire in his bosom and his clothes not get burned?*

JUST THE idea of travel made Hector sweat. He was out of his element. When not in control of his surroundings, he felt disoriented, irritated, and downright uncomfortable. But when the FBI called, you went, especially if Martin Belmont was the only link you had to your prime suspect, who was now dead. Hector had nowhere else to turn.

He had asked them to do a DNA test on Martin. It too was not a match to the skin under Lois' fingernails. This bit of evidence was looking to be as elusive as any sense to this whole case.

He told Psych of his plans to interview Martin in Nashville. Psych advised him to see the full-sized replica of the Parthenon and the statue of Athena—the goddess of wisdom and of war, of the arts and the law—an ironic if not conflicted soul. Unsure if he would have time for sightseeing, Hector nodded politely as Psych spoke so passionately about something entirely uninteresting to Hector.

Making his way through the airport, an agent met him at the baggage claim. He had always wanted to see his name on a sign held by a man in a chauffer's uniform. He got half his wish. A young woman with short blond hair and a gray business suit held a sign bearing his name. She barely acknowledged his presence before hurrying to the car and ferrying him to FBI headquarters.

Hector observed the interview from the next room. He argued his case for being in the room to interview Martin himself, but the Division Chief—a buzz-cut, furrowed-brow tough guy—refused to budge. Faced with either watching from afar or going home, Hector chose to watch.

"Precisely where were you when your wife died?" inquired the female agent who met Hector at the airport.

"I already told you, I was at the jail. I saw my wife burn to death. Frankly, I don't know what I'm doing here. I've got clients—"

"I don't care what you've got. We just have a few questions. If you cooperate and answer them to our satisfaction, then you'll be free to go. Did you know Lois Myers?"

"Of course I did. She was my wife's aunt. Since she was the only family Mavis had left, we visited her as often as our schedules allowed."

"Were you aware of your wife's two recent trips to Shoestring?"

"Well, I just found out about the first one, but I knew about the second." Beads of sweat formed on Martin's forehead. He ran his hand through his hair. Having interviewed his share of guilty criminals, Hector knew that sweating was a likely indicator of guilt. Martin certainly was being less than entirely honest.

"Actually, we know you're lying. You followed your wife to Shoestring the very next day. We have the ticket info right here." The agent waved a piece of paper in front of him. Martin knew that the police often tried to coax a confession out of a scared, intimidated suspect through the use of manufactured evidence. Somehow that knowledge escaped him as his blood pressure shot through the roof.

"I... I...I—" Martin stammered. "It's not a crime to follow your wife to the place she was raised."

"No, that's not a crime," replied the young woman with a note of triumph in her voice. "Lying to the FBI, now that *is* a crime."

I CALLED Franny to tell her I would be in Austin in the morning for the budget meeting, but that I wanted to spend the afternoon with my wife and Michael.

Angie seemed to be much calmer now that Michael was apparently out of the woods and would fully recover. They were slowly bringing him out of the chemically-induced coma. He became agitated and restless, his bed becoming a battleground, which was painful for us to watch.

"Lois...Lo...what..." Michael tossed and turned in his bed. I looked at Angie; the words seemed not to register with her, but they were the shock of my life. Here was my son, my beloved, hanging on to life by the slimmest of threads, and he's moaning in delirium about a dead woman he had never met, and did not know existed until I got involved in this case. This whole thing was getting stranger and stranger, but I needed to tell Hector what I heard. I was sure he'd think I was crazy too.

I got up, told Angie I was going to get some air, and went to the nurses' station.

"Has Michael had any other visitors besides us since he's been here?" I asked.

"No, sir, not that I'm aware of." The nurse looked at some papers. "Oh, wait, his pastor has been here a few times. I remember him. A good-looking fellow, in good shape for a minister."

I wanted to ask what she meant by that, but refrained. I had a much bigger mystery than the state of a minister's physical fitness. I had to unravel the mystery of who was visiting my son and posing as his pastor.

HECTOR WANTED to leap through the glass and shake Martin by his shabby lapels, but there was another agent sitting with him, which forced him to calm down a bit.

"Why did you follow your wife to Shoestring, Counselor? It's a simple question." The blond agent sat back and smirked.

"I wanted to see what she was up to. She had just lost her aunt. I was worried about her."

"You don't seem very broken up about losing your wife, sir."

"I don't know what to feel. I watched my wife burn to death in a jail cell. And now I'm being detained and interrogated by federal agents because you think I had something to do with her death. I don't know if I should be afraid or grieving. I'm very confused right now. I think I want to see my lawyer."

Hector observed Martin begin to twitch. He wondered if the agent picked that up. He knew it was helpful to have two people in the interview room because one person can detect non-verbal cues the other might miss. He ached to be that other person, but for the time being, he knew he had to remain patient.

"You mean you followed her because you didn't trust her?" asked the blond agent.

"She didn't tell me she was going. That's not like her. We tell each other what we're doing. We have no secrets from each other. So naturally I was curious."

"So you left all your commitments and all your precious clients in Nashville because you were 'curious'? Why didn't you just ask her, if you trust her so much?" She took her glasses off and started to clean them, blowing on them and then using her shirttail.

"Look, I've answered your questions, and you said you were going to let me go; you've got nothing to hold me on." He stood up as if for the first time, tentative and unsure of himself.

The agent shoved him down with a violent jerk.

"Just answer a few more questions, and we will—I promise." She straightened herself and waited for Martin to catch up.

"She was leaving me. She wasn't going to check on her aunt; she was going to live with her while she figured out what to do about us."

"And you hated her for that. Maybe you just lost it because you were losing her, and you wanted to end the pain."

"You see, that's why I didn't tell you in the first place. I knew you'd jump to that conclusion, but then why would I tell you now if I had done it? It makes no sense."

"When passion and hurt feelings mix, there's no telling

what will happen. Martin Belmont, you are under arrest for the murder of your wife—"

"What? How can you? I was as shocked as anyone when that cell blew up! I want to see my lawyer."

"We've got a source that says you put a hit on your own wife."

"He's lying."

"Actually, it was a woman, someone in the same cell block."

"Well, then she's lying, there's no truth to any of it."

An officer came in and stood Martin up. He cuffed Martin's hands behind his back, reading him his Miranda rights as he led him away to be processed.

Hector was stunned. He sat back as he watched Martin leave the room. He shook his head and clenched his teeth. "Swift justice..." he whispered.

"That's how we do it in the FBI," said his companion as they departed the room.

CHAPTER EIGHT: Harassment

I NEEDED to talk to Hector, so I called him on his cell. I heard various noises in the background that I couldn't make out.

"I'm at the airport," he offered. "I'm coming home. They've arrested Martin Belmont for Mavis' murder. Said they had testimony from a fellow inmate of hers who claimed Martin put her up to it."

"That doesn't sound right at all," I said. "Besides, I've got something here that's just as puzzling." I told him about Michael and how he was moaning Lois' name as he was coming out of the coma. "I don't know what that could mean."

"I don't know either, but when I get home, I'll come by the hospital, and we'll figure it out together."

I watched as my son battled with himself, battling with his regained consciousness, unaware of what he'd done to my own fragile grip on reality. A shadow descended upon me and I felt myself slumping in my chair, slipping away.

What does it mean that my son has the name of Lois on his lips in the middle of a drug-induced delirium? I can't even remember if he heard about her death before he fell ill.

I began to daydream. The next thing I knew, I was a giant mosquito happily flying around our backyard. I had just bitten a bird, and of course she was helpless to stop me. Flying high about the house, I spotted my son tending burgers on the grill.

Filled with a great sense of mission, I made a beeline—mosquito-line would be more apropos—straight for Michael's neck. The next thing I know, I am infecting my son with the potent West Nile Virus as he reaches behind his neck to end my life.

I snap to attention, nearly falling out of my chair. Looking around, I see no one but Michael. Still in the bed, he was calmer now, breathing rhythmically, making me calm and more certain of my surroundings. I remembered where I was and what I was doing there.

I thought about calling Angelica, but knew she would be in class at least until 11:00. Since it was only 10:00 a.m., I would have to wait until then. I was certain that dream would haunt me until I had a chance to figure out its meaning. I thought about Kafka's *The Metamorphosis* in which the main character becomes a massive cockroach, but I hadn't read that since college and had never thought about it until this very minute.

I suppose it is a part of my Scotch Presbyterian nature to feel a sense of guilt over what Michael is going through. And I certainly wanted to take his burden on as my own; any parent would.

I shook my head and ran a hand through my salt and pepper hair. I thought about taking a walk. My roommate at Seminary used to say something that stuck with me: "Never trust a thought arrived at while sitting down." So I decided to take a walk before heading home and seeing how Angie got through her day. I needed to consider whether this dream had anything to do with the murders and why Michael would ever say Lois' name in the first place.

AS SOON as Hector got home from Nashville, he headed out to Canyon Lake. He needed to clear his head and try to make sense of all he'd been through since being appointed police chief. He'd settle for the last twenty-four hours if it came to that.

He spent the day on the lake, with the sun kissing the rippling waters with a touch of warmth. The weather was supposed to change soon. Fish are incredibly sensitive to such things and prepare for that change before the fact. Needless to say, he didn't catch anything, except his breath. The stress of his job demanded that he take these breaks every now and then. If he didn't, he surely would have gone crazy long ago.

He had done all the figuring he could. He was shocked when the FBI ended the investigation of Lois and Mavis' murders by arresting Martin. That seemed too easy. It was as easy as Hector's own "swift justice," pinning Lois' murder on Mavis. He needed to atone for that rush to judgment. He would talk with Angus tomorrow, but for now he needed to see his priest. The phrase sounded strange to him, "His priest." He stopped by the rectory on the way home from his day on the lake.

He pulled up to a modest house built of blond brick. The yellow roses on the side of the house indicated that someone cared very much for them, and for the house as a whole. Hector rang the doorbell and a pleasant woman in a checkered apron opened the door. She reminded him of his wife with her open face and unsuspecting air. His nostrils also had the treat of being greeted by the smell of oranges.

"Can I help you?" she asked.

"I'm Hector Chavez, here to see Father Paul."

"Yes, Chief, I know who you are. You solved the murder of that poor Presbyterian minister last year. You did such a wonderful thing for that family. Won't you come in? Right this way." She led him to an agreeable room with a big black chair, a large wooden desk, a file cabinet, and plants festooning every possible surface. One wall had a copy of Rembrandt's famous painting of the homecoming of the prodigal son, with the son kneeling before a grace-filled older man with a long, white beard who was cradling his son's head. Off to one side, in the shadows, stood the elder brother, angry and scowling at this sweet scene. Hector had seen it before and always marveled at the grace, love, and forgiveness he witnessed in the painting.

Father Paul came into the room with a big smile and his arms open wide. "Hello, Chief," he said, giving Hector an uncomfortably vigorous hug. "To what do I owe this unexpected pleasure?"

Father Paul sat behind his big desk in the black chair, Hector looked around for somewhere to sit, and found a small chair across the room.

"I was appointed to attend to the safety of a small town, and in the space of two years time we've had four murders. This is more than I can handle, and frankly, I need all the help I can get."

"You certainly do get right to the point! I appreciate that. And I feel privileged that you thought to come to me for help." He leaned his head in his hands, his piercing blue eyes wide with interest and sympathy.

"I had no one else I could talk to. I don't know, Father, maybe this was a mistake; maybe I've taken up too much of your time." Hector stood to leave, his hat in his hand.

"No, no. I don't have anywhere I'd rather be. Please, please, sit. There's a good man. Now tell me all about it."

"It's the most frustrating thing, Father. All the evidence pointed to Mavis Belmont being the killer, and then she dies in a prison fire and we're still trying to figure that one out."

"Yes, I heard about that. Nasty business. What a way to die." Father Paul got up from around the desk and came to sit in an identical chair next to Hector's. "What can I do to help?"

"All this murder is starting to get to me. I'm confused, and feeling just a little bit guilty. I thought Mavis was the killer, and then she ends up dead. I'm just so frustrated by all this."

"I don't doubt that for a minute. You left the big city to get away from the stress, and it seems to follow you here. What are you doing to take care of yourself?"

"I go fishing with my son, when I can."

"That's a good start."

"And I'm here talking to you."

"And I'm glad for that. I'm glad you thought you could come to me."

"Did you know Lois Myers at all, Father?" The shift in focus was so abrupt, it seemed to surprise Father Paul for a moment, but then he seemed to recover.

"Please call me Paul. No, I didn't. This is a large parish, and I never got around to seeing everyone. She kept to herself and caused no trouble. Besides, she didn't get to mass that much. So, no, I didn't know her well."

"Is there someone here who might know about her movements, her activities?"

Father Paul wrote down the name of Jed Price, who was the deacon in charge of pastoral care. He told Hector that he worked at the Chevy dealership as a car salesman.

Hector cleared his throat. "It all seems just too easy, Paul. I'm stumped. I had settled on Mavis before I had really examined all the clues. Then she dies and Martin runs and the FBI tied up the investigation with a neat little bow, like a Christmas present or something. There's got to be something we're missing."

"You might want to check out Lois' neighbors. Your men interviewed them, but they might reveal something more that they didn't tell you the first time."

"I interviewed them myself, but that was right after the fire. After a couple of weeks, they might remember something more. Not a bad idea, Fa...er, Paul."

"But tell me this, Hector. Your suspect is dead and the FBI thinks they have their man. So officially, the case is closed. How long before it really is closed?"

"Like I said, I'm just feeling uneasy about how simple all this was. I'll check out the neighbors, probably talk to Angus once more, and then I'll feel better about moving on."

"Angus?" Paul's brow furrowed.

"Angus McPherson. His son's in the hospital with West Nile virus."

"Oh, yes, of course. How silly of me. How's his boy doing?"

"They say he'll be fine, that he's come through the worst of it."

"That's splendid! That was certainly a close call, wasn't it?"

"Well, it was touch and go for a while. Thanks for this, Paul. I'm feeling so much better."

"I'm glad to be of service. Come by any time."

AS SOON as I got home, I challenged Angie to a game of tennis. Neither one of us was any good. We mostly tried to see how many times we could get the ball over the net without faulting.

We came out here for the exercise, and to feel the cool breezes of early October. Being out here at all is a gift of the place where we live. They wouldn't dream of doing this in Scotland, where they can't dig themselves out of the snow until the end of May.

After the game, we returned home, showered, and started to fix dinner. We decided we were in the mood for omelets, and set about to get the eggs, cook the bacon, and toast some whole wheat bread.

I told Angie that I heard Michael say Lois' name while awakening from his drug-induced coma.

"That's shocking," she said with a worried look.

"That's exactly what I thought."

"What could it mean?"

"It could mean a couple of things. It might mean that he heard us talk about it and he's just now bringing it to mind, or that someone had visited him in hospital and told him about her."

"Either way, it's kind of strange that he would utter the name of a recently murdered person who was a stranger to him."

"I agree," I said, chopping onions.

AFTER DINNER, we went to see Michael at the hospital. He was awake, but not fully conscious. The nurse was changing an IV when we walked in the room.

"These must be your parents," said the nurse, who was heavyset with liquid brown eyes.

Michael struggled to smile as we came in. "Yes, Mom and Dad, this is Celia. She saved my life."

We shook hands with Celia and thanked her.

"He means I've been here for him."

I was startled by the sudden appearance of Jessica standing in the doorway. She was holding a cup of coffee in one hand and a bag in the other. Her face reddened as she spotted us.

"I just went to get some dinner; I'm famished." Jessica was a petite brunet. Her picture could appear in the dictionary under the word "perky." She put her offering on the bedside table and hugged us, long and hard.

I had only been thinking about how Michael's illness had affected Angie and me. I hadn't thought about what it would have done to Jessica. Maybe that's why we're not the only ones in the room, that life happens to other people, and a part of our job is to learn to care for everyone as though they're a part of us.

ONLY SIX people in the jail were "guests" of the county at the time of the fire. All six had been interviewed and, of course, no one knew anything about what had happened. But one of the guards had said that one of the most recent inmates, Dorothy Melon, had a passing acquaintance with fire in her past and may have known how to set something up that resulted in the fire that took Mavis' life.

Hector sat across from the heavyset woman whose one eyebrow stretched across the width of her broad, stern face.

"Dorothy, I suppose you know why you're here?"

"No, no, I don't, Slick. Why don't you tell me?"

Hector reminded her about the fire and the death of Mavis Belmont.

"I understand you have a history with fire," Hector remarked.

"So?" is all she said.

"So, I can charge you with murder and arson and destruction of government property and you'll do serious, hard time. This being Texas, we can probably seek the death penalty in this case."

"You're wasting your breath, Slick."

"We picked you up on C Street attempting to distribute at the elementary school. Personally, that's the same as murder in my book, but the state takes a much dimmer view of murder than it does intent to distribute. So, I could get you a deal if you're willing to talk."

"Like I said, Slick, I can't help you."

Without saying another word, Hector closed the folder he had in front of him and stood up. There was nothing he could do to make her cooperate. If she got closer to a murder wrap, it might open her mouth, but not now. Hector would have somebody follow up with interviews on the street. The only thing on his side now was time, but even that was slipping away. Dorothy had been sentenced to six months, and she'd already served three. Once she got back on the street, they would lose leverage with her, unless they harassed her into telling them what they needed to know. And even though he didn't like to, he wasn't above harassment if it led to the right result.

CHAPTER NINE: Something to Hide

MARTIN'S MOOD began to sour. Sure, he was stuck in a jail cell for the second time in his life, and he wore the orange jumpsuit that itched—not because of the fabric, but because somebody else had worn these clothes before him. He was peculiar that way.

He remembered those old prison movies where the inmates made a ruckus, scraping metal cups across the bars. Now they got plastic cups. He didn't want to cause trouble— he just wanted to get out. Then a thought struck him. In those same prison movies, there was always an escape. Elaborate planning and days of preparation usually resulted in escapees being caught in a swamp or being killed before they could make it to the wall. But maybe he'd be different; maybe he could do it. He certainly couldn't prove his innocence in here, especially with the legal representation they'd dug up for him. Actually, he'd be better off dead. He shuddered at the thought.

PSYCH WAS in the squad car out in front of the home of Lois' neighbor, Josh Manning. He was about to take one last sip of his mocha latte from McDonald's when he got a call on his cell phone. He dug furiously in his pocket to catch it before it went to voice mail, and in the process spilled his coffee on his uniform. Psych let loose with a string of profanity as he started his car to return home to get his other uniform. It was a good thing too because the call was from his wife of three years, Marcia.

"Marcia, you know I don't like you calling me at work," he snapped.

"I'm sorry, Sweetie, but I wanted to remind you about the diapers. We need them badly, and you know I can't get out."

Marcia had experienced a difficult pregnancy and was slow to recover. Psych apologized. He still worried about her and how she was adjusting to being a mother.

"I have to come home and get my other uniform," he said haltingly.

"Why?" She sounded surprised.

He told her what had happened and she laughed. Aside from the fact that it was her fault, it sounded pretty funny to him too, and he was able to breathe a little easier. Besides, it felt good to hear his wife laugh. It's something she hadn't done since the baby had arrived. He lived only a few blocks away from the station and he'd be back here before he knew it.

"DO YOU remember anyone coming to talk to you about Shoestring and what happened there?" It felt awkward, but I wanted to find out what Michael knew about the fire in Shoestring and how Lois died. I knew he was my son, but unconsciously he was a potential witness in a murder investigation. Besides, I had to know.

Angie's frown communicated all the anger I could

handle, but my need to know outweighed my fear of her disapproval.

"No, Dad, I don't remember a thing before they put me under. I remember seeing a couple of nurses and a doctor or two..."

"But did anyone ask you about Shoestring or Lois Myers' death? I mean someone had to plant the idea of 'Lois' in your mind in order for you to repeat it in your coma." The smoldering look from Angie erupted into a full-blown conflagration.

"Angus, really! He's not some suspect that must be interrogated. He's your son. Do you have to press him this way? He obviously doesn't know anything."

"Mom, it's okay." Michael reached out his hand to take Angie's. "I want to help in any way I can. If I said the woman's name, I'd like to know why myself."

Michael paused, and his smile faded as he turned his head toward me. "You know, Dad, I'm remembering the first time I heard her name—Lois, I mean—was from you. I remember all that stuff from Shoestring, the last time somebody got murdered there. Then when it happened again, maybe I got scared and that's why I said it as I was coming out of my coma."

I felt uneasy with this explanation, but was willing to live with it for now, if I knew what was good for me. The look Angie gave me now reminded me of looks I got from my mother when I confronted my father after he'd come home drunk once too often. You know, "If looks could kill..."

Michael's explanation certainly was plausible, if far too simple. I needed to let it go for now because I didn't have anything else to go on, and Angie was frustrated with me and worried about our son. I wanted to employ the tactic my dad used when he incurred the displeasure of my mother—leave. But since Angie and I had come in the same car, I couldn't leave her here, except Jessica could take...*No, be a man, Angus, and take your wife home.*

But even worse was waiting for her to prepare to leave Michael. Now that he was awake, she was glued to his bedside. We talked about plans for Thanksgiving and about when Michael and Jessica would get married—one of Angelica's favorite topics.

I HAD decided to meet Hector in Shoestring at the Golden Fork. I was beginning to obsess about these murders, as I had the first time, and I knew that was dangerous. But I couldn't help myself. Franny was covering the office well enough, and I was staying in touch with Sam, the troubled pastor in Cuero, by e-mail. I did miss a budget meeting, but I couldn't have added any wisdom to an already dismal picture. I told myself it was okay because I would be preaching in Shoestring this weekend.

"What'll it be?" asked Ruthie as she handed out menus. Hector ordered a cheeseburger and I the roast beef, mashed potatoes, and green beans. Ruthie came back with our drink orders, and Hector asked her a question.

"When Mavis came here the first time, Ruthie, what did you remember about her? You knew her from when she was a little girl, didn't you?"

"Yeah, I did. That was quite a shock."

"How do you mean?" asked Hector.

"Well, I was just surprised to see her after all those years."

"Did you remember anything about her dad that was unusual?"

"Just that he taught history in the high school. And that him and her would come here for breakfast every Saturday."

"Did you recall any rumors floating around about him back then? Did he ever talk about trouble in the family? Had you ever heard of Lois before she moved here?"

"Whoa, whoa there, Chief. I haven't worked here all my life. I was young once too, you know."

"Ruthie, what about when you saw her the first time when she came back?" I asked.

Ruthie's expression changed. "She seemed worried. Maybe it was about Lois. Maybe it was about getting caught. But she definitely was worried about something."

After that, Ruthie was off to wait on other customers. Hector looked at me with concern. "What's wrong, friend? You look like a cat dragged backward through a mouse hole."

Surprised to see how I was coming across, I took a quick inventory. Mavis was arrested for murder, and then murdered in her own jail cell. Her husband attempted to run and was caught in Nashville. My son contracted West Nile virus and mentioned the dead woman while awakening from a drug-induced coma. Also, I was feeling guilty about neglecting my work in favor of this sleuthing. What could possibly be wrong?

"It's nothing, Hector. Nothing at all," I said finally.

Hector took a sip of his coffee and then produced two photographs from his pocket. One was a picture of a charred clay sun with the verse from Rev. 8:8 on it. The other was a picture of the Celtic cross found in Lois' hand.

After a long silence, Hector said, "Martin's in custody

in Nashville. The FBI thinks they've wrapped up the case with his arrest. But last time I checked, following your wife to Shoestring is not a crime. The two pieces of evidence that don't fit Martin are this passage from scripture and this cross. Have you been able to come up with anything else that might shed light on what makes these important?"

Hector was beginning to take on my worried aspect. It was as if I were watching Hector disintegrate right before my eyes. I could not let that stand, but felt helpless to do anything about it.

"I have racked my brain for what they could possibly mean, but still the only two options are that either this is a message from Lois about the killer or a warning from the killer about what's to come."

"Is there anything else it could be?" asked Hector, urging me to think harder.

At that moment, Psych walked into the diner where he was silhouetted in the doorway by the sun behind him. He took off his cowboy hat, and the sun's rays danced all around him.

Psych sat down and his whole countenance fell. Both Hector and I noticed and exchanged troubled glances.

"What's wrong, amigo?" Hector asked, placing a hand on his shoulder.

Psych looked at both of us with deliberate solemnity.

"I went to interview Lois' neighbors again." He paused. "And one of them, fella by the name of Doug Able, said they saw Tom Branch carrying a gas can around Lois' house the day before the fire."

"Did you check it out with Branch?" asked Hector, his frown completely shadowing his face.

"Not yet. I knew you guys would be here, so I thought

I'd let you know before I did anything."

Hector's frustration grew into full-blown annoyance. "There could be a hundred explanations for it, on top of which the guy could be lying. Ever since that day, I didn't like that guy; besides, his hand was burned."

"Don't you remember, Chief? His story checked out. He said it was a stupid grilling accident. His wife verified."

"Psych, how long have you been a policeman? She could be lying to protect her husband, couldn't she?"

"Yes, Boss, she could, but I believed her. You always taught us to go by the book, but to pay attention to our gut. My gut said she was telling the truth."

"How pretty was she?" the Chief asked, smiling.

"She is pr..." Psych caught himself, smiling too. "But that has nothing to do with it."

"Anyway, we owe it to Lois to check out the neighbor's story. I'll take it from here, Psych. Thanks for following up."

"TOM, YOU just can't seem to stay out of trouble," Hector said, as he walked into the city manager's office. All of these offices were the same, never mind that this one had an oriental rug on the floor, indirect lighting, and a wet bar. Hector knew the mayor was jealous of that, which made for interesting if somewhat tense politics at City Hall.

Tom looked confused. He saw Hector smiling, but didn't think his words were very funny. "If you're joking, Hector, you have a strange way of showing it."

"Tom, it's just that I keep hearing stuff about you and in spite of my being an officer of the law, I find it hard to be impartial where you're concerned." The cadence of his comforting speech began to falter.

"What have you heard?" Tom asked sarcastically.

Hector sat down. The brown leather chair was soft and comfortable. He looked at the chair, running his hand over the armrest. *What is it about leather?* he thought.

"Hector?" Tom said again.

"Sorry, Tom. Psych went and checked out the site again, talking to neighbors. Somebody said they saw you with a gas can. What with the fire going on, you can see how everybody's jumpy about that."

"As it happens, Hector, I was mowing her lawn; I used her lawn mower."

"But why wouldn't somebody say that if they'd seen it?"

"I don't know, Hector. Maybe somebody's got something to hide."

"Maybe. And, by the way, your DNA matches what was found under Lois' fingernails."

CHAPTER 10: The Fifth Trumpet

MY HEAD hurt. I checked with Franny only to find out that the Cuero session voted to leave the denomination. The Presbytery had put in place a procedure to accomplish this with supposedly as little pain as possible. But as usual, if somebody wants to do something, nothing you can do will change that. I called the chair of the Pastoral Care Committee and told her to assign someone to be Sam's mentor through this ordeal. Then I called the stated clerk and asked her to get a discernment team together to walk Cuero through what they would need to do to leave the denomination. After that, I headed home. As Angelica probably wouldn't be home from school yet, I decided to go for a ride before she got back.

There's an appeal, something earthy yet somehow spiritual, about the smell of a stall of animals that you love. I've always considered the irony of God's making his entrance into this world in a manger, among animals that were usually slaughtered to feed people.

Dixie was glad to see me, playfully nudging me as I put a saddle on her. The air was crisp and brilliant as the fading sun hid behind the fir and oak trees that uncomfortably shared the pasture space. Nothing like a horseback ride to bring you back down to earth, keep you grounded, and refresh your spirit at the same time. I spotted nothing that even hinted of coyotes, and the ride itself was calm and uneventful. My whole body heaved a huge sigh, relieving any anxiety as I connected with an animal I loved while appreciating the gift of the land. The scenery here might not be as gorgeous as in Scotland, but for me today, this surely was God's country. As I was putting Dixie up, Angie pulled up in the drive.

"You're home early," she said after parking the car in the garage.

"Aye, I spent the day in Shoestring again, and ... oh, forget it."

Angie smiled and the sun was setting behind her. I couldn't decide which was more beautiful. "Come on," she prodded. "What's on your mind?"

"I just can't shake all the business in Shoestring. Why all of a sudden is that small town shrouded in death?"

She hugged me and we held each other for a few minutes. The silence filled with wonder, and I was once again the young man who intended to turn the world upside down.

"I see you went for a ride without me," she finally said, breaking the silence as she patted Dixie's head.

"I hope you don't mind, Love. I needed to clear my mind and get centered again. Nothing does that like being on the back of a horse. How was your day?"

"Maybe if I took my class horseback riding it would calm them down some. God knows I don't know what else to do."

"I'm sure you're doing just exactly what needs to be done."

It was as if awakening from a dream. The clouds parted just enough to let the dying sun shine through, throwing light all over the sky the way a third grader would splash color on a page with joyful abandon. I felt my smile fade and color drain from my face.

"Honey, what's wrong?" Angie frowned at me.

"'What needs to be done!'"

"What does that mean?"

"The killer is desperate. This is not an urge to kill for the sake of killing. This is killing with a purpose."

"Killing is killing. What purpose could he possibly have?" Angie's brow furrowed even more.

"It's in the Bible quote. He burned her because that's what he does, but he's also angry. But I think there's even more to it than that. His anger is global. I believe he wants the world to pay for whatever it did to him. That's the effect of the passage from Revelation. It's not just personal. He thinks whatever he's doing is going to have eternal significance. He's interested not just in affecting the lives of one or two poor souls. He wants the world to suffer."

"That's awful!" Angie's jaw dropped. "But there's no indication that something so large is even developing, let alone set in motion."

"What's worse, Love, is that I think the killer has a particular interest in me."

"Again?" Angie turned away and walked over into the shade of a live oak by the fence. "How can you be so sure?"

"Think about Michael."

"I do nothing but." Angie's face showed equal parts shock and worry. Her sparkling eyes darkened.

I smiled and crossed to her, and we embraced.

"Of course you do, Love. I think the fact that he contracted the West Nile virus is no accident."

"You mean someone gave it to him deliberately?"

"That's exactly what I mean."

"How?"

"Of course I don't know that. But the killer wanted us to suffer, so he went after the one thing we love more than anything."

"I guess what you're also saying is that it's someone who knows us, knows our son, obviously, and doesn't like us very much."

"It's not a question of like or dislike. He wants us out of the way so that he can fulfill his larger purpose."

"Larger purpose? What on earth could that be?"

"I am afraid we may soon find out."

"HOW MUCH vacation do I have coming?"

"Boss, you know you've got all the vacation days you want," Franny said, with her hands on her hips.

"I just wanted to hear you say it," I replied. "Could you book a flight for two to Scotland?"

"Scotland? That's rather sudden, isn't it? This is the first I've heard of this."

"Yes, I know. But it can't be helped. The investigation requires it. We believe Scotland holds the key to several pieces of this puzzle."

"When are you going?"

"In a couple of weeks."

"That's right before Thanksgiving. The prices will be through the roof."

"Yes, I know. But this time, it can't be helped. It's the only time I can get away, and we need answers we can only find in Scotland. Now, will you please book a flight for two to Scotland?"

"You're the boss. Do you think you need to clear it with the Council?"

"Of course, of course. And get Sam on the phone for me while you're at it."

THAT NIGHT, Angie and I talked about our trip. We would take it in a couple of weeks. We'd fly to London then take a train to Edinburgh and take a car to the university. There, we'd meet with the eminent entomologist Professor Gou about the insect theory, as well as look into the origins of the Celtic cross. Michael was on the mend and we felt that he was in capable hands. Even though I knew we needed to go to Scotland, I dreaded the trip. My life there was filled with such pain, and I wasn't sure I could take it.

We decided to drive out to Shoestring for a Sunday service. I needed to connect with the place that had so recently turned my world upside down for the second time in two years. That night, I woke with a start. Angie was shaking me, gently calling my name.

"Angus, wake up."

"Wha...how...huh?"

"Amour, you've had a dream. You were calling for Rex...you wanted to go riding..."

The cobwebs were clearing from my mind. "I was being chased by giant insects. They were catching up to me. All I had was my family crest and Rex. I couldn't get him saddled quickly enough, so I jumped on him bareback. One of the insects grabbed the crest and devoured it. It was frightening."

"Are you sure you want to go to Scotland? It's bound to dredge up a lot of painful stuff for you."

"This isn't about Scotland! It's about the end of the world."

"You mean your world, don't you?"

"I suppose so."

THE NEXT Sunday, we went to church in Shoestring where all the usual suspects were gathered. The first to greet us was Paula Snodgrass.

"Oh, Reverend, it's so good of you to come back to see us. After Pastor Pete died, you know, I was devastated. I've had a chance to reflect on that, and I'm in a much better place. I see his widow, Connie, and we're becoming..."

She went on chattering about how much better things have been this past year. It made me appreciate the distance I have from such banality in my isolated office in Austin. What was I thinking that I wanted to pastor this church? More importantly, what was God thinking?

I didn't see the associate, Beth McKinley, until the service started and she greeted all of us and opened with announcements. Then Beth spotted me, her face lit up, and I knew what was coming next. She introduced me and invited me up to say a few words.

I could feel my face flush as I rose to accept her invitation. The place erupted into applause. Now I was not only embarrassed, but surprised. I had forgotten how much of myself I gave to this church last year when they lost their pastor so cruelly. I had forgotten how much this church had meant to me as Hector and I searched for Pastor Pete's killer. It seems they hadn't forgotten. And I was grateful. When I reached Beth, she asked me to introduce Angelica. When she stood, there were new waves of applause, and we lapped them up like thirsty travelers, fresh from the desert.

"Your affection for Angelica and me is wonderful and deeply appreciated," I said. "What we went through together, only a few communities would really understand, thank God. That your town is again visited by the dark shadow of 'mysterious death' is too much to bear, and my heart goes out to you. I say again to you what I said last year. I will not rest until the persons responsible for this are brought to justice."

The congregation sprang to its feet and thundered with applause once again as I took my seat with Angie. After the service, as we were shaking hands, Tom Branch made his way over to us and gave us a hug.

"So you decided to go slumming today, I see," he said, extending an oily hand.

"Why, Tom, what do you mean?"

"You know what I mean. Say, I'd like to have lunch with you sometime this week. I've got some information you might find useful."

"Have you shared it with Chief Chavez?"

"He wouldn't know what to do with what I've got."

We agreed to meet Wednesday for lunch.

On our way home, we started planning the trip to Scotland. We decided we would visit Edinburgh and Glasgow, my home town of Dumfries, and be home before Thanksgiving, but we would have to have it at one of the other boys' house. We acknowledged that we were going during the coldest part of the year, but it couldn't be helped, had to be done, and speed was necessary. We also talked about getting all new cold weather gear for the adventure in the frozen north.

I was feeling a mixture of dread and excitement. I was excited to go back home, to see all the familiar places. I was looking forward to discovering any new clues about the current case. What I dreaded was the traveling. Once I'd come to Texas and settled here—I considered myself home. And home I would stay. Angie got me out of my Lazy Boy to visit her parents on occasion, but other than that, I only traveled for work, but usually preferred to stay home. And we were going at the exact wrong time of year. But if justice were to be done, I would have to take one for the team and just be a good soldier and go.

I phoned Hector and told him about our plans. I would see him after lunch on Wednesday and let him know when we'd be in Scotland and why. When he heard I was having lunch with Tom, all he said was to be careful. I wanted to ask him what he meant, but I was in hurry, as usual.

WEDNESDAY FINALLY came and I headed to Shoestring after letting Franny know where I'd be. I didn't know what Tom Branch had in mind, but I've learned never to be surprised.

I met him in his office and he suggested the country club, and I didn't object. If I was going to do a difficult thing, better to do it over good food.

Tom looked nervous as we placed our orders and settled in with chit-chat. The weather had turned cold, which was always a topic of conversation in Texas, because it so rarely happened.

When our drinks and salads arrived, I could tell Tom was very agitated.

"Tom, what is it?" I asked with genuine concern.

"I know why Lois died," Tom blurted out, his face flushed with color.

"This is something you should be speaking to Hector about. There's nothing..."

"Will you stop that? I'm here now with you. There's very little time left. We have to act."

The waitress came with our orders, two steaks and a baked potato with all the trimmings—which passes for fine dining in the States. When she'd left, I leaned into Tom.

"What do you mean, 'little time left'?"

"I mean the prophecy in Revelation 9. The fifth angel blew the trumpet and locusts riding horses and wearing armor would devastate the land. They wouldn't harm the grass or trees, only those who weren't faithful."

"Oh, Tom, you're talking nonsense!"

"Well, you see, I thought a minister would understand."

"Understand what?" I replied a little more loudly than I intended, and people began to look in our direction.

"The end of the world, Reverend. The end of the world." His eyes grew dark as he averted his gaze from me to the floor.

"When? What? Why?" I sputtered.

"Calm down, Reverend. All will be revealed. All will be revealed."

"Do you know something about Lois' death? If you do, you must tell me or Hector, and do it soon."

"I was putting away the lawn mower at her house one evening. It was the night before the fire. That night, I had decided was the last time I would mow her lawn. It was hard enough to mow mine. Anyways–I was putting away the mower and I saw someone in a plaid shirt and blue jeans. He ran when he saw me, and I didn't get a good look at his face.

"I told Lois about the guy, and she got real nervous. She said she may have seen something she shouldn't have. She didn't tell me much, only that she was worried. Then she said something that really spooked me. She said 'It all will burn.' I asked her what she meant, but she just repeated, 'It all will burn.'"

I called Hector later and told him about my strange lunch with Tom Branch. Hector informed me of the toxic nature of politics at City Hall and that Tom's wife was leaving him. He suggested Tom might just be suffering from stress. I assured him that I hoped that was the extent of it, but that Tom might need some mental health help. Hector agreed to look into it and wished Angie and me a good trip.

CHAPTER 11: Flight of the Phoenix

I HATED TO FLY. It had something to do with being high up, without any net. But it's more about the lack of control and trusting someone else to know what to do in case of an emergency. I've heard flying described as hours of boredom, punctuated by a few moments of sheer terror. During these moments, I'd like to be in charge. That I'm not is a matter of faith. Coming from a man of faith, I know this is a mark against me.

We had already conferred with Michael and his doctors. Jessica was now in full charge of his care. He would be home soon, anticipating a full recovery. We could leave, resting easy in the knowledge that the worst was behind him, and he would return to full health.

According to Angie's research, it was cheaper to fly into London Heathrow and take a train to Edinburgh, so that was the plan. The plane's takeoff was delayed, which added to my anxiety. However, Angie's patient presence proved extremely reassuring. Once airborne, the pilot reaffirmed the fact that although we'd gotten off late, we would make it up once we reached altitude. I couldn't help wondering what he meant. Would he be going faster than normal? Would the plane fall apart? Of course, I knew I was being ridiculous, but I couldn't help myself.

We changed planes in New York for the flight across the pond. I couldn't help thinking of cattle being led down chutes in the slaughterhouse. I didn't care to hear about flying being the safest form of travel available. For some reason, I thought of that great movie with Jimmy Stewart, *The Flight of the Phoenix.* A group of World War II soldiers crash land in the desert, and they escape by building another plane out of the wreckage of the old one.

Once we landed in London, we were herded about with fellow passengers and found a link to the train. Rushing to make our connection, we lugged our bulging suitcases on board only to find standing room on the train was enough to fray the nerves of the sanest of travelers. Once the train reached the London station, the crowd had thinned enough for us to sit down. We decided not to stop in London, but to head straight for Edinburgh.

The train headed through lovely market towns and passed sheep farms before stopping at York, where the spires of York Minster Cathedral were visible from the train. What assaulted my memory as we passed from town to town was the lush, deep green of the place; the Emerald Isle of Ireland had nothing on this verdant land. Later, we passed Berwick on Tweed and caught glimpses of the North Sea and the craggy coastline dotted with black-faced sheep as we climbed higher and higher into the border territory of Scotland.

When we arrived in Edinburgh, with its dark, gray stone buildings, it was as if I'd been transported back in time. I was twenty years old again. My parents dead, my past a blur, I was heading to a new life and a new adventure. Having completed my schooling here, my next stop was America. I was leaving my past behind. I shuddered at the memory. I realized this was going to be harder than I thought. It was my first time back since I'd left all those years ago. I could see my aunt, her disheveled red hair bobbing as she waved goodbye. If I was here to catch a killer, how could I operate when haunted by a past I thought I'd left behind?

We found a beat-up yellow cab with fringe on the dashboard, driven by an Indian man dressed in a red-checkered coat and turban, and incense wafting from the open ashtray, which was quite pleasant under the chaotic conditions of travel. It was a wild ride through the rainy streets of Edinburgh until we stopped in front of a modest hostel. We paid the man and took our luggage up the stone steps.

Edinburgh is a dark city, filled with ancient walls and murky gray buildings. The city lies between two castles on either side of town. It was an excellent place to begin our journey because the town matched my mood, dark and brooding.

Once we reached our room, which was modest but clean, I had an overwhelming urge to sleep, but if I were to get my body back in rhythm, I knew I had to resist and fight through the fatigue. Since it was too late to make our inquiries, we decided to take a walk. Angie was eating this up. She had never been out of the States. She seemed to have energy to burn while I was dragging seriously.

This was an unfamiliar part of town. We got out Angie's umbrella and walked arm in arm. Her smile now was as innocent as a schoolgirl's. It was the most genuine contentment I had seen in her in some time and I relished it; it eased the tension I felt as I dreaded going back to my old haunts.

After our walk, we decided to stop at a corner pub. The food was Italian, and the waiter was a comedian, playing up to the tourists. Filled with spaghetti and Chianti, our walk home was through emerald lights. These next few days would be trying and difficult. But for now, we were in heaven.

I awoke refreshed and revived. Angie and I spent the morning consulting our maps and planning our day. First stop was the University of Edinburgh and Professor Gou. After that, we would seek out more information about the original Celtic cross. We finished our proper Scottish breakfast, heavy with beans and sausage, and set off for the bus ride.

Set in the middle of Edinburgh, the University was an imposing array of turreted and steepled buildings constructed of gray and yellow stone. Some gothic, some more modern, all were dour and serious. We found the science hall and looked on the directory for Professor Gou's office. We were told that classes were on holiday, but that he would be in his office alone.

We knocked on his door and the sound within came to us like the voice of Scrooge's Ghost of Christmas Present. We opened the door and the effect was complete. Gou had huge mutton-chop sideburns and bushy white hair. The walls were covered with every type of bug from moths and butterflies to more exotic types, all in glass cases, all coded and classified. His desk was piled high with books and papers, and he himself seemed to be the happiest man on earth.

"What can I do for ye?" he asked, looking down his nose through the small pair of glasses perched on the end of his nose.

We introduced ourselves. "Thanks for agreeing to meet with us," I said. "We're here to test out a theory about a situation we have back in the States."

"What's your theory?"

"The first theory," said Angie, stepping forward, "is that the Druids were wiped out inadvertently by an insect eradication."

"I've heard that theory, Mrs. McPherson, and I'm not saying I agree or disagree. I just don't know. No one does. Blackburn, the fellow who put forward the Druid theory, was a bit off the beam anyway."

"Are you saying he was mentally unstable?"

"You didn't hear that from me," he said, putting his index finger against his nose. "But you know how rumors fly in the scientific community."

Professor Gou scratched his sideburn. The way he scratched like a dog made me wonder about the order of the brain of the man before me. However, we pressed on.

"The second part of our inquiry is that we suspect something like the Druid scenario may be in the works, only on a much vaster scale, with more dreadful consequences."

"Please explain," said Gou. His face darkened as he leaned into me, staring intently.

"We think someone is planning to bring about the end of the world by getting rid of all the insects."

William Gou leaned back and roared with laughter. Angie and I looked at each other before I replied. "We're quite serious, sir. We have reason to believe that such a scenario is not only plausible but likely, given what we know. You are familiar with Jonas Salk's quote about if the world were rid of insects, then life as we know it would end, but get rid of humanity and the world would flourish?"

"Yes, I've read the quote before. Don't think I hadn't thought about putting the theory to the test, but that's all it is, a theory. Besides, Salk wasn't an entomologist and was speaking on something of which he knew very little."

"Be that as it may." Angie stepped forward, looking with puzzlement from me to Professor Gou, "We need to know how such a thing could be possible, and if it were instigated, what could be done to arrest it?"

"No! No, it's out of the question. Nothing like that would work, and therefore, I wouldn't begin to know how to stop it. I've heard about the Druid die-off theory, which I dismissed as so much nonsense."

"You mean we've come all this way for nothing?" I looked at Angie, then back to Professor Gou. "Could such a thing, the Druid die-off, be replicated in an experiment?"

"Well, you'd have to have just the right conditions. The wood, the heat of the fire, even the weather may have been a factor."

"The weather?" asked Angie.

"Surely. Suppose the weather was cold at that time, which is a safe assumption. The temperature of the air mixed with the temperature of the fire had to come together perfectly to effect a die-off of the magnitude you're suggesting."

"I understand, from when I Googled your name, that you did a visiting professorship at the University of Texas a few years back," I said.

"Yes, yes. I really enjoyed myself. I can see why you settled there. It reminded me very much of my home."

I looked at Angelica for a long moment. The silence exuded a sweet fragrance that touched our time together with grace. "That's exactly how I felt."

"And I found my colleagues intellectually stimulating and the students extremely curious."

"Was there anyone who stood out from the rest? It could be important?" I asked.

"Why do you ask?"

"Someone is dead. In fact, two people are dead, and we have reason to believe it all goes back to insects. Actually, it's much deeper than that, much more twisted. But that's where it starts, we think."

"It all sounds so mysterious and exciting." Professor Gou rubbed his hands together.

"And deadly," Angie interjected. Her face darkened. I hated to see that happen to such a bright light. I saw that same look in the hospital while we prayed for Michael's recovery.

Professor Gou looked intently at Angie. "Cheer up, Lass. We'll find out whoever's doing this and stop them before they can kill again."

"Was there anyone remarkable that stood out: a student perhaps?"

The silence slipped through the air like a slow-motion swing and miss, followed by a furious exhalation of air. "There were several chaps who clamored for my attention. You know, it's all so competitive in the States. I don't know how they can make the study of insects competitive, but they managed it quite nicely.

"I remember one young man. He stood out because he was rather tall. It's interesting that most of the entomologists I know are short in stature. So I noticed him. He was fascinated with mosquitoes and bees mostly. I vaguely remember us discussing the Druid theory, but I can't be sure."

"Do you remember where he was from?" asked Angelica.

"Lass, that was probably twenty years ago at least." Professor Gou smiled at her.

"I know, Professor." I straightened up. "You've been very helpful. We're staying at a little hostel near here. If you think of anything else, could you perhaps contact us?"

"Are you referring to the Embassy Arms Hostel?"

"The very same."

"I know it well. In fact, I'm about to have lunch. May I drop you back there on my way?"

"We aren't going back. We were going to have lunch as well and then head over to Whithorn to see one of the oldest—'

"Celtic crosses!"

"You kn—"

"Know it, Laddie! Besides insects and my wife, they are the passion of my life; she and I both have studied and visited all the most ancient ones in Scotland."

"The only thing is it's quite a distance from here. If we drove, we wouldn't get there until late evening. I suggest we get an early start so that we can be fresh."

We?" I asked, raising one eyebrow.

"Certainly! You need someone to guide you. Whatever it is you want to know about the Celtic cross, I can help you. Does it have anything to do with these murders?" Professor Gou looked from me to Angie and back again with wide eyes and an expression of pure delight mixed with concern and sympathy.

"We think so, yes," I said.

"I will meet you tomorrow at the Embassy Arms at 7:00 a.m. You'd best pack an overnight bag because we're going to have to spend the night."

"Actually, we hadn't thought that far ahead." I shook my head. "We were lucky to get here in one piece."

"And it's just my luck that you did! And to ease your mind, the trip is on me."

"Oh, we couldn't do that! Besides, don't you have classes tomorrow?"

"Dear boy, that's why we have graduate assistants; besides, we're on our holiday break. So, I'll see you bright and early in the morning. I must go home now and prepare."

He shook my hand and hugged Angie a little too tightly, but he meant well. We left lighter than we had come, and more hopeful than ever.

Aside from preparing for the trip tomorrow, one other task remained for our afternoon. That was to visit my boyhood home.

CHAPTER 12: Misguided Lust

HECTOR CLEARLY didn't know what to do. Tom Branch was becoming unstable. He could not be serious about all that "end of the world" stuff. He had asked Tom about his DNA being under Lois' fingernails. He said that she was talking to him about her lawn; she fell and Tom reached out to prevent her fall. That's how she scratched him. Hector decided to take that at face value, but now he needed another kind of help. He thought about Father Paul, and how helpful he was during the last series of murders that stirred Shoestring. Hector decided he needed to pay another visit to the priest.

He met Father Paul in his office. It looked very similar to his own, except without the largemouth bass hanging on his wall. Hector also did not have the colors of the rainbow streaming through a stained-glass window. He thought about how distracting that must be to serious, sustained thought; then again, he was not that religious and did not know what motivated the truly devout.

Actually, that was not quite true. He knew they were under orders just like he was; that Father Paul was interested in seeing justice done the same as he; and that most of all, he would do anything to see that the oppressed were treated fairly.

The same painting dominated the room, *The Return of the Prodigal* by Rembrandt, and he could not take his eyes off it. As Father Paul greeted him, inviting him to sit down, Paul noticed Hector admiring the painting.

"It's either 'The prodigal son,' or 'the Return of the Prodigal Son,' depending on who you read. Do you like it?"

"Oh, yes, definitely, I would say it's very powerful."

"And I would say you're very astute. Of course you know the story, don't you?"

Hector nodded, hesitating.

"This boy..." Paul pointed to the kneeling figure, "this boy asked for his inheritance *before* his father was dead, saying, in effect, 'You are dead to me.' The old man agrees, which is amazing in itself, and of course the young son wastes his life, and all his money. He is penniless and stuck with nothing but pig food to eat. Then scripture says, he 'came to himself' and decides to return to his father and ask to be made a slave. But the father surprises the boy by throwing this great party for him."

"And the oldest son was none too happy about that!" Hector beamed a childish grin.

"That's right, and it means that both God's mercy is boundless and that our judgmental attitudes know no bounds either."

Hector cleared his throat and after a pause, decided he needed to proceed.

"Father—"

"Hector, please call me Paul."

"Paul, thank you, Fa—" Hector stammered, "I want you to tell me if you know Tom Branch?"

"Yes, yes, I do."

"Have you had any occasion to talk to him recently?"

"Well, no. He's not one of my flock and I don't have much occasion to run into him in my daily rounds."

"That's fine. It's just that he's been acting strange lately, and I was wondering if I could ask your advice about how to handle this?"

"What's he been doing?"

"He's been talking about the end of the world, quoting Revelation and generally scaring me to death."

"I can see how upsetting that might be, but you'd probably do better talking to his doctor, or to him, not to the local Catholic priest."

"Yes, sir, you're right. I was just hoping maybe a fresh set of eyes might help me see the situation differently, or give me a better path to follow."

"I see." The priest's smile vanished, his mood darkened. "I'm not a psychologist," he said after some time. "But the end-of-the-world enthusiasts come in all shapes and sizes. Some think they're doing God's will, while others simply want to make sense of an often senseless world by bringing order and an ending to the chaos and pain. A third group, and these are the most dangerous, are so angry, so rabid in their rage that they want to see the whole mess end just to satisfy their misguided lust for justice and to end their own pain. I don't know if that helps you, Chief, but that's my take, just off the top of my head."

As Hector was about to leave, he remembered something and turned back to the tall priest. "One more thing, Reverend, the Bible quote, from Revelation—Rev. 8:8."

"'The second angel blew his trumpet and something like a great mountain, burning with fire, was thrown into the sea.'" The priest quoted the scripture, looking up the entire time.

"So you know it."

"Yes, my people have an unhealthy curiosity about the end times, so I teach this book a lot. It draws big crowds. Everyone wants to know how this whole thing will end."

"No doubt, no doubt," Hector scratched his head. "But what do you make of it appearing in Lois' hand as she lay there dying?"

"Come to think of it, she was one of those who had an insatiable curiosity about the end. Every time we offered a study of that book, she was there. It seemed she couldn't get enough."

"It's curious, don't you think, that she had this verse with her, and then she died in a fire?"

"Are you saying this might be suicide? What a way to go."

"Yes ... indeed; suicide or murder." Hector put on his hat, thanked the Father, and left.

CHAPTER THIRTEEN: The Prodigal Returns

FOR SOME reason, I was reluctant to go back home. My only cousin remained. Certainly it would be good to see her, but other than that, most of my memories of the place are full of pain and plenty of anger.

We boarded the train at the central station for the short ride to Dumfries. The look on the faces of the people on the train were worn, almost frightened. Did they know something I did not? Was there an impending doom I knew nothing about? Or was it the universe telling me I could not go back home, that only disaster and misery awaited me as I alighted from the train? I looked over at Angie, who was drinking in the countryside as we hurried toward our destination. I'm sure she had never seen such a green terrain as this, emerald against the low, gray clouds.

She was the dark beauty at the center of my soul. Watching her made me calmer and more hopeful. Maybe I needed to see my home through her eyes and not trust mine as much, at least at first.

We arrived at the station at Xenquiar, a few miles from Dumfries and the site of the mines where my father once worked. The chaos and noise were disconcerting. But the first thing I noticed was a familiar sight, the first unpleasant memory I'd had to confront on my trip back home: the low hanging cloud of soot that clung to everything and everyone. Even the taste of the air was bitter and rotten. We stepped out into the air at Xenquiar during the brief stop, and then we proceeded on toward Dumfries.

Humans are extremely adaptive. We can get used to nearly everything. That's the only reason these thousands of people continued to choose to live here—that and the fact that the coal company paid them to do the company's dirty work.

We continued on into Dumfries. When we descended from the train, we collided with the rush of bodies getting to where they needed to be, and cabbies vied with vigor for our attention. We only had a few hours before we had to get back, but I decided we would walk around first in order to get our bearings and to figure out what to do. It was close to lunch time, and we looked for a place that showed some promise for good food. As much as I loved my homeland, Scotland and good food were usually not uttered in the same sentence.

We found a pub called the Globe Inn, and settled into its dark and welcoming interior. This was the pub where Robert Burns, the author, spent many happy hours. A song about his true love was written above the philosopher's chair in which he often sat. I quoted the song to Angie, and those around us toasted to our love. We ordered haggis, and I fairly drank in the smells and the taste. There is, of course, nothing like it in the States, and neither Angie nor I would know the first thing about how to make it.

Near the Globe Inn is a mural of Dumfries' other favorite son, Robert the Bruce. He was famous for the battles he won in the fourteenth century for Scottish independence and for the murder of a rival for the throne. He later sought and received forgiveness for this act from the church; back when everyone cared what the church thought.

After lunch, we lingered awhile in the warm womb of the pub. At that moment, I was transported to another time. My memory came rushing toward me with the force of a raging river. I had been in this place many times as a lad. I remember pleading with my dad more than a dozen times to leave this place and come home. I stood up like a rocket and told Angie we were leaving. She was confused and slow to respond. I started to leave, but she caught up with me.

She grabbed me by the arm and swung me around to face her. "Angus, what is it?" she asked, her eyes drawn up in worry. I told her of the realization assaulting my senses. Then I said, "I told you this was a bad idea."

"Nonsense," she replied. She ordered two more pints and persuaded me to join her back where we were sitting. We took our time. Mostly I was silent, and Angie waited patiently for the story to unfold. I told her about how when the mines closed here, Dad was laid off. That's when he started drinking. He tried to find other work, but he didn't know anything but mining. By then, drink had a firm grip on him, and never let go. He eventually found work in the next town over, Xenquiar, which required a train ride, and occasionally a night's stay in some seedy motel. But the best of my dad had been stolen by his unrelenting love affair with booze.

In those days we could not afford much of a place to live, but it was home. We lived above a bakery, but now it was a travel agency. A Tudor-style building in white stucco and dark brown crisscrossing beams stood in the middle of the block just a half mile from the Globe Inn pub.

Memories inundated my consciousness. I closed my

eyes tight; saw my father yelling at Ma, his face still black from coal dust. But I also saw us in happier times, like when Dad brought a puppy home, and how we named him by placing names on slips of paper and the first one he stepped on was his name. The first name he stepped on was "Scotty," the name I wrote down.

After a few minutes, I came back to myself. I noticed that the house hadn't changed much since I left it.

I saw Angie looking at me with concern etched in her eyes. "Mi hijo? Are you all right?" she asked, touching my arm.

"Yes, Love, I'm fine. I just had a wave of memories about Dad's abuse, but I have many happy memories as well."

"Of course you did. And although I know you've done it many times before, maybe this is another chance to forgive your parents and perhaps yourself for the past."

I looked deeply into Angie's red-rimmed hazel eyes and hugged her as if my life depended on it. I never even saw the people passing by on the sidewalk. I took a couple of deep breaths and turned to take a look at the street where I had lived until I left for the States all those years ago.

Towering over all the houses and the shops that dotted the ancient streets on this side of town was the steeple of the Kirk of Scotland I had attended as a boy. We wended our way to it and stopped outside the red brick edifice with its white trim and a bronze steeple.

I didn't want to go in, even at Angie's urging. I was a lost boy in a vast ocean without a life preserver. I remembered my call to ministry, which occurred during the funeral of a young pastor who had lost his life in one of the worst mining accidents in the twentieth century. He'd gone down into the mines to support those who were in his parish and he paid with his life. That kind of courage and compassion was something I aspired to. This too was a battleground for my parents. Mom knew I was a very spiritual child and wanted me to explore ministry for a profession. Dad knew that the church was a magnet for hypocrites and couldn't stomach a son of his associating with the likes of them.

This was also where Robbie Burns was buried, and we paid our respects to his memory and to all that was beautiful and holy in the land of my birth.

I suddenly felt much better, like I wanted to go on, like I could discover and focus on the puzzle set before us. It was after 4:00 p.m. and our train left at 5:10, so we decided to head back. We couldn't find a taxi and decided to walk the few blocks to the train station. We sat on the train until it was ready to leave and rode back in silence.

PROFESSOR GOU met us in the lobby of our hostel at 7:00 a.m. the next day. While we looked a bit worn out with eyes at half-mast, he was wide-eyed and full of energy.

"Good morning, Laddies!" he practically shouted. "Have you had breakfast? No time right now; we must be off. We'll get something on the way."

The mistress of the hostel said there was no need to stop on the way. There was an assortment of breakfast breads and coffee in the common room. We took advantage of the offer and each took a coffee and pastry as sustenance for the journey ahead.

The first part of the trip was made in silence. I was still trying to process yesterday afternoon. I had not wanted to go back home, but was glad I did. The range of emotions I'd experienced astounded me.

"I have a confession to make," Professor Gou confided, leaning across the train sofa as we trundled toward our destination. Angie and I looked at each other in wonder and disbelief. "I wasn't entirely honest with you back there. I had heard of the Druid insect die-off theory and how the end of the world would come from the extinction of all the insects. In fact, I'm fairly certain, I lectured about both those theories while I was in the States."

"But why..." I stammered.

"Prying ears, dear boy, prying ears," he said with a wink. "That's one of the reasons I came on this little jaunt. I wanted to give you a clearer picture of what I know. The University wants all its professors to tow the orthodox line. They don't want any theories which stretch the imagination. Here we can speak freely."

The countryside was again soothing and invigorating. Eventually, the three of us began to chat about Scotland, the cold weather, and the search for the Celtic cross. I didn't know what we'd find, and that made the search all the more exciting, if somewhat frustrating.

The trip to Whithorn was filled with tales of Scottish lore, and Professor Gou even knew about the Civil War in the States and the role the Scots played in it. He made a rather convincing argument that it was the Scots who started the Civil War because they had come to the new country seeking freedom from British rule, and their dander was up when Lincoln had to revamp their whole economy around the idea of freed men, rather than the slave culture.

Whithorn was very much like Dumfries—green and picturesque. St. Giles Church exuded age and a long-forgotten grandeur. I could see why these old churchyards gave rise to ghost stories and superstitions. The cemetery next to it was as old and unkempt as the church. We found a caretaker next door, and he directed us to the Ruthwell Cross. It was in the back of the cemetery by an ancient stone wall. We headed up the uncertain stone steps, taking several turns to reach the top.

The cross we had been looking for was located at the top of the hill. Sixteen feet high, it stood with only a round circle of granite left to indicate what type of cross it was. At its base was a plaque which described it as it must have looked when it was first erected over 2,500 years ago.

Professor Gou took out his camera and started taking pictures. He snapped photos of the cross itself and the artist's rendition of what it looked like originally. I was glad he was taking pictures because I couldn't be sure what I was seeing. In the twilight of early morning, shadows became form and form became shadows. While it would be equally hard to tell them apart in a photo, later, with study, perhaps we could ascertain more about what we were seeing.

Professor Gou pulled me over to see the depiction of the cross at its base. "These cross pieces and the circle," he said, "were aids in navigation for the Druids."

I nodded, even though I already knew that.

"And the snakes represent fertility for the Druids, but sinfulness for Christians," I said.

"Not sinfulness, Reverend, temptation. There's a difference." We smiled at each other.

Then Professor Gou did a double take. He bent down to the plaque, lifted his glasses, and squinted. "Look here, Laddie," he said, tapping his finger on the bronze plaque.

Angie and I came over and bent down to look where he was pointing. All I saw was a word that I did not recognize.

"What do you see?" he asked, ever the teacher.

123

"It looks like 'golack,' if that's what you mean."

"Aye, Laddie, it is. Have you ever seen that word before?"

"No, never."

"Well, now," Gou said with a smile while straightening up to his full height, "I laughed at you when you first told me your suspicions about the end of the world coming from the eradication of all insects."

"I remember that," said Angie with a frown.

"I do too." I smirked.

"Well, that word, 'Golack' is Gaelic for insect."

"Really?" I said, eyes wide.

"Yes, indeed," he repeated. "Now, I'm not an expert in the language, but I know someone back at the University who is. Maybe he can tell us what the rest of the inscription says."

"Well done. It seems this has been a very good day," I said, hopeful.

THE PHONE rang with an insistent, shrill tone. We had made it back to our lodging in the early morning hours. Professor Gou had assured us we would hear from him the next day about what message the cross inscription had for us. I stumbled for the phone on the other side of the bed.

"Yes," I whispered.

"Good morning, Laddie!" trumpeted Professor Gou.

"Dear Professor, we're still asleep."

"Sleep...Sleep is for the uninformed. Life is short, Laddie; life is short."

"So you haven't been to sleep yet?"

"Oh, no. I've contacted that friend of mine, the Gaelic expert."

"Yes?" I said, rubbing sleep from my eyes.

"He says it's some sort of recipe."

"Recipe?"

"Do you have a parrot, or what? Yes, a recipe."

"What sort of recipe?"

"It appears to be for reintroducing insects into the ecosystem."

"Excuse me?"

"That's what I said when he told me."

"How would Druids know what to do in such a circumstance?"

"Apparently, they were intelligent enough to figure out how it happened in the first place, and they tried to reverse the process but just ran out of time."

"So Salk was right? Once the insects go, humans aren't far behind."

"Apparently so."

"Do you think it would work?" I asked.

"We have no way of knowing without running some experiments. It might be as complicated as reprogramming and engineering their DNA."

"What's the easy way?" I inquired.

"Introducing some gestating hermaphrodites and letting nature take its course."

"That's the easy way?" I asked in disbelief.

We agreed to meet for breakfast in a couple of hours to go over what he'd found and what it meant for our investigation. When we came down, Professor Gou had already ordered and was drinking tea, happily flirting with the waitress.

"Aye, Lad and Lass," he boomed as the entire breakfast room turned in his direction. He stood and held out a chair for Angie as we both sat down.

"A great day to be alive, eh, Laddies?"

"Aye, indeed it is," I said, as I poured coffee for us both from the carafe on the table.

Our host came and took our orders as Professor Gou showed us the translation his friend had worked out last night.

"It's basically just the smoke from a particular tree. Actually, my friend had an intriguing theory. Instead of just the tree's bark, it could also have involved tree sap."

Angelica's brow creased and her eyes darkened. She looked at me with an intense gaze.

"I appreciate the fact that the Druids hastened their own demise by burning a certain kind of tree that eliminated insects from that region; all that is fascinating. But what does that have to do with Lois burning up in her own house, and Mavis dying in a prison cell inferno?" asked Angie.

"Well," I sighed, "it continued with Michael getting the West Nile virus. Since he was nowhere near the range of those mosquitoes and he hadn't been outside much prior to his infection, I thought it had to be deliberate. I told you or Hector at the time that I didn't know how it was done, but that I thought it had to be premeditated and done purposefully."

"But how do you get from that to ridding the world of insects?" The professor leaned in on his elbows.

"It's a short trip, really," I said. "It was the Celtic cross. I had never seen one like it. The snakes, the Sun God, and the cloud were telling a story I was only partly familiar with. You and your friend confirmed what I was thinking, so I think we're on the right track."

"But that's what I want to know," said Angie, shaking her head. "What track is that? Leading where?"

"Somebody's trying to bring about the end of the world by getting rid of all the insects."

"Whoever that is, their rage must know no bounds."

CHAPTER FOURTEEN: Meaning Escaped

A NGIE AND I prepared ourselves for the journey home. Trans-Atlantic flights always begin at dusk, the idea being that you spend the time asleep, so passengers won't be too disoriented when they arrive at their destination. That's the theory anyway, but it rarely works for me. We had a connecting flight in New York, so our journey wouldn't be complete once we crossed the pond.

I decided to splurge and paid for an upgrade to first class, never having had the experience. The increased leg room was worth the extra cost on its own, but to throw in champagne, a New York strip steak, and the best part, a warm towel before sleep was a nice bonus.

These luxuries couldn't make me forget about the experience or allow me to sleep. My demons danced on the edge of my brain.

OUR TIME in Scotland yielded much fruit. We now knew more about the cross and the clues about the Druids, how they caused the localized extinction of insects by accident, and how they tried to rectify the calamity but ran out of time.

We knew that Professor Gou had a student when he was a visiting professor at the University of Texas who fit the profile of the man we were looking for. He was obsessed with insects and fascinated by the story of the Druids. Frustratingly, we were still no closer to a killer than we were before.

I looked out the window of the plane, where clouds flew by and lights in the distance signaled we were nearing Austin. With Michael home from the hospital by now, and this whole investigation and the turmoil in the church, maybe a trip to Scotland was a bit too much. But our "vacation" was coming to an end, and I needed more time to decompress.

Normally, this time of day—the time just after a long night and right before the coming of the light—was my favorite. Usually, such a time is so full of possibilities, pregnant with new choices, new adventures, and new directions. But now all I could muster was exhaustion.

All I could think about was Michael. We couldn't drop by this early in the morning. Besides, we weren't fit company for anyone until we'd had a shower and maybe a nap.

Angie was still sleeping beside me. She always could sleep better than I, the sleep of the innocent. I hated to wake her, but we'd be on the ground soon, and would need to move fast if we weren't going to get run over.

Then it came to me. It was so powerful I had to sit down, with luggage and gifts plopped on my lap. Angie looked surprised and concerned.

"What's wrong, mi hijo?" she said.

"What? Uh, oh, Sweetie, I'm sorry. I think I've just had a new insight. It's about Lois. We've gone to Scotland to find out about the Celtic cross and about insects and the end of the world, but the whole thing started with Lois. Why did she have to die?"

"She's the reason we went to Scotland. The two clues we began with were the cross and the scripture, Rev. 8, wasn't it? You noticed it was a strange cross with unusual symbols. That's what led us to Scotland. Now we're closer to figuring this out, if not closer to knowing the killer's identity."

"I know all that, but one of the things I haven't paid attention to was Lois herself. Aside from her connection to Mavis, and now Martin, I'd never asked about Lois' history. What else is there about her past that got her killed?"

"Sounds like we need to see Hector again."

"Aye."

When I looked up, the flight attendants were staring at us. The plane was empty. They were waiting to clean up, and we were in the way.

AFTER A few days on the job, I figured a trip to Shoestring would help make the findings of our trip to Scotland fit together and make better sense. I decided to go on a Friday and Angie gladly took another vacation day to go with me. She could talk to Silvia, and maybe Hector and I could go fishing. That's exactly what we did.

"I LIKE to keep my work and personal time separate," I said as we walked out to what in Texas they call a tank. In Scotland, it's a loch, or small lake or pond. My guess is they call it "tank" because it's manmade. But then they stock it with bass or catfish (which, by the way, don't get along well together). Hardly seems sporting.

The day on the "tank" the sky became overcast, and according to Hector, that is good fishing weather.

"My trip to Scotland left me with several holes in my knowledge. For instance, I know that Mavis and Lois were related, and that according to the FBI, Martin killed them both, which on the face of it just sounds ridiculous."

"It does to me, too," said Hector, casting his line in a shimmering arch of silver and hissing spray. "It's like fitting a round peg into a square hole. Instead of finding order in this chaos, they're forcing puzzle pieces to make them fit. Lots of military types suffer from this 'Imposing Order Syndrome.' 'IOS' I call it."

I smiled. "Who knows, with all the new disorders they're discovering every day, maybe someday it'll catch on." After I reeled in my lure with no hits, I tried yet again.

"I found out some things about the cross and the insects, but I want to know more about Lois."

Hector removed his cap and brushed back his black hair with his free hand. "There's not much to know. She'd lived in that house for ten years. She was one of three sisters and a brother, who are now all dead. She was a Catholic who went to church occasionally. And she was a retired elementary school teacher."

"Then you know quite a lot about her," I declared.

"Yeah, I suppose we do."

"But what does it mean?"

"We've thought about that too. We've checked out the school and the Catholic Church and discovered nothing in either place. At school, she was a decent teacher who didn't socialize with others much and it was pretty much the same at the church."

Meaning escaped us as we sat in silence for hours trying to lure fish onto the shore to no avail. It appeared that meaning wasn't the only thing eluding us today.

CHAPTER 15: A Silence in Heaven

PSYCH WALKED into the Golden Fork for breakfast on a crisp late November morning. Ruthie greeted him with a wide open grin and a little bow.

"Welcome to our humble establishment, kind sir," she said.

"Why, Ruthie, you'd think you've gone high-brow on us."

Psych sat down and Ruthie poured him a cup of coffee and said, "Two eggs over easy, hash browns, bacon, and whole wheat toast?"

"You got it," he said, grinning.

Psych looked around the little diner. Pleasant seaside pictures graced the walls, along with pictures of 1940s movie stars. It was a mix that didn't quite work, but it had been that way for so long that he couldn't imagine it any other way.

The bell on the door announcing the next customer awoke him from his reverie. Psych didn't know him, but watched him all the same. Shoestring is a small town, but Psych didn't know everyone, even though he was born and raised here. That didn't mean the man who entered was a stranger—just unknown to Psych.

When Ruthie brought his order, Psych leaned in a

conspiratorial manner and asked in a whisper if she knew the man seated over by the door.

"No, but we can fix that right quick."

Psych watched as Ruthie did her stuff. He marveled at how at ease she was with strangers. He was just a bit jealous of her because he was so guarded and cautious.

After a few minutes, Ruthie came to Psych's table, beaming like a love-struck school girl.

"His name is Rudy—Rudy Garza," she said, puffing up her ample chest.

"Well done, Ruthie." Psych glanced over at the tall, thin, dark man who was staring in their direction. A cold chill came over him as he returned to his conversation with Ruthie.

"He hasn't been here long, but he works over at St. Mary's."

"How did he decide to come here?"

"You're the one that wants to be a detective," she answered with her hands on her hips. "I'll let you do the rest. Now, let me do my job!" And she was gone, almost spilling the coffee out of the pot she was holding.

Psych smiled as he watched her leave.

SUNDAY WAS always difficult for me. After becoming a General Presbyter, I gave up having to lead worship every week so I could sleep in, ride horses, or go on overnights with Angie. But my guilt and sense of duty wouldn't let me. Then Angelica suggested we go to church with Hector and Silvia, so we stayed with them Saturday night, and we were starting to stir to get ready for Sunday.

To wake up in a strange bed in a strange house is to

be completely disoriented. Often, I'll wake up in strange places, not knowing where I am for a few minutes. It's one of the oddest sensations I know. That's why I consider it a spiritual discipline. Anything that gets you out of your comfort zone and shakes you out of your routine is liable to help you experience God in a new way.

That's what got me thinking about Scotland. I hadn't had a chance to process the trip, to review what we'd learned, and to see if we were any closer to catching this killer.

We had coffee and pastries on the deck as we watched the world awaken. Birds preening and singing, trees swaying in the breeze, and a rooster crowing to summon the world from its slumber made it feel as if we were experiencing creation for the first time. It's hard not to take such things for granted because they happen every day, but because we're in a different setting, adjusting to a different routine, things seem new and fresh, and we see the world in a whole new way.

After we finished our pastries, we took the dishes to the kitchen. Hector asked, "So, did the entomologist shed any light on the theory?"

Silvia shot him a look and said, "Hector, you promised. No talk about work before church."

"Sorry, Honey, I was just curious," Hector apologized.

"You're right. There's a time and a place for all this. Maybe later this afternoon would be better?" I suggested.

Hector and Silvia looked at each other. Silvia smiled. "I'm sorry. I just like to keep 'work' away from the weekend as much as possible." Then she leaned toward me with a mischievous grin. "I am interested in that professor. He sounds like quite a character."

"That he was, that he was," Angie smiled back at Silvia.

"He initially dismissed the idea, but then I told him about the Druids and the research already being done, and he began to come around."

"We also discovered that Professor Gou was a visiting professor at UT, and there was one student who was almost insistent on discussing this theory about wiping out insects as a means to kill the human race. But he couldn't tell us anything about that student," I broke in.

"That's too bad," said Silvia. She looked at the clock and announced that it was time for mass.

I showered and dressed and we made our way to church. The day was chilly and overcast. I felt the expectancy of rain and the frustration of it not coming. As we found a place to sit, I began thinking about kneeling. In a Catholic church they have long, low padded benches called kneelers which swing down to allow one to kneel at the appropriate time.

Most Presbyterians do not kneel. We feel that because we've been set free, no one can make us bow. But there's something that feels right about kneeling. It says I'm vulnerable, I submit, I'm begging, I'm pleading. Self-esteem is arrived at by humility, not arrogance. It allows us to know we are not the center of the universe, and God knows we need to be reminded of that from time to time.

Whenever I'm in a Catholic church, I always watch Angelica. You can take the girl out of the Catholic Church but you can't take the Catholic out of the girl. She followed me willingly to the Presbyterian Church but at heart she would always be a Catholic. There is either a great sense of loyalty or guilt in being a Catholic; if you've left, you'll always wonder if you've done the right thing.

The service started, but Father Paul was nowhere to be found. They had a priest from the diocese come in. It was all very last minute. The deacon in charge assured us that Father Paul was fine, but was simply called away.

After mass, we decided to go out to eat lunch together. In Shoestring, the options were slim. We could eat at the Golden Fork, but that's not fit for Sunday dining. The town, however, was lucky enough to have a Western Sizzlin' steak buffet, so we headed there.

The clouds were clearing and the sun shone as we entered the restaurant and found a place to sit.

"I wonder where Father Paul was this morning," said Hector.

His son, Jorge, rose to the bait and almost shouted, "If I were him, I'd be fishing."

PSYCH WAS surprised to see such an old car move so fast. The first thing he thought of was drug runners. They found the ugliest cars and spent a lot of time and money on the engine so that, if need be, they could outrun any danger encountered, most likely from the cops. This time they weren't running from danger; they were inviting it. Some cops go into law enforcement so they can drive fast legally. Psych couldn't deny that there was a certain logic to the argument, but like most characterizations, it was only part of his motivation.

Psych tried to enlist prior to Desert Storm, but flat feet kept him out of the military. The next best thing was the police academy, where he excelled in all they put him through. When he graduated, the only department he tried for was the Shoestring Police Department. Hector was newly hired, and Sean was Hector's first hire as a deputy. He'd been "Psych" ever since.

He rarely got a chance to turn on the siren in the small town of Shoestring, so now he thoroughly enjoyed it. The old car sped down Broad Street; the beat-up '65 Plymouth Fury screamed to attention as soon as the driver heard the siren. Screeching tires turned onto First Street near downtown. As Psych pursued, he began to worry about pedestrians getting in the way. This was Tuesday, which is court day at the courthouse. The driver of the Plymouth probably made the move in hopes that civilians would provide cover for a getaway.

Psych radioed Max at police headquarters for some help with the chase. Max told him that another car would be on the scene shortly. Worried it would come too late, Psych asked Max to run the plates from the speeding suspect's vehicle.

Max reported back what he'd found. "The car is registered to a Mavis Belmont of 432 Sycamore Lane."

"Mavis Belmont..." Psych let that sink in. "From Nashville?"

"The same," said Max.

Just then a police car came to a cross street. It was Seventh Street, the busiest street in town. The fugitive slammed on squealing brakes. Psych was forced to do the same before nearly hitting the beat-up Plymouth. He quickly drew his weapon, pointed it at the car, and shouted for the driver to get out. The car door opened with a creak, and out stepped the man he had just seen at the Golden Fork—Rudy Garza. Psych and the other officer rushed the car and placed Rudy under arrest. Psych put him into his car and radioed the impound lot to come get Rudy's car. They rode together back to the police station in silence. The radio chirped to attention and Psych answered it. It was Hector.

"You have Rudy Garza in custody?" asked Hector. "I'll be at the station in a few. You reported the car was registered to Mavis Belmont."

"The same."

"Good work, Son."

Psych knew he had done good work, but it's nice to hear from the higher ups. Whenever the Chief called him "son," he knew he had done well.

When they got Rudy to the station, they began to process him and put him in a holding cell until they figured out what to do with him.

"There was silence in Heaven for about a half hour," Rudy said, staring intently into Hector's eyes.

"What are you...?"

"There was silence..."

"I get it, I get it." Hector got up. "You know what? Just sit here a while and think about your future." Hector left the interview room.

"I don't get it," Hector told Psych. "I know Rudy and his family. I've gone fishing with his father. Rudy was always a wonderful kid. I don't get it and yet I do. War does things to people. He served in the second Gulf War. Frank, his father, told me he came back pretty messed up. He saw things no young man ever should see."

"You don't know if he's done anything yet," said Psych.

"Being in a high-speed chase with a cop isn't nothing."

"You know what I mean, Chief."

"Yes, yes, I know what you're talking about. Has he made his one phone call yet?"

"Nope."

"Well, let's help steer him in that direction and see if we can get anything out of him."

CHAPTER 16: Another Weed in the Garden

ON OUR way home from Shoestring, we called Jessica to see how Michael was doing. There was silence on the other end of the line.

"Jessica? Are you there?" Angie's look said all I needed to know about what was going on.

"Oh, what does that mean?"

"What does 'what' mean?" I asked. Angie put up one finger indicating I should be patient, something I had difficulty doing my entire life.

"Is there anything we can do? Does he need to go to the hospital? Have you called the doctor?"

Angie was silent as she listened, her eyes blinking back tears.

"What's going on?" My voice rose in frustration.

"Well, keep us informed. We don't want to be a bother, but you know we'll come over in a heartbeat if you needed us."

There was a pause. Angie said, "Uh-huh," and closed the phone.

"Apparently, Michael has a fever. Jessica called the doctor. She told her it's common for West Nile to hang around, even after the initial symptoms disappear. They're going to monitor him closely to make sure it doesn't get any worse."

"Does he need any more meds that maybe we can pick up and bring by?"

"No, the doctor said to give him ibuprofen and keep an eye on him."

"Wouldn't you like to see for yourself how he's doing?" I suggested, expressing my anxiety.

"Yes, I would, but Jessica's in charge. We have to let them live their lives."

"Yes, but what if it costs him his?"

"Angus, please relax, will you? You're making me nervous."

I said nothing more, except a silent prayer for my boy and his bride to be. We decided to stop by their place on the way home.

Michael and Jessica lived in an apartment in East Austin. It lay on the border between the decay of a dying section of town and the staunch defense of encroaching chaos. Perhaps it wasn't so dire, but that was just how I saw their place.

Michael's work with a computer start-up company kept him tied to downtown, but Jessica was a freelance writer, which meant she could work anywhere.

We spent a few pleasant hours with our son and Jessica. The color had returned to his cheeks and we both could see him regaining his strength. We promised not to stay long, both because Michael could only take company in small doses and because both of us were exhausted.

On the ride back home, my phone rang and Angelica answered it. "Hello, Hector," she said, with a great smile spreading across her face in a wave of pleasure. "We so enjoyed our time with y'all. You'll have to come to our place soon."

"Yes, he's right here, but he's driving so I won't let him talk on the phone. Is there a message I can give to him?"

"Sure, I'll tell him." She shut the phone and put it in the center console. "That was Hector."

"Yes, I believe I got that much," I said. "You know, your no-talking-on-the-phone-while-driving is..."

"Do you want to hear what he said?"

"Yes, yes, of course."

"They have Rudy Garza in custody. He's saying some strange thing over and over again. Hector thinks you may be able to help them understand him."

"What's he saying?"

"There was silence in heaven..."

"'For about a half hour...'"

"Yes, that's right."

"It's from Rev. 8. It's part of the same chapter that was with Lois when she died. They are obviously connected. But you didn't let me tell him I want to help."

"You can call him when we get home. But first you must rest. You can go there tomorrow," said Angelica.

"That's if the other drill sergeant will let me go."

"Oh, and who's that?"

"Franny."

I CALLED Franny when we got home, told her what I was up to, and she cleared my calendar. She told me Sam Horn had called. They're having the vote about leaving the denomination in a couple of weeks. After that, it was six months of discernment about whether this was the thing God wanted them to do. It seemed backwards to me. Do the discerning first, and then vote. Besides, I could tell you that God does not sanction their leaving. Not the God I worship, anyway. I could see God wanting a woman to leave an abusive relationship, but how could God condone a church leaving over a disagreement about policy? It made no sense to me, besides making me angry.

I told Franny I would call Sam and let him know we would be there for him. We would find him another call if that's what he wanted.

About that time, Adam, our gray, short-haired cat, found his way onto my lap. He seemed to always find me wherever and whenever I needed him most. I relaxed most when I just petted him and most especially when I heard him purr. Such contentment is so very rare.

"There was silence in heaven for about a half hour..." John of Patmos was always so symbolic with all his images, but he got very specific with this one. "For about a half hour."

It sounded like he's leaving his wife a note about going to the grocery store. "Be back in about a half hour..." But more troubling still is what connection would Rudy have to the quote? Why would he choose that quote to repeat over and over? It's as if someone had programmed him with that response, and that's the only thing he could say.

I remember some of the talks with the miners in the pub about the IRA. They'd always quote the scripture about not worrying what to say if you're taken to the authorities because the words would be "given to you." It felt very much like these words had been given to Rudy. So it was all very calculated and very casual at the same time. That's why it was so confusing to me.

"You're thinking about Hector's call, aren't you?" Angelica said, putting her hand on my arm.

"How'd you guess?" I said. "Hector knows this boy. Said he served in the Iraq War ~ a very stable lad. Then he leads Psych on a high-speed chase and starts spouting this Revelation nonsense, 'There was silence in heaven for a half hour.'"

"Sounds to me like some kind of instruction."

"I was thinking the same thing."

"I DON'T have a problem swimming upstream on this." Sam Horn seemed very calm for being a rookie in a very tight situation. I wondered how I would respond in his shoes. "The thing I struggle with is not taking it personally."

"Oh, you can bet this isn't about you," I said with a confidence I did not feel. "There are some very fine people there, but it only takes a few to spoil the whole batch. Heck, it might be only one person."

"I know who it is. James Beecham. He's the one stirring this pot."

"What's that old saying? My church is fine—nothing that a few well-placed funerals wouldn't solve."

Silence drifted over the telephone like a heavy fog.

"A little dark for some, but clergy humor nonetheless," I said. "I just want you to know that the stated clerk will be there to moderate the meeting, and whatever happens, we are with you in this."

I hung up the phone. Not my finest hour. One of the difficulties of ministry is to stay focused on the other. Jesus did that so well. Whoever was in front of him was the center of his world. He gave his all every moment. With so much going on, it's been hard for me to focus on one thing at a time. Here I am in the center of more mayhem in Shoestring

145

when I should be focused on my job, on the well-being of Sam Horn in Cuero. But Hector needed me too. If I had to take vacation days, I needed to help him find this killer.

That night as Angie and I talked after dinner, I told her I was going back to Shoestring; I needed to find out where Rudy was getting this Revelation talk, and why he was speeding.

THE TRIP to Shoestring, took longer than usual; the one lane roads, and the unusually heavy traffic made me more than impatient. I stopped by the church to see how Beth, the interim pastor, was getting on. Since the death of their pastor, the congregation has been in deep grief. It's not that they felt such a great connection to him. It's just that he had represented a good start in turning around a ship headed in the wrong direction. I have taken on the job of working with their pastor nominating committee whose job is to seek a new permanent pastor. It's a way for me to feel connected to a place that has become very important to me, while I still do my job.

Hector greeted me with a hug, a cup of coffee and a Danish. We chatted in his office about golf and fishing.

"Well, you didn't come here to talk about fishing, or to find out how my golf lessons are going," Hector quipped, leaning forward with his elbows on his desk. "I need your help with Rudy. I haven't gotten a thing out of him except 'the heavens were silent...'"

"I don't know what I can do, but I'll sure give it a try."

THE INTERVIEW room smelled of urine and body odor. When people are at their worst, it's hard to mask the smell of decay. All the Lysol in the world won't get rid of that.

Rudy looked up and sneered as Hector and I entered the room.

"When will the silence end?" I asked as I sat down. Hector looked puzzled by the question.

"In about a half hour," replied Rudy.

Hector's eyes got even bigger.

"The man speaks," said Hector.

"What's at the end of the silence?" I said, ignoring Hector.

"The destruction of our world; the defeat of the great Satan; and the peace that passes understanding."

Hector and I looked at each other. Hector smiled at me and, I think, at himself. Who knew what would happen when a stranger comes seeking truth?

"We know you are the janitor at the Catholic Church." Hector leaned in. "We've called the priest, haven't been able to get him, but he knows you're here. Maybe he'll let you sit and rot here; stew in your own juices."

I put a hand on Hector's arm.

"Is there someone we can call for you?" I asked Rudy.

"You can call my mother...you son of a bitch," Rudy sneered. He looked like he was both pleading and angry at the same time, like someone caught between emotions, unsure where to turn or what to do.

"How can we get ahold of your folks?" I said without blinking.

"There was silence in heaven for about a half hour." Rudy was back on autopilot.

As Hector and I left the interview room, Hector said,

"We'll try to run down the good priest, but something seems wrong about that too."

"What?"

"I don't know. We've always had contact with Father Paul. The church staff has always known where he was. They always could find him. Now he's just gone."

HECTOR HAD paperwork up to his eyeballs, but never liked doing it. "If I wanted to work with paper, I would have been an accountant," he often said. Not that there's anything wrong with that. He was elated to be a policeman; working puzzles was what he was all about.

He decided to pay a visit to the Catholic Church to see what he could find out about Rudy as well as the missing priest.

He entered through glass doors into a very secular looking foyer, except for the gold crucifix on the wall in front of a wall of water. It was a striking image, both for the message it conveyed as well as the expense it represented. Hector had come here many times, and the message was always the same. Someone around here had deep pockets.

He made his way around the corner to the receptionist's desk. He asked to see Deacon Jed. Hector had called ahead because the deacon was a volunteer position. Jed had to be called away from his pharmacy to see Hector at a prearranged time.

Deacon Jed was a short, stout man, with thinning gray hair and horn-rimmed glasses. He stuck out his hand and Hector received his weak and brief handshake.

"You want to know where Father Paul is?" asked Jed

in his squeaky voice. "Well, he's...not to be disturbed...he's away on retreat."

"Can you tell me when you expect him back?"

"In a few days, I should guess."

"You're guessing. Don't you know?"

"Well, when he goes on retreat, he often doesn't know how long God wants him to be by himself."

There was a pause.

"He told me he hoped to be back for mass on Sunday."

"So, bottom line, he should be around at least by next Monday?"

Deacon Jed looked all over the room and nodded his head hesitantly.

"Do you know Rudy Garza?" Hector decided to charge into a new topic without any preamble to see if he could rattle this poor man's cage just a bit more.

"I know *a* Rudy Garza. That's a fairly common name among the Hispanics in this community."

Hector smirked. He hadn't figured the man had it in him.

"The Rudy Garza we have in custody is the one I believe—in fact, I know—is your janitor!" Hector could feel his blood pressure rising as he waited for something to break, waited for something to become clear. He was about to take it out on this poor sap when the phone rang and the receptionist answered it. After a brief exchange, she said, "Excuse me, Chief. It's for you. It's Father Paul."

CHAPTER 17: Martin's Meltdown

MARTIN COULD stand it no longer. He had been in the federal prison in Nashville for a week, and as far as he knew, there was no reason for it. He was growing poorer by the minute. His loyalty to his dead wife evaporated little by little with every indignity and institutional meal he was forced to endure. Finally, he told his jailer he wanted to talk.

They gathered in the same room where his trip through hell began, with the same woman on the other side of the table, but this time without Hector.

"Look," he said, leaning forward. The chains that held him made a sharp, clanging sound and the grip on his wrists grew tight and extremely uncomfortable.

"Look," he said again, adjusting to the chains, breathing calmly through his nose. "I've been here about as long as I care to be."

"Oh, I'm sorry, shall we get your car, or would you like a plane instead?" The blond agent folded her arms on her flat chest. "You're not going anywhere, pal."

"I know, I know. I'd like to talk to a lawyer. It appears I could use some help. But mainly, I want to talk to you about Mavis. You see, I followed her to Shoestring because she had been acting like a crazy woman. She was obsessed with Lois.

After Mavis' father died, she wanted to know everything about Lois. She flew to Shoestring on weekends. I think she made like six trips there in the last six months."

"That's right," said the agent, as she leaned back in her gray chair.

Martin looked at her as if for the first time.

"She went to church with her, took her shopping, and bought her some clothes. We didn't have any children. It's as if she was trying to mother that woman."

"Do you have any idea why she was doing all this?"

"Probably because she was the last family member she had. She wanted to stay as connected as she could to her."

"But something happened that changed her. What was that?"

Martin looked at the agent for the longest time, trying to stare a hole right through her. His eyes began to redden, water forming at the corners. He bowed his head.

"She did change. She got so I hardly recognized her. Often, we would be talking about little things, like the weather, or what to do about dinner, and she would light into me like a freight train. We'd been married eleven years, and I'd never seen her like that."

"Did she say anything that gave you an idea about what was happening to her?"

"It's not what she said!" Martin looked up, shaking his head. "It's what she *did*."

"What was that?"

"She had kept all the stuff she had collected on Lois in a drawer in the kitchen and on the refrigerator. When I came home a couple of weeks ago, all the stuff was gone. Not a trace of Lois anywhere."

"Did you ask what had happened?"

"I'm not an idiot, agent." He glared at her. "Of course I asked her."

"What did she say?"

"She didn't say anything. That's when I really got worried. She just totally withdrew from me, from her life. She became a hermit. Wouldn't go anywhere or see anyone, until that last trip to Shoestring. That's why I followed her."

"Is that when you figured she had to die?"

Martin bowed his head again. He raised his head slowly.

"Is that all you got out of this, agent? No, and for the last time, I didn't kill her. I was concerned about her. I wanted to find out what was troubling her. I wanted to try to save her."

"So you went to Shoestring because you were worried about her?"

"Yes!"

"But we have a witness who saw you arguing at the café there in Shoestring."

"Have you ever tried to talk someone out of the worst mistake in their life?"

He paused.

"How'd that go? So she told you what? What was the worst mistake of her life?"

Martin's head bowed again.

"She was going to leave me," he whispered.

"And you argued?"

"Yes," he whispered again.

"Is that when you decided to kill her?"

"What is it with you? I am innocent. I never touched her. I left the café by myself and went back to Nashville the next day."

"Why didn't you tell us all this before?"

"I was afraid of how it looked. I sounded guilty, even to myself."

"Now, that I believe."

I AM a creature of habit. It's just that some habits are better than others. I managed to quit smoking a couple of years ago, and although I suffered no ill effects from the habit, I have managed to stay away from it without much effort. On the other hand, I have managed to maintain my walking habit, even through the birth of three boys and the 24/7 life of a minister. I am rather proud of that.

My life up to now would be considered pretty routine by most standards—and pretty predictable; but not now. Things have started to unravel. My son had come down with West Nile virus and almost died. Two people connected to Shoestring perished under suspicious circumstances, and Hector needed my help again. And there seemed to be evidence enough to think that whoever did this had bigger ambitions in mind—like the total annihilation of the human race through some bizarre scheme of getting rid of all the insects. It was preposterous on the face of it, but a dangerous, ghastly plan if even remotely possible.

Angie came slowly downstairs at just that moment. The effect of spending all day with first graders was etched delicately on her face.

"Have you heard from or seen Michael?" she asked, and then we kissed. She went looking for a coffee cup in the cupboard over the sink.

"No, not since we both saw them the other day."

"You think someone did this to him deliberately?" Her forehead furrowed and her eyes grew dark.

"I do indeed."

"Well, that's just sick and twisted." She paused. "And awfully tricky. It means that whoever did this had to cultivate West Nile mosquitoes, trap one alive, transport it to Michael, and get the damn thing to bite him. Or they would have had to isolate the virus and somehow inject Michael with it without him being aware of it. There are just too many 'ifs' to make either scenario believable."

"I can't argue with you there."

"Then how was it possible? Or better yet, what possible motive would they have?"

"I'm not sure about motive, but I've been thinking a lot about what happened to him. It all seemed too neat, too planned, to be a random act of nature. I mean, Lois died in what looked like arson, then Michael comes down with West Nile, and then Mavis died. I believe they're all related somehow. The connection between Lois and Mavis is obvious because they were family. And whoever did this probably knew about my involvement in Pastor Pete's investigation last year and wanted me out of the way for this one, and so cooked up something that would keep me occupied and unable to put much energy into the investigation."

Angie put her cup down and came over to where I was sitting and sat on my lap. She hugged me and then gazed intently into my eyes.

"I want you to get this bastard. I don't care if you lose your job because you're spending too much time on this investigation. You get whoever's doing this, and you crush him." She was agitated, but soon resumed her calmer, more serene disposition.

"I will, Lass. I will."

We fixed breakfast together. I prepared the eggs—over

easy for me, lightly scrambled for Angie. She popped some bread in the toaster and zapped the bacon in the microwave. We sat with the sun streaming through the window where a gecko darted in and out.

We turned on the TV while we fixed breakfast, and it didn't take long to shock and sadden us. The lead story was about 20,000 bees dying in some Central American country. Authorities didn't have an explanation, but they did report that fires had broken out in the area beforehand. Angie and I both looked at each other and I shut off the TV.

This being Saturday, we saddled the horses and went for a ride. The air was crisp, with the faint smell of fire on the breeze. I'd thought of the wildfires in the Dallas area this fall, and hoped it was nothing major. It seemed I remember some large number of insects dying as a result of that as well.

Then I thought about all the fires I'd seen as this case had unfolded. I've heard that smoke inhalation gets to you long before a fire burns the flesh. I wondered if that's how it worked for those "witches" the church burned in the not so distant past. Were they spared the excruciating death of burning flesh by first inhaling smoke? Why do these horrible thoughts come to me unbidden?

We went on this ride to clear our heads and to reconnect with all that's right with the world, and all I could think about was gruesome deaths and what they mean.

Then Angie looked at me and said, "What are you thinking?"

"I'm smelling smoke," I said. "I'm hoping it's a planned burn and nothing random or...sinister."

"I smell it too. Do you want to check it out? It seems like it's coming from over there."

We rode hard for a few minutes, feeling the wind in

our faces and adrenaline in our blood. We both spotted the smoke coming from beyond the trees across the road, behind a fence on our neighbors' property. Bob and Linda Bundick, an elderly couple who had no kids, have become quite close to us.

We rode down their drive and saw smoke billowing from the barn. The sirens from the volunteer fire department's trucks spooked the horses as we turned to watch them barreling down the farm to market road, and onto the Bundicks' property.

They seemed to be well trained. Each volunteer knew his job and went about his work efficiently. Our horses were quite another story. We tied them up at the front of the property so they would be as far from the fire as possible. We went looking for the Bundicks.

They were on the porch of their home, in their rocking chairs, seemingly oblivious to the chaos all around them. As we approached, Bob was the first to acknowledge us.

"Well, lookie there, Mother. Angus and Angie come to call," said Bob, with his balding head, wide face, and bushy eyebrows. Linda stared straight ahead blankly.

As we made our way up the steps of the porch, I asked if they were all right. Linda looked at me with fire in her eyes.

"Do we look all right to you?"

"Mother!" Bob looked shocked. "These are our friends."

"I'm sorry, Linda, of course you must be shocked and worried," I said, raising my hand in surrender.

"We're fine, Angus. Thanks for asking." Bob looked at Linda sternly. "I woke up this morning and, in fact, went to the barn to check out the Model T. I was actually thinking about starting to rehab her today." He paused with a faraway look in his eyes. "I guess that's going to have to wait for now." Bob's eyes became red and ringed with water.

We sat with them in silence on the porch. At one point, Angie reached over and took Linda's hand. I watched Linda squeeze Angie's hand until the blood had drained from it. The only evidence that anything was wrong on this very pleasant morning was the sound of fire crackling behind us along with shouts and water streaming onto the blazing structure of the barn as well as the acrid smell of painful smoke filling our nostrils.

I was anxious to see what was going on, but felt I was more needed right where we were. Plenty of people had come by to see for themselves, and to let the Bundicks know how much they cared. Then they were gone.

About an hour into our vigil, the fire chief, Ralph Crenshaw, came to find us on the porch. He sat down in the seat I had occupied, at my insistence.

"The fire investigator's been called, and I'm officially supposed to wait for him before I say anything."

"Say what?" asked Linda.

"Well, Ma'am, I've been doing this for ten years, and I think I can tell the difference between arson and a natural fire."

"Which was this?" Angie asked.

"Arson, definitely arson."

WE GOT back home, took care of the horses, had showers, and were beginning preparations to put some steaks on the grill. The phone rang. I was outside getting the grill ready, and Angie handed me the cordless phone. It was Hector.

"Are you sitting down?" he said.

"No, as a matter of fact, I am not."

"I think you'd better."

"What's up, Chief?"

"I just heard from Father Paul."

"So he finally surfaced."

"Yeah, he heard about Rudy and wanted to let us know that he was posting bail for him."

"That's a good thing, right?"

"That depends."

"On what?"

"On whether we can make the charges stick. I've let him go, but I can't sweat him any more when he's free."

"You think his speeding was more than a joy ride?"

"Rudy is definitely hiding something. He's always been such a responsible person, so respectful and polite. I don't know this person. And for the first time, Father Paul hasn't been very helpful either. He practically demanded that Rudy be released."

After we explored the mystery of Rudy for a few more minutes, I shared what my afternoon had been like.

"The fire chief gave us a very unofficial cause of the fire," I said. "He called it arson, unmistakably arson."

"Who would want to burn down this old couple's barn?"

"Who indeed?"

AFTER DINNER I headed back over to the Bundicks to check on them. The Fire Chief started down the stairs, and turned back to the group gathered on the Bundicks' porch. He took a plastic bag out of his pocket. Inside it was a large flat stone.

"It has a scripture carved on it," Ralph said.

"What scripture?" I asked.

The Chief took out his glasses and squinted at the stone.

"They surround me like bees..."

"They blazed like a fire of thorns." I completed the verse. "In the name of the Lord, I cut them down."

They all looked at me, surprised.

"I found it when all this started. It tied the fire and insects together for me. It's from Psalm 118." I stood and went to the west side of the porch. I could see the barn still smoldering, and men with dirty faces spraying water and making sure this unrelenting enemy was at bay for good, for now.

The blood rushed to my face, then vanished. I was angry and numb at the same time. I wanted to chop this murderer's hands off, to open his mouth and feed him all the fear, disgust, and panic he had caused us.

It had been awhile since I'd asked the most self-centered question people ask in a crisis. I wanted to stuff it back down my throat, but the question was too strong, too persistent.

Why me? This started in Shoestring. Why take the fight to me? Why not Hector? I guess he's used to it. I'm just a country parson. What do I know about arson and death or murder?

He obviously saw me as a threat. That's why he's coming for me. But my neighbors? What have they done to him? Bob's precious Model T is now a charred ruin. He couldn't restore it if he wanted to.

Angie came over to me and put her arm around my waist.

"Are you okay, Corazon?"

"Now I am." I smiled. "Now I am."

CHAPTER 18: THE LAST GOODNIGHT

THE NEXT morning, the phone rang. Angie answered it while we were on the deck enjoying the awakening day. It was Hector.

One of the great things about all the death and evil we have confronted is that we now have discovered great friends. I don't know what I would do without Hector, Silvia, and their kids Jorge and Maria in our lives. Friends are one of the greatest gifts. They help us to get through tough times and to focus on what's important.

I wasn't much of a student in grammar school. The one thing my teacher said on my report was, "He chooses his friends wisely." I've never forgotten that. The trouble is, in the ministry, you're a 'professional friend' and therefore have very few real ones. Hector and Silvia have been as real as they come.

Angie turned the phone off and put it on the table.

"Why didn't you let me talk to him?" I asked.

"He said he couldn't talk. He only had time to tell us something he heard the county sheriff had found at the fire next door."

"What was that?"

"A note they found in the Model T. It said, '48 hours 'til the last good night.'"

"So he's giving us time to find him."

"Then what happens, Angus?"

"The end of the world."

Angie gasped, and then laughed at the preposterous sound of this statement.

HECTOR AND Frank, Rudy's father, went way back. They were classmates in high school. Hector went on to college while Frank enlisted in the army, but whenever they were in Shoestring they'd look each other up. They felt it was important to maintain a connection, once they had cemented their relationship in high school. Now that they had jobs and families, they had lost touch.

Hector remembered that as one of the worst mistakes he'd ever made, and one of the most thrilling. Hector and Frank were part of a group of friends who always wanted to push the boundaries. One night they were roaming the streets and found a car with the door open and the keys inside. It was a car that simply begged to be stolen. The leader of the group, a big dumb boy named Juan, egged on the younger boys, Hector and Francisco, to boost the car, which they did. There was a chase, and the boys were arrested, fined, and served a one-month sentence.

The experience changed them both forever. Hector went into law enforcement, and Francisco changed his name to Frank and landed a job in the oil field.

With Frank's boy in jail, Hector reached out to his old friend. They met for coffee at the Golden Fork.

"Thanks for meeting me here, Frankie. I didn't want to talk to you at the station, not after all we've been through together."

"Thanks, Hec. I appreciate it, but I want to see my boy. What's he done?"

"You will, you will. Your boy is in a lot of trouble, Frank. He was speeding—"

"Everybody does that. Especially teenagers." Frank winked at Hector. "You remember, don't you, Hector?"

"Sure I do, Francisco, but Rudy's hardly a teenager. He's twenty-one. We also have him on resisting arrest and possession."

"Possession! You've got to be kidding me. Possession of what?"

"Cocaine."

"Look, Hec, you know my boy. He served with distinction in the Iraq War. Did two tours. He's having some trouble adjusting, but a lot of kids do that. I'm sure there's a logical explanation for all this. Have you talked to his boss?"

"That's next on my list."

"WHAT DOES it mean, '48 hours 'til the last good night'?" As we drove back to Shoestring, Angie's face darkened like the clouds outside.

"Remember the Jonas Salk quote about what would happen if we got rid of all the insects? Do you also recall the research on the extinction of the Druids caused by burning a certain type of wood in the forest at a certain time? Even though he laughed at it, Professor Gou took it seriously enough to help us find some answers to all our questions."

"Of course I remember. But so what? What's going to happen in 48 hours? And what does this have to do with the murders?"

"I believe that first Lois, then Mavis, found out about the plot to kill insects and they paid with their lives."

"But who would do such a thing? It would be a massive undertaking. We would have to be looking for a huge laboratory. Someone smart enough to put all this together."

"And don't forget subtle. Very subtle."

HECTOR WAS in Father Paul's study. Books lined three walls, but in the place where his desk stood, behind him was only a mirror, so that those who sat in front of Father Paul had to look at themselves. Paul Sanders had, of course, done that deliberately. While the Catholic Church had relaxed somewhat on the idea of confession, Father Paul always thought it was a good thing to encourage those who came to see him to engage in a little self reflection.

"Paul, I'm sure you're aware that we still have your custodian, Rudy Garza, in custody," Hector stated, trying hard not to look at him.

"Yes, I'm aware," Paul replied without emotion. "He's a good kid and a conscientious worker. He's been through a lot and appears to have a deep faith. But what does that have to do with me?"

"We were hoping you could shed some light on why he would go off the deep end the way he has."

"I have no idea. Perhaps I could talk—"

"I'm afraid that's not possible, Father."

"Oh, I see."

"If you could just tell me anything about Rudy, anything at all that might be helpful."

Father Paul told Hector about Rudy's upbringing, about his poverty, about seeing the military as a way to get out of the mess he was in. He told Hector about his bravery and the honors he'd achieved. Then he described his obsession with insects. And that's when Hector began to pay attention.

"He came to me and asked if he could use a room at church to observe insects in their environments. You know, first it was a simple ant farm. Then he conducted lab experiments to see how hot and cold affected different ones. Pretty soon, he had a real collection of stuff. It was all very interesting and baffling to me."

"Baffling? How so?"

"All he'd ever been interested in when he was growing up was sports, cars, and women; then this sudden fascination with insects. It seemed to be out of character for him."

"I get that. Where is all this paraphernalia you're talking about?"

"Would you like to see it?"

"Yes, I would."

Father Paul took Hector to a small, dark room in the basement of the church. There was a sink and a table with a light suspended above it. On the table sat a microscope, a collection of insects stuck with pins, and a Bunsen burner. Hanging upon the walls were extension cords, mop heads, light bulbs, and glass cleaner. It was a janitor's closet.

"It's from here that Rudy conceived the idea of ridding the world of insects?"

"I only discovered his interest in all this fairly recently, Hector."

"I wonder what Rudy would say about all this?"

"I wonder that too, Hector."

HECTOR LEFT Father Paul and headed back to the station. When he arrived, he had two surprises waiting for him: one good, one bad.

The good surprise was that Angus and Angelica were waiting for him. They talked briefly about what was happening. Hector called Silvia and they arranged for them to stay over with them. Hector told Angus about his visit with Father Paul, and wanted to get Angus' take on it. Angus told Hector that he'd like to have the chance to talk to Rudy if possible.

Whether or not he'd have that opportunity had everything to do with the bad surprise. Rudy's father and his lawyer were waiting in the lobby to see Hector.

The sight of lawyers always tied Hector in knots. Each of them represented the law, and that's supposed to be a good thing. But the law in the hands of certain calculating people could be a real annoyance. If you were skilled enough and knew enough, you could bend the law into anything you wanted. That's why Hector didn't mind bending the law from time to time to get the right outcome.

Hector met with Frank and his lawyer. Frank was sweating and bleary eyed; his lawyer was slick and greasy with a limp handshake. He introduced himself as Waldo Withers. Hector knew most of the lawyers in town, but not Withers. The immediate question sprang to Hector's mind. What self-respecting parent would name their child "Waldo?"

"I'm here to see my client," Waldo stated. Frank nodded, saying nothing. "If you have violated my client's civil rights, I'll have you brought up on charges."

This is exactly why Hector hated lawyers. You'd think they were there to help him do his job—putting bad people away from the rest of decent society. Most lawyers couldn't care less about that. All they wanted was to focus on their client's rights. Hector knew that was important too, and being the good cop he was, he took pains to see to it that most rights were not violated. But that's also why, whenever he saw a lawyer, his gut tied up in knots.

Hector went back to his office. Angus and Angie went to his house, but Angus had agreed that after supper they would come back and Hector would let Angus talk to Rudy, provided Rudy was still in custody.

Hector rubbed his temples and shut his eyes hard, so hard that he saw colors swirling in the darkness. He had left Austin for this very reason—too much violence and heartache. His ulcer couldn't take it. He and Silvia had talked about him getting out of this business and becoming a security guard or something. Hector listened, but knew that sitting and watching was just as stressful as too much action, so that was not something he saw himself doing anytime soon. Besides, he really could not abide the boredom. He needed stimulation, and boy was he getting it now!

He looked up and saw Frank and Waldo standing in the doorway. Hector heaved a huge sigh and stood up, showing the two men to the chairs opposite his desk.

"What can I do for you, gentlemen?"

"Chief," Waldo said, stretching his arm across the front of Hector's desk. "My client is in fear of his life."

"He'd better be, Counselor. He endangered himself, my officer, and the driving public by reckless operation of a vehicle, resisting arrest, and being in possession of a controlled substance with intent to distribute." Hector threw that last one in just to see if Waldo was paying attention.

"If you charge him with intent, I'll have you fired."

"That's fine, Counselor." Hector smiled. "I just wanted to see if you were paying attention."

"Oh, don't worry, Chief. I'm paying attention. I've got my eyes on you." He put two fingers up to his eyes and then turned them toward Hector.

Hector wanted to laugh so badly he closed his eyes and turned his face away. Maybe Waldo thought he had intimidated him; if that was the case, then so much the better.

Waldo finally said, "See you on Monday, although I may be back here tomorrow to confer with my client. Have a good night."

Hector knew that Monday was when Rudy would be arraigned and the bail set. At least, Waldo knew enough to know that he couldn't get Rudy released without appearing before the judge. That was something.

Hector left the station soon after Waldo. It was dusk and the sky was beginning to change. The crisp, blue sky was beginning to turn a deep purple and pink, and the cold breeze was more severe and biting.

Just what I need, thought Hector; *a good slap in the face.*

When Hector got home, he heard laughter before he walked in the door. His mood brightened with the light at the front step and got brighter as he greeted his wife and their good friends.

He joined them with a beer, went to his bedroom to change, and couldn't wait to get back to his guests to let this day—this dreary, irksome day—seep through the floor of his existence and into the ground water beneath his feet. What a curative thing good friends could be.

He knew his friend had asked to see Rudy tonight. If he asked, he would certainly do it. But he prayed that Angus would not ask, because that was the last place he wanted to be tonight.

At the end of the evening, they told one another goodnight. As Hector was getting ready for bed, he said a quiet "Thank you," out loud.

CHAPTER 19: Angus' Dream

I WOKE up to a buzzing sound; then I saw it. It was an iridescent monster with six-inch wings—a cross between a mosquito and a dragonfly, but twice as big. I swatted at it to no avail. It came below me and I tried to drop my pillow on it. It flew overhead and I tried to use both hands and merely clapped as it went by. I woke up with Angie shaking me.

"Did you just clap your hands?"

"I must have...been dreaming," I said, very unsure of my bearings.

I told her the dream. She asked, "What do you think it means?"

"It means I'm preoccupied with insects."

"Sounds like you're afraid of them as well."

"Yes, yes, that too, I think." I didn't want to tell Angie how afraid I was, especially after the Bundicks' fire. That fire was sending me a definite message. I was worried now about my family's safety, which was exactly what the perpetrator wanted me to do. I was also much more aware of dreams when sleeping in a strange bed.

Angie and I dressed and headed toward the kitchen where I smelled coffee brewing. Silvia was starting to fix breakfast, while Hector sat at the kitchen table. He stood and greeted us and offered us coffee and sweet rolls, which we gratefully devoured.

After we settled on the deck with eggs, bacon, home fries, and biscuits, Hector asked us how we had slept. I told him about my dream.

"The fire at your neighbor's really has you spooked."

"'They surround me like bees?' Seems like a strange choice of verse, unless it was specifically about this case and my involvement in it."

"But why did the killer burn your neighbor's barn and not yours?"

"I might be more inclined to back off if I knew he would hurt those close to me. Going after me would just make me mad."

"And…" Hector paused. "What are you afraid of?"

"Why does everyone assume I'm afraid of anything?" The anger in my voice surprised even me.

"That dream just screams fear," Silvia said. "And, hey, your neighbor's barn just burned down, and it was an obvious message for you. You have Angie and the boys to think of. Who wouldn't be scared? Give yourself some room to feel this."

"You sound more like my therapist."

"Yeah, I suppose she does," smiled Hector while looking at Silvia.

"ARE YOU in Shoestring again?" asked Franny over the phone.

"Yes, I am. Apparently I'm the only one who can get Rudy to talk. I'm needed here."

"Well, you're needed here too, you know," she said, desperation rising in her voice.

"Yes, okay. I'll call Sam. Who else needs me?"

"You mean besides me? Well, Bill Brown called, asking for you. I told him where you were and he hit the roof. I was able to calm him down, but I'm sure he'll be on the war trail."

"That's 'path,' 'warpath.'"

"Right. Anyway, when are you coming back?"

"I'll be back there before lunch."

"See that you are." She hung up.

I decided to send Franny some flowers. Even though Administrative Assistant's Day (which used to be Secretary's Day) wasn't until April, she shouldn't have to put up with abuse from frustrated bean counters like Bill Brown.

After breakfast, I rode with Hector to the police station. Rudy was waiting for us in the interview room. The stale smell and depressing atmosphere put a damper on a fine meal shared with friends in a wonderful setting.

Hector and I sat opposite Rudy, who looked sleepy and lethargic.

"So, Rudy, we saw your lab. Pretty pathetic, if you ask me," said Hector.

"Who's asking you?"

"What do you know about the barn burning at the Bundicks' place?"

"The Bun-who?"

"Bob and Linda Bundick."

"I don't know anyone by that name."

"Sure you do. You set fire to their barn on Saturday."

"How could I do that when I was in here, smart guy?"

"Oh, right, right. My mistake." I looked at Hector and he responded.

"And you're not going anywhere until Monday," he

said, standing up. "And after Monday, we'll probably still have the pleasure of your company." Then he leaned down into Rudy's face. "You'd better take that time to tell us what we want to know, or you'll rot in this cell for a long time."

Rudy's veneer began to peel.

"Look, I've told you everything I know. The cocaine was a mistake, but the lab and all the rest—I know nothing about that."

"We'll see if the judge thinks the cocaine was just a mistake or something more serious. As for the lab, I'm not buying it."

IT WAS time for me to leave. The chat with Rudy didn't go quite the way I'd hoped, but we made progress nonetheless.

When I got in the car, it suddenly dawned on me that I hadn't been by Lois' house since right after the fire. Something compelled me to revisit that desperate scene, and if I've learned one thing in this life, it is to pay attention to these unbidden urges. Women call it their intuition; men say they're following a "hunch"—whatever that means. So I was following a hunch.

The house itself was just a ghostly shell. I thought that kids could get hurt playing around a ruin like this. I wasn't sure I knew what I was looking for, nor did I even have a real idea of what I hoped to find. I just tried to go there with an open mind.

I felt inclined to go back there, even drawn there, as though the house had some unfinished business, some additional secrets to divulge. I remembered the Celtic cross with the snake and Adam and Eve. I also recalled the verse from Rev.8:8 about the fire and the mountain. But there are no mountains in this part of Texas. The only mountains are miles away in Ft. Davis or in Big Bend.

None of us put any stock in the "mountains" angle. Fire seemed to be the most obvious clue because now there had been three of these. If the scripture was planted by the killer, then mountain would mean one thing. If it was left by Lois, then it was a clue to her killer, or maybe it was just hyperbole, as I had first suspected.

I just sat in front of Lois' house ruminating on this gallery of stray thoughts. I was drawn from my reverie when my cell phone rang.

"Well?" Angie said. "Are you finished up at the station?"

"Yes, Angie, but I wanted to take another look at Lois' house."

"What on earth for?"

"Call it a hunch, Sweetie. Anyhow I was just thinking of calling you. I've been thinking about this mountain business."

"What mountain business?"

"From the first fire; the scripture, Rev. 8:8. We all thought the focus was on the fire. But maybe the mountain image could mean something other than what it appears. Now, I want you to do some research for me. Look up the Fort Davis Mountains, as well as other things about mountains. See what you can find out in scripture about mountains and fires."

There was a pause.

"Sure, Love," Angie replied.

"In a half hour, I want you to call me and make sure I'm okay. This place is just an accident waiting to happen," I said, immediately regretting my choice of words.

"Oh, that makes me real confident about you prowling about over there alone."

"I'm sorry. I was just thinking out loud. I've got to stop doing that. Call me in a half hour. I really need you to do this research. I'll be fine."

She hung up to get started on her research. That's what we were doing here~pursuing the elusive truth. I guess that's what any detective wants to find—the truth of the matter.

Finding and bringing a killer to justice is one thing; finding the truth is quite another thing altogether. Finding the truth is not even all about facts or even principles. It's about discovering the essence of a situation. The truth about this killer is that he or she is obsessed, driven, or motivated by burning. Perhaps it's about purity, purging the darkness with an all-consuming fire.

I share that fascination with fire. I could stare at it for hours, but I'm grateful for the limits we place on it, and am careful not to go beyond them. This is about someone who has either no fear or no concept of such limits. Either way, it spells trouble for those trying to find the truth.

Lois' house had a vaporous feel—mysterious, ephemeral, foreboding, and dark. Each step was an adventure, grinding scorched memories into the dust. Lois' presence fairly screamed at me. Every sound and dank, acrid smell spoke of death and destruction. The pain was palpable as I made my way into the remains of her bedroom where the cross and scripture were found.

The windows were broken, and what was left of the curtains hung akimbo part way across the windows. The bed springs groaned as I bent down to look under them. Carefully, I brushed the burnt debris aside and found something surprising underneath. I took my handkerchief out and placed it in the center and wrapped it. It was badly burned and almost unrecognizable, but being an aficionado myself, I recognized—a cigar band.

I nearly leapt out of my skin. Knowing the CIF to be a thorough man, I was astounded that he had missed something so significant. Surely, Lois wasn't a cigar smoker, so it obviously had to be an intruder. And being in the bedroom suggested a level of intimacy that said he wasn't just a deliveryman.

Just then, an icy wind brushed the back of my neck. I turned and saw nothing, instinctively lifting my hand to the back of my neck. An idea came to me instantly—look in the basement. But there was no basement in this house. There may be a crawl space, but certainly no basement. This was Texas, they don't build basements. I looked through the rest of the house, which was depressing enough. I was sorry that any human being had to suffer this way, and sorrier still that we could not have prevented this tragedy.

I decided I should look under the house just in case, but wasn't dressed for it. And I didn't have a flashlight; plus, I get nervous in close quarters and think twice about putting myself in those situations. So, I would have to return later to finish that little task, but now I needed to move on to other things.

I drove by the police station. Hector was gone. I told Max about the cigar band and gave it to him. I also asked him if he knew if they had looked under the house. He was sure someone had, but wasn't sure of what they might have found. I told him to let Hector know I was here and that I would like to talk with him when he got back.

I drove by Hector's house to see if Angie was ready to leave. When I pulled up into the driveway, Silvia and Angie were pulling up right behind me. I told her we were about to leave, so we switched places in the driveway. I went to retrieve our overnight bag and said our thanks and goodbyes to Silvia.

My cell phone rang. It was the treasurer, Bill Brown.

"Still chasing your little mystery, I see," he said.

"Hello, Bill. How are you?"

"You want to know how I am? I'm angry, that's how I am. Nero plays his fiddle while Rome burns."

"I know you think what I'm doing is crazy. But this is every bit the Lord's work as tending to the budget."

"If you were a police chaplain, maybe so. But you are the General Presbyter for our Presbytery, and the budget needs your immediate attention! Get your butt back here and tend to your business."

The line went dead. It's too bad too because I had just thought of that line from Dicken's *Christmas Carol* about business, "Mankind is my business..." But nobody believes that. Even in the church, it's all about the bottom line. Maybe that's why the church has lost its soul. We've forgotten what business we're in.

As we pulled out of the drive, Hector drove up in the Shoestring white and blue cruiser. He got out and came over to me, the sun shining brightly behind him on the metal of his car.

"We got the cigar band, and we're processing it now. Great find, Angus. Really, very helpful. But what was that about looking in the basement?"

"I was hoping you wouldn't ask me that. Call it a hunch, and let's let it go at that."

"Besides, there's no basement in that house. Anyway, I'm sending Psych over there to have a look."

We said our goodbyes and we headed for home. Angie looked at me until I finally noticed her steady gaze. It was patient, confident, and concerned.

"What?" I asked.

"You want to talk about it?"

"Talk about what?" I knew what she meant. And no, I didn't want to talk about it, and no, I didn't want to tell her that. So I was between a rock and a hard place.

Finally I said, "I'm meeting with the budget people in an hour. Bill will be there. We'll work this out. There's nothing to worry about."

"I'm not worried." Angie smiled her Mona Lisa smile, and everything was right with the world. How did she do that? I don't know, and I guess I don't care, just as long as she continues to be by my side.

I asked her about what she found out in her research about mountains. She told me there wasn't much.

"I did find out one very interesting thing, though, from the Bible. A lot of divine revelation takes place on mountains. You know, Moses and the burning bush, the Ten Commandments, Jesus and the Sermon on the Mount, and so on. Very interesting."

"So, either Lois or the killer wants to 'reveal' something."

"Yeah," Angie looked out the car window at the passing trees with birds flowing like fingers through long, blue hair.

We got home; I dropped Angie off, and made my way to Austin in record time. I was angry that I let little men pull my strings; that I bowed and scraped like a court jester for the amusement of those who think they are my superiors.

I saw Franny in the front office.

"Don't even start," I said.

She put her hand up. "Not me, Boss. Oh, by the way. The meeting's over. They all went home, and I have some good news."

CHAPTER 20: Trail of Tears

MARTIN PACED in his cell as his agitation grew. He should have been freed by now. *They know they have nothing on me*, he thought. *They know nothing about why Mavis was killed.*

Martin had heard that the one suspected of Mavis' death had not told them anything. What they did know was that someone put her up to it. Beyond that it was a dead end.

He needed to talk to his lawyer, to see what the holdup was. He knew too that he would devote himself to finding out what Mavis was up to and what she knew that got her killed.

He asked a guard if he could contact his lawyer. The one thing he realized was that he couldn't defend himself. But he didn't know whom to contact. Although he had a lot of lawyer friends in Nashville, he didn't want any of them to defend him. He chose someone he did not know, almost closing his eyes and choosing the one his finger first landed on in the phone book.

As it happened, he chose a woman—Phyllis Cuthbert, just out of Vanderbilt Law School. Martin knew it was a long shot, and that Vanderbilt had a good reputation, but he couldn't afford anyone else, especially since he'd been stuck in here for a week.

They met in the drab, gray and green visiting room at a plastic table surrounded with benches bolted to the floor. Phyllis was in her mid-twenties with chocolate brown skin and bright hazel eyes. She had short, curly hair and wore a bright dashiki in orange, green, and blue. She smelled of daffodils.

"For having picked you out of a hat," said Martin smiling, "I think I did pretty well."

Phyllis smiled back. "But you don't know if I can lawyer my way out of a paper bag."

Martin opened up. He told her everything. How he'd noticed that Mavis was acting strangely, that she was becoming obsessed with her Aunt Lois, that she'd made frequent trips to Shoestring, and that when he'd followed her the last time, he'd confronted her. They had a fight. He came back to Nashville. The next day, Martin found out that Lois was dead. It pained him to say, but he was afraid that she might have killed Lois, but he couldn't begin to figure out why.

Phyllis labored hard to figure out the workings of the system on the fly. She used her rookie status to her advantage. On Monday, Martin appeared before the judge, and the charges were dropped because of a lack of evidence, and Martin was once again a free man. The hug he gave Phyllis was more than a victory hug—it was profound relief and letting go. Martin almost cried. Tears welled up in his eyes as he contemplated the last week of his life.

He received his cell phone before leaving the jail and noticed that it was dead. He needed to get back to his place to charge it. This was his lifeline. He had to find out if there were any money-making opportunities he had missed while he was incarcerated.

Before doing that, he thanked Phyllis profusely for what she had done.

"I've got to figure out what happened to Mavis," he said, his eyes as sad as sundown. "But I need your help. Can I buy your lunch, and you can help me figure this out?"

"I'll buy yours because I know you have no money, and yes, I'll help you."

Martin and Phyllis ended up at the Hermitage Café. The name came from the home of Andrew Jackson, the seventh president of the United States. His major claim to fame was the forced relocation of the Cherokee Indians to the Oklahoma territory known as the Trail of Tears.

They ordered and Martin looked out the dirty window at the light clouds floating innocently by. Phyllis cleared her throat.

"You know, I'm here on your dime. I know you want to try to resurrect your career, which I can help you do, but if we're going—"

"Yes, yes, of course."

"What was out of the ordinary for Mavis before she went to Shoestring that last time?"

"I can't recall anything very strange about her behavior. I could tell she was very nervous and pretty quiet. I was usually the quiet one, and she talked all the time—"

"But before she left, what put you on to her—what prompted you to follow her?" Phyllis interrupted.

There was a long pause. You could see Martin's eyes move as if he were watching a slideshow of Mavis' last days. Then he stopped; his color grew crimson red. He leaned forward, his eyes burning with intensity, looking around the crowded, noisy café.

"I remember getting so worried at one point I decided

to check her laptop for her browsing history. One site really scared me. It's the reason I decided to follow her."

"What was it?" Phyllis leaned toward Martin, her face shining with anticipation.

"She was looking up a book by Joseph Wambaugh called *Fire Lover*. It was about John Orr from California, who was a fire investigator and an arsonist."

"What did that mean to you?"

"It meant that Mavis was thinking about fire. Maybe she wanted to learn from this Orr guy about how to do it."

"But he didn't get away with it, did he? And besides, the question you have to ask before all that is "Why?" That's one of the reasons you're a free man, because you couldn't help them figure out why she would do this, if she did."

"I don't think she did. I know for a time, I couldn't help thinking that she had done it. Now I'm positive she did not. And I'm sorry if she didn't trust me enough to confide in me, but I think she went to Shoestring not to kill Lois, but to protect her."

"From who?"

"That's from *whom*, Counselor." Martin smiled for the first time. "Maybe she suspected the Fire Investigator, Miles–what's his name?"

"She'd have to have knowledge of him to suspect him," said Phyllis, as she ate her catfish and Martin ate his burger.

"She went to Shoestring several times. It's a small town, maybe they met at the coffee shop or the library. They could have met after Lois was killed. Maybe Mavis wanted to check on his findings. She could be very thorough and persistent."

The conversation drifted to other things; Phyllis and Martin also started talking about how practicing law without a partner could be very difficult. They actually started to think about what it might mean to form some sort of partnership. They even talked about how much money each of them would bring to the venture.

He had to let his assistant go because he could no longer afford her. Phyllis had a few steady customers with big families, and Martin had two well-heeled clients who always seemed to be in trouble and needed his help. Together, they just might be able to survive, when separately they weren't strong enough.

Fortified by the lunch and their conversation, Martin felt better than he had in months. The grief he'd felt about his disintegrating marriage shockingly morphed into grief about Mavis' tragic death, which exploded into his arrest and then release by the FBI. *If he had any talent or time in this area*, he thought, *he could write a book.*

But for now, he concentrated on retaining his two clients, and thought about what he needed to do next to clear his wife's name. He thought *if I do that, then maybe I can get a fresh start too.* That night, for the first time in a long while, he thought of someone besides Mavis. He thought of Phyllis, and he slept peacefully for the first time in weeks.

CHAPTER 21: Christ the King

TWENTY-FOUR hours before "twilight time," and we were no closer to figuring this out. I called Hector and told him that I would come to Shoestring and ride this out until the end.

He said that was fine with him—he definitely needed my help. I then called Franny and told her where I was going. She grudgingly accepted what I was doing, although she did not understand it. I told her that made two of us.

I've spent so much time in my jeep lately that I've begun to wonder if there's a better place on earth. I was surprised by this, but it's become a kind of sanctuary for me. Then I had a really strange thought: Maybe that's where road rage comes from.

People have no sanctuary—a safe place where they feel secure, like nothing can touch them. They discover that place in their automobile, and when that is violated, they feel cut off and just go off into rage.

It says something about sacred spaces—the need all humans share. It had never occurred to me before like this.

I GOT to Shoestring, my head clear and my heart strong. Then an idea struck me so violently that I almost had an accident. It was the same feeling I had at Lois' house, only this time, stronger, more prominent and persistent.

"*Check the basement,*" was all it said. I say "it" because I didn't know what else to call it. I managed to pull over, breathing heavily, taking in gulps of air.

"*Check the basement.*"

The last time I got that message, I was at Lois' house, and I asked Hector if he'd look into it. He told me he had Psych go over and look under the house in the crawl space. He reported that he found nothing except the remnants of an old wasp nest, abandoned after the fire.

I decided that before I met with Hector, I would stop by St. Mary's. Ever since Hector had arrested Rudy Garza, I had so many questions about his role in all this: What connection did he have to Lois or Mavis, for that matter? Father Paul vouched for him, and I believe him. But the vision of the janitor's closet with lab equipment was suspicious at best. I didn't think Rudy was the one behind the insect die-off but I figured he knew who was.

WHEN I arrived at St. Mary's, I discovered no cars in the parking lot. I am a law-abiding citizen and would not break the law, but if you suspect someone of possible foul play, it's better if your presence on the premises is unknown. The other lucky thing is that they haven't changed universal lock technology for some time; the locks I'd picked in Dumfries would be practically like the same locks I would pick right now. And so I made short work of the back door, asking for God's forgiveness as I did it.

If I were caught, I'd just say I saw the door open and

entered the premises to see if everyone was all right. It's worked before.

I entered the darkened hallway and paused to let my eyes adjust. Having only been in Father Paul's office, I had no idea if and where a basement might be in the building. It occurred to me that I should have done that first—search for an outside entrance.

Moving in the opposite direction from the church offices, I found the kitchen. In a little hallway off the kitchen, I found the door I was looking for, conveniently labeled "Basement." It was locked, but again it's easier to ask for forgiveness than permission.

Obviously, I was not well prepared for this adventure because I didn't have a flashlight. Thankfully, there were windows down here. I could make out much of what I wanted to see. I stumbled my way through the seasonal props that adorn churchyards throughout the year. Soon the crèche and the Mary and Joseph figures would be up with the camels, the Wise Ones and the Shepherds. It made me think of the holiday too soon to be upon us. It always began with Christ the King Sunday. It was my favorite Sunday. It's the Sunday right before the first Sunday in Advent, and signaled that one season was ending and another was beginning. Christ the King was the hinge in time, the connecting link, communicating that no matter what was taking place in your life—like your son infected with West Nile Virus, or the end of the world as we know it, or murders of two innocent women—we are not alone, a power greater than us was not only present, but in charge. For now, that was a wonderfully reassuring thought. I also couldn't help thinking that I hoped I would be able to celebrate this wonderful time of year with those I loved.

I made much too much noise as I made my way around the outside walls of the basement. I passed the janitor's closet where Rudy had set up a makeshift lab to experiment with permanent pest removal chemicals. I had my suspicions about that. But I didn't find what I had hoped to find, evidence of complex experiments with pesticides and insects. What I did find led me to more questions. While three sides of the basement were concrete walls, one side showed two-by-four studs and sheetrock facing out. Another room was divided from the rest, but there was no door from this side. This struck me as odd.

Disappointed, I made my way back around the room to the door I'd originally entered. I opened the door and found Deacon Jed holding a gun.

"Welcome to St. Mary's Catholic Church," he said, smiling. "Come with me," he continued, his smile turning to a sneer. He held the gun like a wet dishrag. He tried to look intimidating and menacing, but he didn't have the face for it. If I pushed him, he would either fall over or break. Falling over would be preferable; breaking would not, especially if he broke in my direction.

He led me to the janitor's closet, tied me up, and closed and locked the door. Now I was alone with my thoughts. If that 48-hour promise was real, I figured I had about 20 hours left.

But then what? It wouldn't be the end. Say he would eliminate all the insects, starting with bees. If he could do that, then it would be several years before humans would start to suffer the consequences, and by then, wouldn't they probably figure out a way to reintroduce insects into the ecosystem?

The Deacon came back. "I wonder how many Hail

Marys you would have to say to atone for the sins you're committing?" I said, once he removed the gag from my mouth. Then he put a pillowcase over my head.

"Come with me," was all he said.

He led me down a corridor; I counted twenty steps. Then we turned right and walked another ten paces. He knocked, and the voice inside bid us to enter. Deacon Jed walked me over and pushed me down into a chair.

HECTOR LOOKED at his watch. *I should have heard from him by now,* he thought. He tried calling Angus' cell, which went to voicemail. He thought about calling Angelica, but didn't want her to worry unnecessarily if he were jumping the gun.

He called Psych and told him to patrol the town to see if he could spot Angus' yellow Jeep. He told both Psych and Max, the desk sergeant, that he was going to the Golden Fork for coffee, and that he had his cell if they heard from or saw Angus.

He drove over and parked in front because there were no cars anywhere. He walked into the café and sat at the counter. Ruthie crossed with a plate of food on her arm, spotted him, and yelled, "What's up, Big Guy? You never sit at the counter."

"Can't a fella change things up every now and then?"

"He can if that's what he does, but you always sit in a booth."

"I just wanted to be closer to the source of all this nourishment," he said, sweeping his hand as he swirled around on his stool. "I came in here for a cup of coffee, but I think I'll have one of your world-famous shakes."

"World famous? Now I know you've been sniffing the fumes."

They both laughed.

Soon, Ruthie came back with Hector's order. He eyed it like a novice poker player looking at a royal flush. Ruthie turned her back to leave, and then stopped. She turned toward Hector again with a look of motherly concern.

"How's that boy Rudy doin', Chief?"

"We still have him in custody. He will be formally charged on Monday." There was a pause. The color drained from Ruthie's face, and Hector saw it.

"We had no choice, Ruthie. The man resisted arrest. Innocent men don't do that."

"But you don't know what made him do that." Ruthie shot a look at him that cut right through him.

"I'm glad you care, but I'm sworn to keep the streets safe for those who obey the law, and that's what I aim to do."

The door opened with a chorus of bells as the whole café turned to look at who'd entered. It was Psych, who looked drawn and tired as the door shut behind him.

Ruthie went on to the other customers, and Psych sat on a stool next to Hector.

"I did what you asked, and never saw a yellow Jeep anywhere."

Hector's features fell, his shoulders drooped, and his face clouded over.

"Boss, I'm just as frustrated with this as you are. I can't figure what happened to him. I looked everywhere, some places twice."

"Let's check with the troopers and see if he didn't have some trouble on the road."

"On it." Psych left the café, leaving Hector alone with his thoughts.

If he's in Shoestring, where would he be? If he was running late, he would have let me know. He looked at the half-drunk chocolate shake and smirked at the idea of "comfort food." He thought of his dad, when Hector was a little boy, sitting on this very stool, drinking the same chocolate shake with Hector next to him, doing the same thing.

Hector felt frozen to this spot; he couldn't move if he'd wanted to. Ruthie came by to tempt him with some pie, and while he loved their pastries, Silvia would not like him devouring pie and a shake on the same day, so he passed it up. Then he thought, *It's nice having a conscience outside yourself to prompt you to do the right thing.*

Do the right thing! If Angus was in Shoestring, he would stop at some crucial place to the investigation. So far, the crucial places were City Hall, the police station, and Lois' house.

Hector's cell phone rang. His ringtone was the "William Tell Overture." Always a fan of the Lone Ranger growing up, he also loved the part Tonto played in their fight for justice.

It was Psych. "We found Rev. McPherson's Jeep, Chief. It was in a ditch outside of town, pretty banged up."

"Get a wrecker out there, and have the boys go over it with a fine-tooth comb."

"It's on its way. Oh, and there was something else. Max got reports of fires started in two pecan orchards about twenty miles from town. And you'll never guess what else, Chief!"

"Please don't make me play a guessing game right now."

"As the fires are devouring the trees, there are reports of massive insect die-offs. You know, I would have thought that would be a good thing, but ever since I got on this case, now I'm not so sure."

There was silence on the other end.

"Chief?" Psych said. "You okay?"

Hector looked at his watch. Twelve hours left to the countdown. What was going on? Was this a trial run with something more sinister and massive when the countdown was up?

Finally, Hector said, "I'm treating the Jeep in the ditch as a crime scene. Don't move it until you call the State boys and CSI. I want them to go over everything. Tell them to do it twice. I'll be there in a few...Oh, and Psych?"

"Yes, Boss?"

"Keep me posted on the pecan grove fires. It seems the countdown has started."

Hector paid his check and tipped his hat toward Ruthie, who dipped slightly in a semi-curtsy, and he was out the door.

The weather was cool and crisp. Hector liked the late fall and early winter. It made him feel refreshed. The sun was so unrelenting most of the time. Getting a break from it made life in Texas a little more bearable.

He drove to the site where the Jeep was smashed into a deep ravine, covered with mud and brush. He examined it without touching anything, since CSI hadn't gotten there yet. He could see nothing out of the ordinary. No blood, no hair, no clothing. Books, papers, and the contents of an open briefcase were scattered everywhere. He would look at the contents of the briefcase when they got it to the lab. Surely there would be something revealing in it.

Meanwhile, he worried, *Where's Angus? What's happened to Angus?* He would have to talk to Angelica soon enough, but wanted something to go on, something solid that would give her hope of Angus being found. Right now, he had nothing.

CHAPTER 22: The Beginning of the End

HECTOR HEADED back to the station. He needed to catch up on paperwork and was worried about Angus and wondering about the fires and the death of the insects.

He could feel the anger welling up from deep within. He wanted to rip something apart. He hadn't been fishing in some weeks. He was too distracted and, frankly, too busy with everything happening now. He had neglected his family, especially his boy, Jorge.

Christmas was just around the corner and by this time Silvia and he would have already gotten Jorge's gift. But they hadn't even talked about it, let alone gone shopping. Hector shook his head. *Focus, mi hijo,* he thought. *Where is Angus? Should I put out a missing person's report or can we handle it from here without getting the media involved?* Taking care of it in-house seemed the best thing.

Hector didn't often think this, but now he needed to talk. He and Silvia had been going back to church lately and enjoying it. Hector thought Father Paul had helped him through the last murder and may now be able to shed some light on the disappearance of his friend.

Hector decided to go to the evidence locker and take a closer look at Angus' briefcase. There were of course budgets and business papers about the church. There were some interesting things about the church in Cuero leaving the denomination, and the disagreement with their pastor about this move. But any clues about Angus' whereabouts were missing.

One piece of paper had something interesting on it. It said "Lois Myers = Lynn Swann." Hector had met Michael's doctor when he had visited him in the hospital, but he had forgotten that she was also Lois' doctor. Maybe he would visit with her again—this time about Lois.

So he had two places he needed to visit. First, he would see Dr. Swann, then Father Paul. As he was at the front desk telling Max his plans, the door blew open and sunshine filled the entrance. As Hector's eyes adjusted to the light, he recognized the person standing in the doorway as Martin Belmont. Hector squinted hard in a double take, not having expected ever to see Martin again.

It was as if Martin had been resurrected from the dead. How did he get out of prison? Why did the FBI set him free? What was he doing here? As soon as he recognized Martin, Hector knew it would be a long interview. He looked at his watch. Ten hours until the "twilight time," his friend was missing, and the "end" was near—at least in the perception of this bizarre perpetrator. But Martin was here for a reason, and Hector very much wanted to hear what it was.

They went back to Hector's office and neither had a clue about how to start this conversation. Finally, Martin broke the awkward silence. "They let me go because they didn't have any evidence to convict me. I mean, it's true that we weren't getting along, and Mavis had become obsessed with Lois, but the FBI came to believe that I was innocent. So they cut me loose."

"So what happened to Mavis when you followed her back here?"

"She had no idea. I was very careful. She had told me she wanted a trial separation, and that she was going to take an apartment in Antioch, a suburb of Nashville. But she took nothing with her. So I followed her. When she came here, I was just so surprised and hopeful. I mean, she wasn't seeing anyone, but why lie about wanting to come see her aunt?"

"That's a good question. Do you have a good answer?"

"Maybe she was ashamed. Maybe there was an inheritance involved. She hadn't thought about her aunt for years, and now, all of a sudden, she comes here twice in a month's time."

"Do you think she killed Lois?"

"Absolutely not."

"Then, what?"

Martin's eyes shifted from side to side, as though he was reading a legal brief.

"Let's try this," Hector said, finally. "What do you think she knew that got her killed?"

"I know she was reading a book about a Certified Fire Investigator who became an arsonist. I found that really interesting reading under the circumstances."

Hector paused. The bass on the wall stared down at him as he contemplated what he did know about Mavis' death. The FBI agent did tell him they were pretty sure who did it, but that she wasn't talking. Her history was littered with fire-related mishaps and accidents, but no death, not until now.

Every fiber in Hector's being told him that Martin was telling the truth. But he also knew having a bird in the hand is worth two in the bush. So he needed to keep an eye on Martin and follow up with Miles Stone, Certified Fire Investigator.

I WAS led to another room. The Deacon told me to sit down, which I did, and he closed the door behind me. I called after him and received no reply. I could tell I was in a relatively confined space, a small closet somewhere. I could smell the faint odor of ammonia and Windex and a mop bucket with old water that splashed when I accidently hit it.

Deacon Jed has clearly gone off the deep end. It's odd that Father Paul has such unstable people working with him. I could feel the panic rise in my throat. *Am I going to die? Is the Deacon going to kill me? Is this the end of the world for Shoestring? But more immediate than all that, will I get out of here? Will I see my darling wife again? Will I watch my fine son marry Jessica?*

I allowed myself a minute or two of such thoughts, and then went about the task at hand. First I rubbed my head against a shelf protruding from the wall and worked it to remove the pillowcase over my head. I looked around the small room. I saw a microscope sitting on a shelf attached to the wall. And then my eyes fell on my salvation. There were two glass beakers standing next to the microscope. Obviously, these people were amateurs when it comes to kidnapping and tying up their captors. It was easy enough to bump the shelf with my head to make the beakers fall and shatter into pieces. If they heard the noise and came to investigate, I would attack them in whatever way I could. So I struggled to my feet, and then bent down to retrieve a piece of glass to see if I could free myself from this rope.

The glass was wet with whatever was in the beaker. It had a pungent odor of sulfur in it. That confirmed two things for me. Sulfur is an element used in making matches and the manufacture of insecticides. There was also fertilizer. My head was a fog of uncertainty, but that smell could only spell trouble for what was about to happen.

I didn't care if I got any of the sulfur on my skin; I'd worry about that when I got free. I picked up a large enough piece of glass and started working back and forth on the rope which tied my hands behind me. Often I would miss the rope and pierce my skin. I knew by now I must be bleeding. But I kept on sawing at the rope.

My forehead was bathed in sweat; *Do I stop to wipe so that I can see, or continue to saw to freedom?* I sawed with that piece of glass thinking all the while of Angie, Michael, and the boys. I said a little prayer for them, and that seemed to help my effort in the moment.

It took me what seemed like half an hour to saw through the rope. Finally free, I bent my head, exhausted and spent. I felt my arms and wrists; they were bleeding badly. My shirt was almost totally saturated in my blood and sweat. I tore the pillowcase in strips and tied them onto my wrists in order to stanch the bleeding.

After a few minutes rest, I started to think about the next problem—how to get out of the room. My first thought was to somehow start a fire, and with sulfur on hand, that wouldn't be too difficult. But I quickly disabused myself of the idea because I couldn't count on the Deacon hearing me and coming running before I succumbed to the smoke.

There must be another way. That got me thinking about the magi in Matthew's telling of Jesus' birth. They came to pay homage to the new king, Jesus, and were warned in a dream to go home by another way. I prayed hard for that 'other way' to show itself.

He had taken everything out of my pockets, so I looked through the closet. I risked being discovered by turning on the light. A janitor's closet always provides a fascinating adventure. Many things have been thrown in there with a promise to dispose of them properly later on. For most of those items, the promise is never fulfilled, and the once promising items become trash, forgotten or ignored.

Feeling around, I discovered an old broken fan in a wire cage that was layered with cobwebs, several computer printers, one computer monitor, an occasional bucket, and several mops with new mop heads waiting on the shelf. I didn't know what I was looking for, but I knew it when I found it.

It was a slug left over from an electrical box used to house a light switch. I said a silent prayer of thanks and tried it on the screw that held the doorknob in place. It was too big for the slot of the screw, but I wasn't going to let that deter me.

I worked slowly and deliberately. At one point I caught it just right and worked the screw until it was able to turn. I scraped my knuckles so hard and so often they too began to bleed. I used a strip from the pillowcase to stop that bleeding. My forehead pounded with the rush of adrenaline, and my brow was pouring sweat.

TIME WAS getting short. Hector really didn't know what to do. He remembered that he was on his way to Dr. Swann's office before Martin came in and side-tracked him. Martin was on his way home, being of no more use to Hector or help in finding Angus.

He was once again on Dr. Swann's trail. He had questioned her as Michael's doctor, but did not know then that she was Lois' doctor as well. But with only a few hours left before the "beginning of the end," he felt torn. He needed to find Angus, but not knowing where to look left him in distress.

Often when he concentrated so hard for so long without getting anywhere, taking a break from it often yielded a pleasant surprise of insight and clarity.

He had Max call Dr. Swann to ask her to clear some time for him; then he drove to her office. It was located in a newly constructed Medical Arts Building next to the hospital. Hector opened the office door and was greeted by a petite, blond young woman with a perky attitude. Hector thought Dr. Swann might have cloned herself—she and the assistant looked almost identical.

Hector introduced himself and she called Dr. Swann. He sat in the light, airy waiting room for a half hour before Dr. Swann finally emerged from the door marked private.

"I'm so sorry to keep you waiting, Chief, but I had to finish with my patient," she said, before shaking hands. Hector said nothing, but noted the disrespect shown an officer of the law for keeping him waiting.

She invited him back to her office and asked him to be seated. The office was as dark as the waiting area was light and airy. She sat behind a large, mahogany desk while Hector was shown to a straight-back wooden chair which was a good bit shorter than the leather chair in which Dr. Swann swiveled back and forth.

Also unsettling was the presence of shrunken heads on the lip of the bookcase behind her. There were no pictures, just her degrees from The University of Texas, as well as an African mask.

Dr. Swann saw Hector looking at one of the heads with a puzzled expression.

"Please don't worry about the heads, Chief. It's just an inside joke about my ex, my shrink, and my lawyer. They all screwed me in their own way. And to your second question, no, they're not real."

"That's fine, if a little disturbing. It must be a bit off-putting for some of your patients, though."

"I never let them in here."

Deciding to move on, Hector went right to the point. "Angus McPherson's Jeep was found in a ravine outside of town. In that Jeep we found a piece of paper with some incriminating writing on it, and I wondered if you cared to comment?"

Dr. Swann leaned back in her chair, looking away from Hector and asked, "What did it say?"

"It simply said, 'Lois Meyer = Lynn Swann.' Naturally, that made me quite curious. What could that possibly mean? Obviously, it didn't mean that Lois and you were the same person because Lois is dead and you're very much alive. It could mean that you were related to Lois in some way. That can be easily checked and ruled out with a swipe inside your cheek, if you'll allow it. But I think that will turn out negative as well."

"I'd be happy for you to test my DNA because you'll find that I am not related to Lois."

"That leaves the third meaning—some kind of connection between Lois and you. Lois knew something about you that you did not want exposed, and you killed her for it!"

She shot out of chair like a rocket, "Really, that's your great deduction, Sherlock? That's your big conclusion from 'the facts'?" She made quote marks in the air, shaking her head. "Lois was my patient. I treated her as best I could, and I take my oath, *do no harm*, very seriously."

"In your professional responsibility, I'm sure that's true, but when an affair, say, becomes public knowledge, that could damage your reputation, to say nothing of your practice."

Dr. Swann's face turned beet red. Hector couldn't tell if it was from embarrassment or anger. She placed her knuckles on the desk, and leaned into Hector.

"Do you think I would jeopardize my practice with a tawdry affair? You're sadly mistaken." She straightened and became very composed. "Now if you'd excuse me, I have patients to see."

Hector stood, and then stepped squarely in front of her.

"Lynn, do you have any information regarding the whereabouts of Angus McPherson?"

"Of course not, Hector," she said with derision. "Why on earth would I know where your precious Reverend is?"

"Because he never told me about any suspicions he had linking you and Lois, which means he had just discovered it. And it must have been of sufficient sensitivity to warrant such discretion. So, I'll ask again: What did Lois know that you didn't want spread around town?"

She tried to push past Hector, but he didn't budge. "It's none of your damn business!"

ANGELICA WAS starting to get worried. She hadn't heard from Angus for some time, and had a feeling that something was just not right. She called the Shoestring Police Department and talked to the desk sergeant, Max. He hadn't seen Angus, but didn't tell her that his Jeep had been found crashed without him in it. Max thought that such news would be better coming from Hector. Silvia, Hector's wife, just happened to be there dropping off some tickets for a Lion's Club Holiday Dance this weekend. She asked if she could speak to Angelica, and Max reluctantly handed over the phone.

"Silvia, no one seems to know where Angus is. It's not like him to not let me know what he's up to," said Angie. "I haven't heard from him in some time, and I know he's in Shoestring because he told me that's where he was going."

Silvia looked at Max as Angie was talking. She sensed that he knew more than he had let on.

Silvia said, "You sit tight. Let me look into this and see what I can find out. I'll call you when I have something."

Silvia handed the phone back to Max and leaned on the counter, revealing a low-cut sweater and her ample bosom. "Now, Max, why don't you start over again from the top, and tell me what you know. We're all on the same team, and need to work together on this," she said.

"But Hector wouldn't like it."

"I'll take care of Hector. Be a good boy and tell me what you know."

CHAPTER 23: Hearing Voices

I 'VE ALWAYS hated confined spaces. I have suffered from claustrophobia, it seems, my whole life. I've meditated about it often, but something about it keeps coming back to me like a plague. Maybe because the feeling of constricted air, the anxiety about where my next breath is coming from, the cold sweats I get until I find my way out of a tight spot—all remind me of my father. And as abusive and hard and unfeeling toward me as he was, he was still my father, and I loved him. Such a conflict always makes it hard to breathe, to panic in the face of uncertainty.

I thought of him now. I needed his strength. The screws were almost out now. I really hadn't planned beyond getting free. I just wanted to get out of here. Then I thought about the sulfur. I remember my dad coming home from the mines often smelling of sulfur. It's what they used to blast holes in the rock.

Now that the door was almost open, maybe I could start the fire. I looked around for something to get the fire going. I spotted a cordless vacuum and thought immediately of batteries. Just as I had hoped, a nine-volt battery! I put some sulfur in a plastic coffee can lid and touched it a couple of times to the sulfur. Nothing happened. I started to panic. It worked that way on the science show I watched as a kid.

I looked around for things to keep the fire going once it did start, and I said a little prayer. God had already answered my prayers about Michael, and I needed divine help again. I touched the battery to the sulfur once more, and sure enough, a spark or two flew up from the plastic lid. I added those things I found to build the fire, slowly and carefully.

Finally, I opened the door as the fire grew more intense. Soon the whole room that had been my cell was now engulfed in flames. I searched for another room where I could hide. I found a classroom a couple of doors down from the janitor's closet, and hid behind the door. I thought about escaping, but wanted to beat the Deacon more than I wanted my freedom. Then I got a surprise.

The sprinkler system kicked in and the whole building was awash with water, as if a cooling rain surely from the heavens refreshed the ground and my soul. I smiled for the first time in quite a while.

Soon the Deacon did come, carrying his gun even more awkwardly than before because he was slipping as he rushed to the janitor's closet. As he rounded the corner, he did slip and fall, now completely wet as he struggled to his feet.

I rushed him, tackling him back to the floor. The gun slid ten feet away down the hall. We struggled against each other. My life flashed before me: all those years of wrestling with my father while trying to protect my mother now gave me an inner resolve I did not know I had. If it came down to one of us surviving, I knew it was going to be me.

He broke free from my hold and made a splashing dash for the gun, and I tackled him again. Now inches away from the gun, we both grabbed for it, desperate for the life raft of the upper hand.

I reached the gun first, got a firm hold on it, and struck the Deacon across the face; the adrenaline from that act of violence surprised me, my chest heaving, gulping in acres of air. He fell to the floor in a heap. I tied his hands behind him with the cloth I'd found in the closet, got him to his feet, and helped him move in the direction of Father Paul's office.

"He's not there," the Deacon said quietly.

"Where is he?"

"How should I know?" I wanted to hit him again, but refrained.

"Well, then, let's go to the police."

I jerked him toward the hallway that led to the front entrance. The deluge from the sprinklers had stopped, but water was still dripping from the ceiling. *There's going to a big repair bill on this building,* I thought.

We were met at the front door by a frantic Father Paul.

"I came as soon as I heard the alarm. What is going on here? Why is my deacon tied up? And why do you have a gun?"

I turned my back to the Deacon to address Father Paul and that was the last thing I remembered. Something hit me hard over the head. Blackness descended as day turned quickly to night.

The next thing I knew, I was sitting in Father Paul's office, tied with the cloth strips I had used on the Deacon. My head was pounding and my vision blurred.

PSYCH WAS frantic. "Chief, you'll never guess what the lab came up with."

Hector could hear his heavy breathing over the phone.

209

"Have you been running?"

"Yeah, I've been in Austin waiting for the results. I ran to the squad car as soon as I heard."

"Well, take a minute. Calm down, and tell me what they found."

"They found a fingerprint, that of one Jed Price. Ring a bell?"

"No, I don't think it does. Do you have an address?"

"Yeah, I do. 521 Sunset Avenue."

"Great; I'll check it out."

Hector found the house, but no one was home. The dark green abode was covered with what must have been asbestos shingles. The shutters hung loose on the sides—drunken soldiers, ready to fall down on the job at the slightest provocation. He walked around the house a couple of times, not sure what he was looking for or what he might find.

Then the radio in his car called him back. He returned to the squad car and answered the dispatcher. It was Max telling him about the fire at St. Mary's. Hector told him to call Psych and have him meet him at the church. Max also told him about the information Silvia got out of him, and Hector let him know he was an idiot.

CHAPTER 24: You Could Get Hurt

THE FOG began to clear. We were in Paul's office, the water still dripping from the ceiling, the prodigal son picture still in its place, and the mirrored wall behind Paul's desk reflecting the fact that I had seen better days. "Paul, thank God. Your man Jed has gone off the deep end. He's waving a gun around like a licorice stick."

"Let's get you out of this bind." Paul bent down to aid my release. "He has been acting very erratically lately. I've been very worried about him. Quick, before he comes back, let's get you out of here."

Paul led me into the hall and across the fellowship hall where our footsteps echoed in the large expanse into the kitchen. Paul put a finger to his lips as he looked around the next hall for signs of Jed on the premises. We made our way around the hall, down the next corridor. We passed the custodian's closet where I had been held prisoner, and the choir room next to that. I could see the door at the end of the hall with light streaming through. I wanted to get out of there as fast as I could.

But Paul stopped right before the door; the look on his face as hard to read as Hebrew.

"I can't go with you, Angus. I have to find Jed. I'm responsible for him. I have to make this right. The fire trucks should be here soon; go out there and tell them what happened here. I'll look for Jed and join you later."

"But he's dangerous. You could get hurt. Let those trained to deal with his type take care of him." I tried to get him to come with me, but seeing that wasn't possible, I wanted very much to get out of there and back to Angie. It's funny, but I thought about my fight with the treasurer, and longed to take up that debate, rather than having my life hanging in the balance.

THIS WAS the weirdest interview Hector had conducted in his five years as Chief of Police of Shoestring. He had known the Certified Fire Investigator, Miles Stone, to be a man of integrity and patience, if also officious and condescending.

"Did you know Mavis prior to the events in Shoestring that led to her death?" Hector was getting weary. They had been at this interview for an hour, and Miles had said little more than almost pleading the fifth.

"No, as a matter of fact, I had never heard of her until I saw her on the slab at the morgue."

"Miles, I know you're lying. I know you had a meeting with Mavis sometime before we caught her and put her in jail. All we need to know is what you talked about."

Hector could tell this was a disciplined man. He speculated that Miles had had military training; his level of focus and control were impressive, if not a little off putting.

A fly buzzed around Hector's head, and he took a swipe at it, knowing that it was hopeless to think about catching or hitting it. Hector just wanted it to go away. Miles watched him with interest; almost assuming that in a contest of wills, Miles was winning this battle, if not the war.

"We know that Mavis had a book in her possession about a Certified Fire Investigator turned arsonist. I find that very curious; given all the fire we've seen around here lately. Why would she, do you think, be so interested in such a strange subject?"

"I'm sure I have no idea, Chief," Miles said with utter boredom, almost with a yawn, his eyes at half mast. "You have two options: charge me or let me go. If you're going to keep me here any longer, I'd like to contact my lawyer. Oh, I almost forgot. I'm very close with the Mayor. I'll let him know how I've been treated here, and we'll see how long you keep your job."

Hector got up from his chair and leaned into Miles face, while Miles didn't move a muscle.

"You are free to talk to whomever you wish. But one thing I know that I share with the Mayor is a strong sense of justice. If you're guilty, you will pay."

ANGELICA COULD not sit idly by and wait for word from or about her husband. She took a personal day from school and drove to Shoestring to meet with Silvia. Silvia had heard that Angus' Jeep was in the impound lot, and they decided to start there.

The Jeep was a muddy mess. Huge clumps of mud were caked on the hood and the roof of the cab. Thick layers of mud encased the tires, and the license plates were covered over so they could not be read.

The front end was smashed; the right headlight was shattered, and the front bumper was hanging to the frame by wires. Angie couldn't help thinking about her missing husband looking the same way. She took a step back from looking at the wreckage and put her hand to her mouth.

Silvia put a hand on her shoulder. "We'll find him, don't you worry."

"Oh, I know we'll find him," she said absently. "I'm just worried we won't find him in time." Then Angie kicked herself for saying what she thought.

They were about to leave when Angie took another look at the tires. It was hard to see because of all the mud, but unmistakable all the same. It was sand.

Silvia said, "That's curious. Sand is all over this county, but not where the Jeep was found."

Angelica put a hand on Silvia's shoulder. "That perhaps means that Angus was caught someplace else and the Jeep brought to the ravine to stage the accident."

"Of course, there's no way to prove that."

"We don't have to prove anything right now. All we need to do is find Angus."

AS I TURNED to open the door, the fire trucks arrived. The yard was a confusion of hoses, men running, and Ralph calling orders over the bullhorn. The air was acrid with the smell of smoke and burned wood. But I took a big gulp of that putrid air; it felt so sweet to me.

I spotted Fire Chief Ralph and was headed toward him when a fireman in a yellow slicker and visored helmet approached me. He insisted I come to the EMT truck to receive oxygen, even after I told him repeatedly that I was all right. By the time I reached the truck and began the oxygen, I realized what a good decision that was. When I turned to thank the man for helping me, he was gone.

As I sat there looking at the scene before me unfold, the view began to blur. The trees looked like men walking around trying to put out the blaze. The men looked like moles, and the hoses became snakes in my mind. I shook my head, trying to clear it of these disturbing images, but that didn't work. I tried to stand, but my legs were oatmeal and I began to fall.

The man, whom I had met before, now told me to lie down in the back of the EMT truck, that I was having a reaction to the oxygen, and that I needed to go to the hospital. As I lost consciousness, all I could hear was the sound of a siren blaring in my ears.

HECTOR ARRIVED just after the fire trucks. As he pulled up to the church, there was an explosion so loud he could have heard it from the police station in town. It shocked him so badly that he took several steps back in disbelief and confusion. The whole crew of first responders had been relaxed and calm. After the blast, they immediately went into battle mode, rushing headlong into the building.

For a moment, Hector sat back, watching the transformation. Then he thought about Angus, wondering what had become of him. He rushed in, not thinking about what lay ahead of him, only about finding his friend alive.

He saw the water everywhere that had resulted from the first alarm. He went to the janitor's closet where the fire originated. He saw broken glass and blood—signs of a struggle. He was studying the possible source of the closet fire when a fireman, all sooty and dripping wet, called to him from around the corner.

"Chief, you're going to want to see this."

Black smoke billowed from the church office. Firefighters continued to douse it with water, but still it came.

"How can you see anything in this?" asked Hector.

"For now, this is what you need to see. We've got our guys down there where the explosion came from. They say it'll be a little while before they have things under control."

"Wait, 'down there'? There's a basement in this building? I'm a member here and I never heard of a basement."

"It's not a basement, as much as an extra room below here."

"So you're saying it's not a basement, something else."

"According to the fellas, it is like nothing they've ever seen before. We should be done here in an hour, and then you can come back and take a look."

"Baloney, give me a respirator so I can go down there and look around. Every second we delay gives the killers that much more time to get away."

"No, Chief, I can't let you do that. You're my responsibility until this fire is under control, and I'm not letting you down there. Please, go study the closet fire that brought us here in the first place; it might help us understand how this all got started."

Hector took a deep breath and sighed. He recognized logic when he heard it, and resigned himself to doing what he could for now.

CHAPTER 25: Fugitive

HECTOR PICKED his way through the scorched remains of the basement. There was water, foam, glass, and debris everywhere. Amazingly, the glass display of insects on the wall was untouched and intact.

Hector began to sweat. One of the things his supervisors had always said about him was how calm he was under pressure. He was feeling anything but calm now. He'd never faced a situation like this; the imminent danger his friend, Angus, was now in as the threat of the coming apocalypse weighed on him. His palms perspired as he attempted to lift a piece of glass from the floor. The normal, painstaking procedure of treating a crime scene with gentle patience was in conflict with the urgency of finding something that could lead to the whereabouts of Angus. The more he fought, the more frustrated he became.

Psych had joined him in the search for clues, and he brushed by a beaker of something on a table and it crashed to the floor, creating an echo.

Hector jumped. "You clumsy fool! Can't you be more careful?" He was red in the face with rage.

"Sorry, Chief! Uh...sorry."

Hector took a deep breath and tried to center himself. Something else was lurking in the darkness of the battle raging within him. It wasn't just his concern for Angus or his responsibility as Chief of Police.

The murder case that had brought Angus into his life also caused in him a crisis of faith, and Father Paul was there for him, helped him see what circumstances wouldn't allow him to see, and he had been eternally grateful to him; and he meant that quite literally.

He shook his head, tried to clear his mind, to focus on the job at hand. He looked down in the dust and the rubble of the dirt floor and saw something written there.

Inscribed in the dust were the letters GR with a smudge, then the letters VE. He remembered the hours he had spent with his grandma watching Wheel of Fortune and guessing what the words were as the letters appeared in the blocks. He smiled at the memory, and knew this was relatively easy. It was either GRAVE or GROVE. The graveyard had been cut out of a stand of trees at the edge of town, but the more likely meaning was GROVE. A grove of pecan trees on the other end of town seemed the most probable place where they had taken Angus.

The radio squawked on Psych's shoulder. He spoke into it and then said, "Chief, there's something you'll want to see. I think we know where Angus is."

HOPE WAS leaking out of Angelica and Silvia like air out of a punctured balloon. Sand was everywhere, and they were nowhere. But they were getting hungry; both of them were so excited about their involvement in this case, they had forgotten to eat. A trip to the Golden Fork seemed in order.

When they got there, they both were assaulted with the smell of bacon, coffee, and grease. Add to that their own anxiety about the turn of events, and they both entered with fear and trembling.

Ruthie, because of all her years in the people business, could read people very well. When she saw the two women enter the greasy spoon, she spotted trouble. Without asking, she brought them both a cup of coffee.

"You look like a couple of cats dragged backwards through a keyhole," she said, smiling. "Here's coffee to set your teeth to rights."

They both looked down at the black coffee swaying in the cups as it was set before them. They offered a whispered thanks and started perusing the menus they were given.

After they had caught their breath, ordered toast, eggs, and home fries, and after Ruthie brought them their orders, Silvia looked at Ruthie and told her where their heads and hearts were.

"That's awful," gasped Ruthie as she sat down next to Angie.

"I was wondering," Angie inquired, "do you know Angus and have you seen him recently?" She described her husband and a light bulb went off in Ruthie's eyes.

"Yes, Darlin', I've seen him before. I remember him from the time the Presbyterians were in the soup about their pastor, and how your husband was able to help them so much; at least that's what I heard. He was in here a couple of days ago."

"Was he with someone?" Silvia leaned forward in her chair.

"I don't rightly recall." Ruthie scratched her chin. Ruthie left them and came back with a pot of coffee. "I remember now, and thought it strange at the time. He was with Rudy."

"Who's Rudy and why was he with my husband?" Angie asked no one as she took a sip from her coffee with two creams and one Sweet and Low.

HECTOR FOLLOWED Pysch to the front of the police station. Psych pointed to the horizon at the dying of the day, which now was ablaze with light not from a celestial source.

"What the..." was all he said. "Get out there and check it out," he said finally to Psych.

"Aye, Aye," said Psych and he was out the door. Hector noticed how quickly he obeyed his order, and was simply shocked. He ran after him and stopped him as he was getting into his squad car.

"Hang on, Psych. I'll go with you. We'll take my car, and I'll drive."

WHEN I AWOKE, my head was aching. My hands were tied around a tree, and the orchard was brightly lit with fire. The Deacon was gone, and all I could see was the night sky ablaze with light and smoke. I inspected the knots as best I could, and struggled against them, but it was no use. The night was cool, but smelled of sulfur and smoke.

Here I sit, tied to a tree.

I've had a rich and varied life, but if this was the end, I would feel cheated out of the best years of my life with Angie.

"O God, I don't want it to end like this." I started to cry.

"What did you say?" A voice from the darkness startled me awake to another reality.

Then I felt something behind me; my ropes began to loosen. I turned my head to see who it was.

It was Rudy!

"What the...?" I shouted.

"Shush!" Rudy whispered. "I'm getting you out of here."

"What?" I repeated, this time more quietly. "Rudy am I glad to see you." As he struggled to free me from the tree, the reality of the situation began to dawn on me. "If I'm going to die, just let it happen here. I'm so tired of this struggle, and I think I've been hit on the head more times in the past few days than ten boxers in their whole careers."

"Will you be quiet? What he's doing isn't right. I know that now, and he must be stopped. If I can save one person, I want to do it. That one person, today, is you. Now be quiet and come on."

"But we'll get caught."

"They're all gone. They're trying to get out of town. We must stop them before this thing goes any further."

"Where did they...?"

"I don't know; first things first."

He untied me and helped me sneak through the field next to the grove. Thankfully, it had rained recently, and the grove was wet. We made our way around the burning trees. At times branches burst from the tree trunks and landed near us as we slogged our way to the river.

"Now what?" I asked.

"We're going to swim across the river. My car's on the other side."

"But where is Jed?"

"Look, I just saved your life. I'm taking you to the

police station where you can tell them what you know, and they'll probably send you home."

"But what about you? You were involved. They'll surely lock you up."

"It's what I deserve. I'll get a reduced sentence. Prison might actually do me good."

"Be serious. Take me to the police, and then take off. I'll say I made my own way."

"And be a fugitive for the rest of my life, always looking over my shoulder, never being able to relax? I want to put this behind me, Rev. Believe me, it's the only way—and frankly, I'm a little surprised you'd lie for me."

"It's the least I could do, after what you did tonight."

"That's what I'm hoping for from Hector. Now get in the water and let's go!"

"Aye, aye, Captain." I saluted him and slipped into the cold water, shocked at first, but considering everything else that had happened, I was too euphoric to notice it much.

As we emerged on the other side, we heard sirens and saw flashing lights on the opposite shore. We looked at each other and smiled. *Do we swim back and let them know I'm okay, or go on to the police station from here?*

I persuaded Rudy to swim back without me, opting instead to make use of his car. I watched as he swam back to the authorities. The wake he made spread out like jewels on the water, reflected from the fire above.

Fire is so primal. We fear it and long for it. We run from its ravaging power and are drawn by the promise of warmth and survival in adverse conditions. It's a sign of judgment and of passion, both of which we fear. This whole case has revolved around fire, which must have been the focus of Jed's formative years. What could it mean? Now that the Deacon was gone, where would he go? Will Hector know where to look? When will this nightmare end?

A tap on the window startled me. It was the Deacon. Apparently, the nightmare continues.

CHAPTER 26: The Nightmare Continues

"ROLL DOWN the window!" Jed ordered.

I shook my head, knowing it might be the last movement of my life. He shot at the window, shattering the glass, but the bullet missed me.

I ducked down, put the car in reverse, and pressed the gas pedal with my other hand. The car squealed as the wheels spun and smoke billowed from the wheel well; the smell of burning rubber assaulted my nostrils.

Jed fired two more shots, the first shattering the front windshield, while the other hit the driver's seat. I heard him yelling as he ran toward me. By now, those across the river had heard and seen what was going on, or so I hoped. Soon this nightmare would end. And if it ended in my death, I knew I was ready; I had prepared my whole life to die a meaningful death. I did not fear it, but I would not hasten it if I could help it.

If I were to survive, I knew I had to keep backing up, get in the driver's seat, turn the car around, and get as far from Jed as I could; all much easier to think about than to pull off. But I gave it a try. I kept pressing on the accelerator as I inched my way up onto the driver's seat. I had traveled approximately fifty yards like that by the time I made it into the driver's seat. Then I heard a shot from far away. The next thing I saw shocked and sickened me. Jed's eyes got big and his hands spread out in benediction. His gun fell beside him before he collapsed head first to the ground with a thud.

Before the significance of what I witnessed really registered, I was broadsided by another car speeding from the opposite direction. My airbags deployed and everything went dark.

HECTOR WAS across the water standing with Psych as he took the shot that dropped Jed. Psych was calm while taking the shot, but afterward, he began to shake. He had always been good with a gun, but this was the first time he had fired it at another person to protect someone else. He got a BB gun when he was eight and a .22 when he was twelve. He had shared his father's fascination with guns and hunting.

Psych had always been fascinated with law enforcement, seeking order where only chance and chaos dominated. Today, he made what he would later remember was the shot of his life.

Hector saw the crash. He watched helplessly as a dark figure got out of the car that had hit Angus and took the unconscious cleric out of the car, before putting him in his own battered car and speeding away.

"Come on, we have to hurry. The only bridge is half a mile from here," said Hector. He and Psych piled into the Dodge Charger cruiser, one of the newest on the force, and one of Hector's proudest achievements because he got it over the Mayor's strenuous objections.

They left the burning pecan orchard behind them and flew down the dirt road, leaving a cloud of dust behind them and fish-tailing as they went. They made the bridge in half a minute and turned toward the river. As they reached the spot where they had seen the driver limp away in his damaged car, all signs of him had vanished. Hector was fairly certain they had not come across the bridge, so they sped down Farm Road 1960, using the spotlight as they drove.

Several miles down one of worst roads in the county, they saw a beat-up Honda on the side of the road; it appeared to be stuck.

Hector pulled up behind it, flashing the spotlight around the area. They cautiously got out of the cruiser and approached on either side, with their flashlights shining and guns drawn. No one was there. Hector saw a gas can and rope in the back seat. They both looked around the car, paying attention to the tracks the two men made as they left the car. The tracks led in the direction of an old house in the distance, but they still could not see either of the men they sought.

"Call for backup," Hector ordered.

Psych hesitated, wanting to say something but all that came from him was silence. Hector shot him a look that wilted whatever confidence Psych had in uttering whatever was on his mind. "Make the call, Psych, that's an order."

"Yes, Chief."

I CAME to in the back seat of the beat-up Honda. It took a few minutes for me to realize what was happening; at first I thought I was home with Angie and had merely had a bad dream. Angie—I missed her terribly. Since we married, we had not been separated for long stretches; now I wondered if I would ever see her again. I thought about what she might be doing right now—I knew that she would be worried, but there was little I could do about that except to be safe, take care of business, stop this craziness, and end this long nightmare once and for all.

My mother also came to my mind. She always told me something her mother had always told her, *"It's always darkest before the dawn."* I'd always wondered about the wisdom of that old saying. Was it a comfort in a dark situation or did it only serve to make one impatient for the light of day? I felt both things were true, and that brought a growing confusion to my awakening mind. It was increasingly clear that I had to do something; even if it was wrong.

I launched myself at the head of the person in the driver's seat. The car swerved and headed for the ditch, coming to an abrupt stop. We struggled for some time before he hit me over the head with his gun. Again, the lights faded.

I CAME to in a dark room with a cement floor and round steel beams holding up what looked to be the ceiling of a basement. My head hurt, and my first thought was that I probably had a concussion. This is what they worried about in American football, as though doctors had discovered this for the first time. Progress toward health, as in all life, comes in fits and starts.

Ever since I started spending time in Shoestring, my health had been at risk. On the other hand, I had discovered a true friend in Hector. I knew he was close by and soon he would stop this madness, and our lives could return to some semblance of order rather than the unrelenting chaos we'd experienced in this terrible ordeal.

I had to figure out a way to get free of this damp, dark basement. I had to find Hector and get back to Angie. And I had to do it now. I looked around as my eyes adjusted to the dimness. I smelled something I had smelled before, and it sent shivers down my spine.

Sulfur. I supposed the smell came from fertilizer and I shuddered again. It wasn't going to be used for the garden, but what fresh hell could they be planning? Maybe they were arranging for my disposal now. Maybe they thought with me out of the way, they were home free.

"Angus, Angus, are you awake?"

It was Paul calling from the dim light above me at the other end of the cellar.

"Paul, Paul, is that you? It's me, Angus. Jed's a crazy person; he's trying to rid the world of insects to teach the human race some kind of sick lesson. Please help me."

"There must be some way to get to you; let me look here."

I looked around, and there were no steps leading to the floor above.

"I've found a rope ladder. I'll have you out of there in a moment." After a few moments, a rope ladder appeared out of the hole in the floor above me. "Do you need me to come down to hold the rope or do you think you can make it up?"

"I haven't climbed a rope since Boy Scouts, but I'll give it a go." My side and my hands had been burned slightly, and stung against the coarse rope, and my perspiration was streaming down my arms making progress difficult. I finally got in a little bit of a rhythm and struggled up the rope slowly and carefully.

"There you go, my boy," the tall priest said as he cut the rope tying my hands together. We gathered ourselves on the floor above and made our way out of the house that had been my prison. The sky above me was a deep dark blue, and the stars interspersed with some clouds.

But the strangest thing to see was the pecan orchard ablaze with fire in the night. I looked at it in disbelief. I looked around for Paul, but he was gone. I looked for my cell phone, but it was gone too. I went around the house looking for anyone or anything that could help me understand what was going on.

Paul came around the corner of the house with a gun in his hand.

"Where'd you get that?" I asked.

"It was Jed's. I found it on the ground near where he was killed."

The fog in my head was starting to clear. I reviewed the last few minutes in my head. The beat-up Honda coming at me, the knock on the head, the being left for dead in this abandoned building.

"It was you."

"What was me, dear boy?"

"You killed Lois, and when Mavis came to town and was about to uncover what you had done, you had to get rid of her as well."

"My dear boy, I just saved your life. What kind of killer would do that?"

"One that was conflicted; I believe the good priest is still there, but this end of the world thing was just too much for you to hide. After all, what's two people when you're going to rid the world of the human race?"

"I've killed no one. I'm just as much a victim in all this as you are, dear boy."

CHAPTER 27: The Fire Starter

"Lois got caught snooping around that basement lab of yours just like you found me. But she wasn't as lucky as I was. You knew lots of people would come looking for me, but not a lonely crazy old spinster like Lois. You decided you couldn't let her live to tell what she had seen, so she had to go."

I started inching my way back toward the house. One more fire; this one could save my life. I stopped before the front door.

"That's far enough," Paul shouted above the roar of the fires just beyond the fence. "Now get in the car." Paul turned his head and bent down to get in the car. I dashed through the house, scrambled down the rope ladder, and went straight for the sulfur. I stacked wood and paper, anything that was flammable on top of the sulfur, after leaving a little trail of the stuff to where I was situated, behind the ancient furnace.

"Angus, I know you're down there. What if I take up the rope, then no one will come to rescue you? You'll die and your precious Angelica will make such a beautiful widow."

Now that I was in the basement, I didn't know how I was going to set the sulfur on fire. I had no matches; so much for another of my great schemes. I waited for some time, hoping it would unnerve Paul, and in a panic he would come down to finish me off. The silence was screaming in my ears.

The sound of gunshots rang out in the darkness; sparks flew as they hit the concrete floor.

Then I heard what could only be described as an answer to prayer. The rope ladder swayed as Paul grunted and puffed his way down. *I'm glad he's as out of shape as I am.*

I made a dash at him out of the darkness, hitting him in the stomach and both of us went sprawling. I had remembered wondering if Paul was a closet smoker. I had seen yellow teeth, remembered the "smoker's breath" more than once, as well as the yellow fingers.

While he lay dazed and breathless, I searched for a lighter and thankfully found one.

"What are you doing?" Paul shouted, coming to consciousness.

I flicked the lighter at the sulfur, but missed. The flame went out. Paul got up and scrambled for the lighter.

"Are you crazy?"

"Yeah, I'm the crazy one." I launched myself at him again, and we both fell hard on the concrete. I tried to wrestle the lighter from Paul. Needless to say, I was losing.

"I'm saving the earth. That's my objective."

"Saving the world? How on earth do you think getting rid of humans would save the earth? What happens if your grand experiment doesn't work? What happens if you do get rid of all the insects—which is preposterous on the face of it—and nothing happens? The human race goes blithely on as before, oblivious to what you have tried to do, and just as destructive and creative as ever?"

"What about the Druids?"

"What about them? One person says their extinction was a result of the insects dying off, and you believe him. I don't buy it."

"That's nonsense. The evidence is irrefutable. It happened just as Professor Gou said."

"So you do know him?"

"Of course I know him. All those interested in entomology know him."

"What about Lois and Mavis?" I called out to Paul through the darkness.

The darkness hung around me like a noose.

"What abou—"

"I, I heard you. Less talk and more dying; I should have muzzled you."

"One of many mistakes!"

"MISTAKES! What do you mean 'mistakes?' The world is about to end, and you're talking about mistakes."

"Killing Lois was a mistake."

IF PAUL made it up that rope ladder and left me down here, I was lost. As I had always known, I was ready to die, but not today, not without a fight.

There we were—both of us breathing hard, exhausted. When I turned toward Paul, he was standing over me with a gun.

"Give me the lighter," he said.

Having no choice, I did as he asked. Paul took the rope I had burned through and retied me away from the fertilizer; then he bent down to the fertilizer and sulfur and set it ablaze. As the flames crackled, he made his way to the rope ladder. He turned.

"I wish this would have ended differently. I really rather like you, but no one can stand in the way of God's will."

"I can!"

Paul stopped, taking his hand off the ladder.

"Blasphemer!" He shouted it.

"If God's will includes the taking of innocent life, including insects, then yes, I will stand in the way of that."

"My dear boy," the priest pursed his lips. "If this whole affair has taught you anything, it should be that no one is innocent."

"You're kidding, right? You're joking. This is all a cruel joke."

"Yes, you're right. Can't you see how we're all laughing?" Paul took hold of the rope and started to climb. The fire grew, getting hotter and hotter. He started to laugh.

Paul climbed the ladder and took it up after him, as I continued to struggle with the ropes, and the fire and smoke grew more intense.

Several minutes later, the rope appeared in the opening, and I prayed a silent prayer of thanks.

I saw a piece of glass that Paul had broken earlier and rolled over to it, toward the flames, grabbed it in my hand and started sawing. Freeing myself, I saw the rope ladder just on the edge of the opening above me. I found a metal can in one corner of the cellar and a broom. I got on the can and maneuvered the broom handle underneath the rope and pulled. The ladder came cascading down. I climbed as best I could, my old bones creaking with every step. I made it to the top, where I discovered he had started the upper floors on fire as well. In fact, I saw him coming down the stairs toward the kitchen. I launched myself at him as he fled upstairs.

We struggled together as the flames leaped around us in this dance of death. I remember in happier times my dad trying to teach me to box, and, though he meant well, all I had to show for it was him beating me up.

I was able to get Paul in a half-Nelson, but the flames snatched at me, and I pushed him away. He fell through the hole in the floor, but caught himself on the edge. He implored me to lift him from danger, saying he would turn himself in, that all this was a horrible mistake. He still insisted that he was innocent of murder, that he didn't kill Lois or Mavis.

I struggled to lift him to the relative safety of the only part of the building that wasn't in flames yet. We both lay panting on the floor; then he swiftly rose and pulled out his gun and laughed.

"You idiot! You sap! You believed me? You took me at my word. You think I repented? Your act of kindness actually fuels my resolve."

"What do you mean?"

"Kindness is weakness. All this 'helping hand' crap the church preaches actually keeps people in a dependent position. If forced by nature, humans become stronger, more resilient, less susceptible to the kind of schlock I poured on you, and you fell for it. It's Darwin's survival of the fittest."

"But Darwin also said that evolution shows that all life is hardwired for kindness. It is kindness that shows we are growing and maturing."

"Garbage!" Paul turned to watch the flames intensify. Then I threw myself at him again, only this time, he moved and I crashed through the floor, and now I was the one hanging on to the ledge.

Paul laughed. "Isn't this rich? Now the tables are turned

again. And will I help you? Why should I? With you out of the way, my plan can move forward, and I can be rid of a major irritant."

"You forget who you are, Paul. You're not a killer, are you?"

Paul's face changed. I saw doubt flash across his countenance like a comet, but it died just as quickly.

"Nice try, Angus. We're both dying today, and there's nothing you can do about it."

"Give me your hand, brother. You don't want to kill me."

"Kill you? I don't have to kill you. All I have to do is leave you there and you'll die on your own."

My strength was giving way. My hands were slipping. I whispered something in desperation. Father Paul leaned down to hear me. I grabbed the Celtic cross that dangled from his neck and pulled with all my might. Father Paul lost his balance and toppled into the abyss. And that surge upward propelled me to a better handhold on the ledge.

I stayed that way for some time, gradually losing my grip. I was about to pass out from all the smoke. I began to think about my life, how rich it had been, how I was a companion to the love of my life, how we had raised good, strong children, and how God had called me to a wonderful work. I even thought of the treasurer and how I had longed to be reconciled to him. I thought of Michael, my son, wondering what he would do with his life, knowing that Jessica was absolutely right for him, and prayed that I could be around to see a grandchild.

I was on the brink of losing consciousness when a hand reached out and grabbed mine.

HECTOR PULLED me out of the hole. I could see the look in his eyes, the terror and the pain. I lay on the hot floor for a minute. Then Hector said, "Let's get the hell out of here."

The flames grew more ferocious as we looked around for an exit. The stairs were consumed in flames, and the prospect of finding a safe space was growing slimmer every second.

Hector left me to see what he could find. He came back with a single mattress that had escaped destruction and said, "Get under here," as he put the mattress over our heads and ran toward the window. Before he did, he told me to aim for the tree outside, which was a good six feet away.

We took a running start and crashed through the window, landing in the branches of the adjoining tree which was by now also on fire.

The scene on the ground was a ballet of chaos and confusion. Sweaty men were trying in vain to put the fire out. Some even attended to us, insisting that we not help with the fire, but sit and catch our breath.

Hector started violently coughing, and then I joined him. Ralph, the fire chief, rushed over, shouting for a medic. It was such a raging battle that it reminded me of Vietnam.

Finally, the EMT rushed over and administered oxygen, apologizing at every other breath. "It's just that they didn't seem to be as exposed to the smoke as we thought!"

"You know smoke victims always receive oxygen first," Ralph scolded, "or do we need to send you back to school!"

The EMT said nothing, finished her work, and went to tend to others who continued to battle the blaze.

"Don't be too hard on her, Chief," I said.

"She should know better. They get trained, and are paid to save lives. It's going in her report."

"Not if you forget to write it." Hector started breathing normally.

Ralph nodded slightly before he left. I tried to sit quietly to process all that had happened, but all I could think of was Angie and Michael. I called them, and hearing Angie's voice was the greatest healing I could have received. I told her about Father Paul, and she was shocked. She told me that Michael was fine, and in fact he and Jessica were getting married. I told Angie I loved her over and over again, and we hung up.

Hector placed his hand on my shoulder; and I told him Michael's news.

"I guess that's the end of this, then?" said Hector.

"Not quite. I'd like to check out Father Paul's place. See if there's anything else that would explain all this. And also see if there's a way to reverse or stop this fire-borne insect die-off business."

Psych came to the EMT truck, his face white with worry.

Hector asked, "What's wrong, son?"

"Father Paul is nowhere to be found."

CHAPTER 28: In The Bone

HECTOR LOOKED puzzled. "Of course, he's missing. He's dead, burned to a crisp."

Psych shook his head, and tugged on his ear. "No, we've looked through the debris of the whole house. There are no human remains to be found."

Hector and I looked at each other, stunned. "Well, put out a BOLO for him, and it seems we do need to go to his place." He said, "Get hold of Barry and see if he'll get us a warrant. Also, alert the bus and the airport."

After Psych left, Hector said, "If you're feeling all right, let's go look at the house."

As we approached, one of the fake shutters came loose and crashed to the ground. I was beginning to feel a lot like this house. It's what Kierkegaard called, "a sickness unto death;" something deep in my bones. I began this investigation in the hope that I could help the police find out who killed an old woman who kept to herself and was a trouble for no one. But now all I felt was tired, a deep weariness that wanted all this sordid mayhem to cease. I knew that none of it would end until we found Paul and the source of all this fire and death.

The fire examiner, Miles Stone, was getting into his gear.

"We meet again, Chief," he said, not looking up.

"What do you know, Stone?" asked Hector.

"I really don't even have to go in to know this was arson. The fire's origin, the speed of spread, the heat of it, all point to its being deliberately set. And I can tell you it's the same person who burned Lois' house."

"Oh, you can? How?"

"Like I said, all those things that tell me this is arson also have a distinct signature. I may not be able to describe it, but I know it. I couldn't prove it in a court of law, but I know it in my bones."

"That's good to know, Stone. Do you mind if we join you?"

"Suit yourself." And he left without waiting for us to finish getting ready.

I felt warm, wet, and weak as we entered the building. After we suited up, making my first tentative steps, I lost my balance and Hector caught me before I fell. All this fire, all this chaos was starting to get to me. I wanted to run from that place, but I was committed to finding this guy and ending the torment.

The sound of church bells filled the eerie silence of these ruins. It was my cell phone. I answered it.

No greeting, no 'How are you?' just "Angus, I'm disappointed. The Presbytery is hemorrhaging money, and you're fiddling around with fire." It was my treasurer.

I wanted to turn the phone off without responding. I wanted to climb into the phone and sock him. I wanted to tell him what I really thought of him, but I took a breath and said, "I'm putting the finishing touches on our five-year plan to get the Presbytery out of debt, and I'll have it to you by next week."

"But that doesn't—"

"We'll get together in a few days and you can let me know what you think." Just moments before I had hoped that he and I could find peace together. This must be God's idea of a little joke, or a test, or both.

We said goodbye and hung up. My next call was to Franny.

"Franny, can you take a look at the figures for the last five years, and start putting the Presbytery on a diet to get out of debt in five years?"

She agreed reluctantly and hung up.

I looked up and both Miles and Hector were smiling.

"What?" was all I said.

WE FOUND just what Miles had suspected at the house that had been my prison, and almost the place of my last breath. This was a rush job; a gas can and accelerant were used to start the whole thing. The house was consumed in flames within minutes; not like the fire at Lois' house. That was carefully planned and executed, with nothing left to chance.

Our next stop was Father Paul's house. We almost despaired of finding anything interesting in the small, plain townhome, until I went into the bathroom.

Underneath the picture of St. Francis was a shelf full of medicines of all varieties. There were amphetamines, barbiturates, valium, and diet pills, all prescribed by Dr. Swann. The thought occurred to me, the same thought that came to the Fire Chief about the EMT. *She should have known better.* I called for Hector to take a look, and he drew the same conclusion.

"There's no way he needed all these. In fact, some of these would counteract the effect of the others, like two bulls playing tug of war."

"It's as if she prescribed them simply because he asked for them, rather than his really needing them," I observed.

"Whatever is going on here, we need to pay her a visit to find out."

Hector called ahead to try to locate Dr. Swann. The receptionist in her office said she wasn't there. Something came up, and we might find her at her house.

When we pulled up to her ranch house, Lynn Swann was outside packing her car. Her eyes grew huge as we both got out of Hector's squad car.

"Going someplace?" asked Hector.

"Why, yes, as a matter of fact; brilliant deduction, Sherlock," she fumed.

"Antagonizing an officer of the law, that's a great way to start the interview."

Lynn's shoulders slumped and she sighed deeply. "I'm sorry, Hector. I'm in a hurry. I have a plane to catch, and I'm late."

"Where you headed?"

"I've been working very hard lately and decided to take a few days to clear my head and get refocused."

"That's funny; your receptionist didn't know about it. All she said was that something came up and you needed to take care of some things."

"That's true. Something has come up and I need to attend to my mental health."

"We've just come from Father Paul's house," I said.

Her eyes narrowed and her shoulders shot back. "So what?"

"We found some very peculiar things," I said, ignoring her outburst.

"Look, that's all very interesting, but like I said, I've got a plane to catch and I'd like to get going."

"I think we need to take a trip downtown to sort this all out. You'll just have to catch a later flight." As Hector took a step toward her, she backed away.

"I told you, I'm in a hurry. If you'll get out of my way, I need to leave."

I couldn't help myself. Ever since I got involved in this murder business in Shoestring, I have found a brazen side to myself that jumps in where the 'old me' feared to tread. I'm not sure Hector fully appreciated this new side of my personality. But when it came to my family—as it did with the first situation which involved Angelica—and now, this one with Michael, I felt a certain freedom I had never let myself experience, especially in the carefully controlled, buttoned-down world of the Presbyterian Church.

I looked at Hector, then at Dr. Swann. "Some of the most interesting things we found in Father Paul's house were in his medicine cabinet, or should I say, closet. A cabinet couldn't hold them all." Hector looked at me and nodded.

"Quite a collection, I must say," I continued. "Many of them disagree with each other's company. Father Paul must be a very confused man by now."

"So, what does that have to do with me?" shot Swann.

"I'd say, plenty," Hector chimed in, "because they were all prescribed by you."

Dr. Swann slumped visibly in the back seat of the cruiser, a wire mesh screen between us.

"Father Paul is a very sick man," she whispered.

"Or you made him that way?" I asked.

She was up against the screen again.

"That's absurd. I don't prescribe...nothing. Not if it's not indicated."

"A double negative," I said to Hector. "That's interesting."

"Are you holding me against my will because of improper use of English? I didn't know that was a crime. Besides, I haven't done anything wrong!"

"No, we're holding you on suspicion of murder." Hector looked squarely at Dr. Swann. Determination and exasperation spelled out across his furrowed brow.

"What!" she shouted. "I didn't kill anyone. Are you mad?"

"No, but we think you are, if you think we'll let you get away with this."

"Away with what?"

"You and Father Paul are somehow together in the plots to kill Lois and Mavis, and are working on a plan to rid the world of insects and to annihilate the human race."

Dr. Swann laughed, a tinny sound emanating from an unpracticed voice. Some laughs are pleasing and warm; hers was irritating and grating.

"Here we are, pinning all this on Father Paul, and now we find who's really behind it all? Of course, he couldn't do all this himself. He had to have help." My Scotch blood was beginning to boil. "Hector killed his deacon, so there had to be someone else pulling the strings."

"Actually, Psych took the shot, and Jed is not dead. He's on his way to the hospital as we speak." Hector pulled the cruiser to the side of the road and put the car in park. The only sound was the rush of the cars as they whizzed by. "Why did you do it?"

"Ah, the ancient question. Why do we do anything? This was all Paul's idea. I had nothing to do with it." The words fell away like scales off a dead fish. Quiet reigned in the cabin of the cruiser like a queen in her court, for what seemed like a lifetime.

"What was Paul's idea?" The icepick of his words broke the frigid calm.

"Why, this whole thing!" She looked first to Hector, then to me, her rage dying with each turn of her head. She settled back into her seat as the darkness enveloped her.

"What whole thing?" asked Hector.

"I don't need to tell you. You've figured most of it out already." If she were a turtle, I was watching her head go into her shell.

"You retrieved Paul from that house fire, didn't you?" I said. Both Hector and Dr. Swann looked at me with questions written on their faces.

She came out of her shell for a brief moment. "Why... yes, yes, I did. What of it? It's not a crime."

"Aiding and abetting a fugitive from justice surely is a crime," Hector shot back with all the sternness he could muster. "Look, time's wasting. Where is Paul? We must stop him. Lives depend on it, or have you given up your oath altogether?"

"I want my lawyer," she said, struggling with her arms handcuffed behind her back.

"Fine, then we'll take you to the station, where you can call him."

"It's a 'her,' actually."

Both Hector and I smiled. "Her, then."

The air in the car became heavy; the hush was a stark contrast to the churning in my soul. Her world was falling apart at the seams as we watched her ponder her fate. I wanted to reach around and shake her, but that would mean she had won.

CHAPTER 29: Sealing Her Fate

"I DID IT."

"Did what?" Hector unbuckled his seat belt, put his hand on the seat back, and turned to face Dr. Swann.

"I got Paul out of the building."

"How?" I asked. "It was an inferno."

"I was already outside the house when it started to burn. I saw you and Paul fighting on the second floor. I heard crashing and didn't see Paul anymore. I heard screams and moaning. I reacted like..."

"Any lover would?" I interrupted.

"Only a fool would go in there," she scowled at me.

"A fool in love," said Hector. "So, where is he now?"

"I don't know."

"Don't play coy with us. We've got to find him, and now, before he has a chance to get away. We've got men at the airport, the bus station, even the cab company. He won't get away. Just tell us."

"He's at a private air strip."

"Where?" Hector shook the cage that separated them from each other.

"At my place."

Hector was on his cell telling Psych where to meet them,

turned on the siren and squealed his tires as he turned his squad car around, racing from Dr. Swann's place.

It started to rain.

"Oh, great," grunted Hector.

The sky blackened, thunder rolled, and lightning streaked across the sky.

They barreled down the gravel drive, spraying mud and fish-tailing through the wet grass to the air strip behind the Greek revival ranch house.

A SINGLE PLANE sat poised on the field with no one in sight. Hector, Dr. Swann, and I got out of the squad car and approached the plane.

Father Paul emerged from behind a car with the trunk lid up. He carried a box and a gun as he came around the side of his car. He was badly burned on his face and arms.

Hector said, "You don't look so good. Perhaps you should have a doctor look at you?" Hector looked at me and back to Paul.

Paul laughed. "I've already had a doctor look at me, and I'm fine. Now if you'll get out of my way, I have work to do." He winced as he walked slowly toward the plane.

Hector drew his gun and crouched in a firing position.

"Father Paul," he shouted over the plane engine's roar. "I'm arresting you for the murders of Lois Myers and Mavis Belmont."

"I didn't kill anyone." Paul moved to the plane, opened the door, and put the box inside.

"I'm warning you, Paul. I will shoot you if you get on that plane."

Paul hesitated to turn around and then quickly wheeled

around with the gun in his hand, grabbed Dr. Swann, and pulled her toward him.

He reached down for an iron pot that appeared to be smoking, and put that on the plane as well.

"Okay, Paul, your next move will be your last, unless it is to give up your gun," Hector yelled through clenched teeth.

"Why do I not believe you?" Paul said, smoothing back Dr. Swann's blond hair. "You and I are going for a little ride, Sweetie, and these good men are not going to stop us." He opened the door again, and Dr. Swann climbed aboard.

"What is the point, Paul? What are you doing? Whatever it is, you won't get away with it!"

"I don't want to get away with it. I'm ready to die, along with the rest of the human race."

"Why? What have we done to you?"

Paul laughed. "You have persecuted our kind since the beginning of time. Now it's time for the meek to inherit the earth."

"But that can't happen through violence," I said, taking a step toward him.

"Oh, yes, Rev. I almost forgot about you. You have indeed been a thorn in my flesh. As I recall, St. Paul couldn't get rid of his thorn, and I guess I can't get rid of mine either."

"Why go to all this trouble?" I asked.

He glared at me through bloodshot eyes, turned and shot me in the leg, and then ran around the plane. Hector fired but missed him. Paul got inside the plane and started to taxi down the runway, with Hector and Psych chasing after.

Meanwhile, having never been shot before, I was left

to writhe in agony on the wet, grassy field. The plane lifted effortlessly into the air as if by magic; Hector and Psych looked to each other and commenced firing. The plane banked sweetly and came back low over the field, as if to taunt them as they continued to fire.

It continued to climb suddenly and then, in a flash of fire and deafening noise, blew up, with an explosion so violent it knocked Hector and Psych to the ground.

THE RAIN began to dissipate and the clouds drifted apart. My eyes were blurred by the rain as well as the pain. Sirens filled the air with an unholy cacophony, declaring that someone somewhere was in trouble. Noting my shallow breathing and my throbbing head and leg, I was reminded that that someone was me.

How did it come to this? How did a quiet life of tending to the Lord's work end in gunshot wounds and planes that explode in mid-flight?

"They surround me like bees; they blaze like a fire of thorns; in the name of the Lord, I cut them down." Psalm 118; definitely not the same comfort as Psalm 23.

"Is he saying something?" Hector was bending down to me.

"Don't strain anything, Angus. Help is on the way. You're going to be okay. We just need to get that bullet out of your leg. Just rest easy."

I was soon unconscious.

I AWOKE in a hospital room. Those standing around my bed filled me with terror. There was a cockroach, a bumble bee, a fly, and an ant. I screamed and woke up again. I dared not open my eyes for fear of what might actually be there. Then, I heard Angie calling my name. When I opened them I saw Angie, Michael, Jessica, Hector and Psych. There was a man in a white coat, the doctor, I assumed.

"Hello, Angus, how are you feeling?" the man in white asked.

"All right, I think I'm fine. I had a weird dream; you were all insects!"

They looked at each other smiling. "Oh, my darling." Angie bent down and kissed me. "You scared us all so much. We thought you might die. I'm so glad you're safe now. "

"My name is Dr. Needleman. Hank. I know, nice name for a doctor. Oddly, no one in my family is a doctor, except me. I'm the first. But I do think we have several tailors in the clan."

Polite laughter filled the room.

"You're going to be fine, Dr. McPherson," Hank said. "We got the bullet, the bleeding has stopped, and you're going home tomorrow. I'll be by to check on you later; nice to meet you all."

And he was gone.

An anxious quiet filled the room as I looked from person to person. "What happened?"

Hector stepped forward with his hat in his hands.

"Do you remember getting shot?"

I nodded. "Then I passed out."

"Right. Father Paul and Dr. Swann took off. But we were able to stop them."

"They're dead?"

"Yes."

"Too bad." I looked at the IV stuck in my arm.

All those gathered exchanged looks. "What do you mean, 'Too bad.'?" asked Michael.

"I know that's an end of it, but I don't think he killed Lois and Mavis."

"Why would you say that?" Hector moved toward my bed.

"Go back to Paul's lab. Look diligently at what's there. Go to his house and see with new eyes. Paul was interested in insects, that's true, and he did try to start the end times, but he didn't kill those two."

"Then who did?"

"Go to the deacon's house. I think you'll find a birth certificate with Lois' name on it. Paul was Lois' son, but she had another son too. I think it was the deacon."

"You know the deacon is in this hospital. He will be arrested after he recovers from his own gunshot wound. We can ask him directly," said Hector.

"That's a great place to start," I said.

Hector and Psych left the room, leaving Michael, Jessica, and Angie behind.

"Thanks for coming, you guys," I said, my eyes at half mast.

"Dad." Michael took my hand. "I want to thank you for all you did for me."

"I didn't..."

"You stood by me; you went after the crooks who gave me the West Nile virus. Without you, I wouldn't be here today. I just want to thank you."

"Thanks for that, son, but it was your mother's prayer, patience, and persistence that got us all through this terrible ordeal." I squeezed her hand.

Michael put an arm around his mother and squeezed her tight. Tears ran down Angie's red cheeks.

"Let's let your father get some rest. I'll check with the doctor to see when they'll let him go, and we'll talk later."

Angie bent down to kiss me tenderly and they were gone. Soon, I was asleep.

CHAPTER 30: A Fire of Thorns

HECTOR AND Psych checked with the guard at the door, then they entered the deacon's room, which was dark; the light from the hallway threw strange shadows on the wall. Jed's face was distorted and misshapen in the half-light. Hector saw that he was handcuffed to the bed and his eyes were closed.

"Jed Price," Hector spoke in a loud, authoritative voice, "I'm arresting you for the murders of Lois Myers and Mavis Belmont. My deputy will read you your rights so that you understand them."

As Psych relished the moment and began to recite the Miranda rights he had so rarely spoken in this small town, Jed's eyes blinked open.

"What's this?"

"Remember, Sailor, don't say something you may regret later on," said Hector, who seemed to be enjoying his job far too much.

"But I didn't kill—"

"Oh, yes you did."

"It's my word against Paul, and he's dead. How are you going to prove it?"

"You are. We went to your house. We found your birth certificate. It had Lois listed as your mother."

"That's a long way from murder."

"We also found papers from the orphanage where she took you."

"Ooooh, I'm getting scared now."

Hector shoved the bed and Jed winced with pain.

"So that's what you're reduced to? Can't get your way so you start knocking me around?"

"I didn't touch you," said Hector, as he shoved the bed again.

"This...is getting...old. Can't you see I'm defenseless? If nothing else, this is harassment and police brutality."

"You're right," said Hector. "This is nothing else. I don't want to give our whole case away, but the last piece of the puzzle is your fingerprint found on a gas can at the scene."

"You're coming to that kind of late, aren't you? And besides, all that is very circumstantial."

"The D.A. doesn't care how circumstantial it looks to us. He worries about how it will look to a jury. And I'm pretty sure this looks like twenty to life."

As Hector and Psych were leaving, Hector turned to Jed and said, "Here's something else to help you get to sleep tonight. With a little help, and a little luck, we think we can get Dorothy to turn and name you as the one who got her to kill Mavis. And it's only a short ride from there to Lois; so, pleasant dreams."

THAT NIGHT I slept fitfully. Hector told me how the conversation with Jed had gone. I couldn't help wondering if he somehow blamed me for all his troubles. I mean, I was the one who had first pointed to Father Paul. I was the one who suggested the police look at Dr. Swann. So by a process of elimination, this plot to end the world was still moving forward, so it had to be Jed—the other member of the "Trinity" of the apocalypse. I turned over, but still couldn't get to sleep.

JED COULDN'T sleep, but for an entirely different reason. He felt all alone. He'd been alone most of his life, but his time with Father Paul was the richest, most rewarding time of his life. And then he read the quote from Jonas Salk and a wild plan was born. He knew Paul had an obsession with insects and could figure something out about ridding the world of them. "They're pests, after all," he argued. He had observed that with large insect die-offs, the human population had thinned as well, so he thought the hypothesis might be a sound one.

The only thing Jed had to do was to convince Paul of two things; first, that it needed to be done, and second, that it could be done. And then there was Lois and Mavis.

Lois had to go. Paul knew that, but didn't have the stomach for it. *I gave him his backbone,* Jed mused. Lois had known about Paul's obsession with insects and in fact fed it. She gave him books and videos on the subject every other birthday, until she put him up for adoption. Paul won a science fair in junior high with his bug collection and a sophisticated paper on their impact on the environment.

But Lois had gotten too curious recently. She had come to church to try to reconnect with her son and discovered his lab in the church basement. When Paul told Jed about that, he knew exactly what had to be done and made sure it was carried out.

Mavis was a total surprise for Jed and Paul. Mavis was coming from Nashville to check on Lois, and Jed knew that would not end well either. But then she was arrested, and Hector appeared to have done Jed's work for him. Jed shook his head. All this reminiscing wasn't getting him anywhere.

But now all that was up in smoke—literally. The prospects for his future were bleak. As the last person alive in his confederacy, he faced a lifetime behind bars, and that's a life he did not wish to live.

The one person he thought had brought his world crashing down around him was lying in a bed in the same hospital, probably on the same floor.

THE GOOD news came in the afternoon. I was going home. Angie and Michael helped get me dressed and packed up. I said my goodbyes to my caregivers and headed for the car, looking forward to the ride home.

"It will be great to sleep in my own bed tonight," I said, from the "shotgun" seat.

Angie looked over at me and smiled. "It will be great to have you there. I missed you. The doctor said for you to get plenty of rest and not to do too much."

I looked out the window as the yellow Cherokee sped toward home. The majestic clouds rose in glorious display, casting images of my mother washing clothes with her ancient machine. I remembered how decent she was and how dreary her life had been, which made me sad and proud at the same time. I said a silent prayer of thanks.

An unbidden, overwhelming sense of peace came over me as I reflected on all that had happened in my life for the past several months; all this hardship and disaster, as we were about to celebrate the birth of our Lord. It was jarring and pleasing at the same time, as well as a relief to know that it was over and our life could get back to normal.

THE NEXT morning at breakfast, Angie looked positively glowing. I remember that look from when she found out she was pregnant with our youngest, Michael. Maybe it was how relieved she was to have me home.

She served me a good Scottish breakfast of eggs, scones with orange marmalade, grilled tomatoes and bacon, and all the while she was beaming from ear to ear.

"What have you done now?" I asked.

"Why, whatever do you mean? Can't a wife cook her husband his favorite meal on his return from the hospital?"

"That look is reserved for when you told me you were pregnant, and when you wrecked the car!"

"I didn't wreck the car..."

"Look, thanks for the breakfast, but something's up, and I won't rest 'til you tell me."

"Okay, okay." She beamed as she poured another cup of coffee, set the glass pot down with a thud, and crossed her arms and rested them on the table.

"Silvia and I went back to the Catholic Church to look around."

"You did what! Do you have any idea how many laws you broke, or how dangerous that was?"

"Remember your blood pressure, Angus." She was still smiling, unfazed by my outburst. "We were very careful. We discovered Paul's lab before the police knew about it. In fact Hector found us there. You see, you were missing, and the days were so long without you. I just got to thinking about what Father Paul and Jed had attempted. They must have had extensive records somewhere. Since his house was too public, we decided to see what he could have left at the church. Besides, we'd heard about Rudy and knew he was connected to the Catholic Church, so we went over there to look around. The basement door happened to be open..."

"So you took it as an invitation?"

"We knew what we were doing was wrong, but I didn't care. If what I was doing helped to find you, I would go to jail for ten years.

"We went through the lab proper, which was difficult because we only had one flashlight between us. We didn't think that part out very well. We actually thought there might be a secret compartment somewhere. That's what we went looking for. Then we saw a butterfly mounted in amber sort of off by itself on the wall. We pressed that and sure enough, we found a small space big enough for a small table, one chair and a computer.

"Then Silvia went to town. She really knows her way around a computer."

She got up, went to the kitchen, retrieved some papers from a notebook, and sat down again. She put the papers in front of me and started leafing through them excitedly, trying to explain the highlights.

"These are all the contacts Father Paul and Jed had made over the years. They were very thorough and methodical. They come from all over the world—mostly in the States, but quite a few in Europe as well. These are the dates they are to drop the sterile bugs and start the fires." Her finger followed the evidence like a bloodhound on a scent.

I looked at all that she showed me. I couldn't believe my eyes. They were really serious. Jed and Paul had planned this down to the last detail. Having only a passing interest in details—who does what when, and for how long—I felt a grudging sense of admiration for what they had accomplished.

Thankfully, besides names and addresses, there was contact information, including phone numbers and email addresses, so the prospect of locating these people and shutting down their operation was greatly enhanced.

The troubling thing, the maddening thing, was the date on which all this was to start.

"The good news is we got to this in time," I said.

"What's the bad news?" Angie asked with a smile.

"The bad news is it starts tomorrow."

Angie's smile faded into a deep, exhausted sigh.

CHAPTER 31: An Acolyte for Death

I LOOKED AT my watch. The tyranny of time now seemed like a cruel joke. I'd been prisoner so many times in the last few weeks, and now I was a prisoner of time.

I called Hector as Angie got on the line and told him how they found the computer and what it revealed. Hector told us he knew all about it, because he had spotted them where they should not have been and he had already called the State Troopers to communicate Jed and Paul's plan.

I thought calling Hector would make me feel better, as though telling him about what Angie found would automatically put an end to this madness about these insects and the apocalyptic scenario. It all had seemed so ridiculous, but now I could see it was not.

How ironic that humankind had spent eons trying to eradicate insects, seeing them only as bothersome pests, but when taken to the extreme, our very existence demands that they survive.

One consoling bit of information at the end of my conversation with Hector helped me rest easier, if not sufficiently peacefully. He said he would contact the FBI about the worldwide nature of the threat and that he would encourage them to bring in Homeland Security and the CDC. Although I wasn't sure about contacting the Center for Disease Control, if we couldn't stop the worldwide demise of the insects, maybe we could figure out how to reintroduce them in order to stabilize the environments where they had disappeared.

"This is all too much for me to handle," I told Angie the next day. "I can't sleep; I can't get all this out of my head."

"But the worst is behind us, Sweetie." Angie embraced me with a soft kiss and a look of complete love and surrender. "Paul is dead, and Jed is in custody. This ordeal is over. We have nothing more to fear."

"Thanks to you and Michael." I kissed her back, looking deeply into her eyes.

"We have to trust that the FBI gets to all those contacts in time."

"They certainly have the resources and reach to do it. It's just a matter of how quickly."

We finished breakfast and put the dishes in the dishwasher. We had decided to take a walk with our dog, Rex. The doctor told me it would be good for me to get out and stretch my muscles and get used to moving around. I told him I was only too happy to oblige.

HE HAD WAITED all night for this, his opportunity to see that justice was done, once and for all. He set to work with purposeful and efficient movements, which was difficult because his wound was starting to bleed. It wouldn't take him long; and it would soon be over. But unlike any other time he'd done it, he wanted his victim in the house. He wanted Angus to die; if Angelica also died, that couldn't be helped; they called it collateral damage. He smiled at the thought. He hadn't wanted to kill Lois, but she just never left her house; and Mavis was just a necessary casualty because she had guessed too much about Lois, and had to be silenced.

He sensed the futility of it all, but was nonetheless resolute in the execution. That's a funny word, isn't it? Execution—getting it done, doing the deed. If he'd thought much about what he was doing, he might not do it. Shouldn't he spend his time trying to get away? After all, he'd had to kill the guard at the hospital to get here to take care of Angus, so what's one more murder. But again, wasn't his hatred for Angus that much greater than the need to escape? *When you're doing what I'm doing*, Jed thought, *your aim is to kill, not to escape*. That realization made him sick. If he'd confessed that to his brother, Paul, or to his mother, he would have felt tremendous guilt. As it was, he was just doing a job, finishing a task, completing a project. Everything else would have to wait.

So he set to work. He poured the gas in the front of the house, assuming they'd return from their walk at the back of the house. The glug, glug sound it made reminded him of his father pouring gas on burning brush that gave him a burn on his left arm. He'd chosen an odorless accelerant to hide it from the dog, and he affixed a fuse to the can he'd left under the house. He would wait until they got back, wait a while longer, and then his wait would be over.

This old house would go up in an instant, so there was no need to saturate the whole house. He got so excited about what was going to happen that in several places there was so much gas that pools had formed. He chuckled to himself when he realized this and tried to be more careful as he laid out what would be certain death for Angus and

Angelica. Just then, he heard the dogs barking, and Angus trying to quiet them. He knew he must leave soon.

He ran into the woods to hide in the darkness, and there he waited. They had come inside with the two dogs. That would make it much easier, and he thanked God for his good fortune. The dogs may bark, but that's what dogs always do.

Waiting was the hardest part. He had waited while his wife died of cancer, just four years after they had gotten married. He waited while his mother died in the flames he himself had set. The mix of emotions and thoughts churning through his brain were so confused and contradictory, he vowed no longer to think. He simply shut off his brain so he could do what he needed, what God had called him to do. He had given his life to God as a young boy, but his faith had been sorely tested when he had prayed fervently, and yet death seemed to win.

So when Paul told him about his research, and about the Salk quote, and what he was attempting to do, he could see that God might need some help starting over with a more obedient humanity. He saw himself as a modern-day Noah, carrying out God's orders to wipe the slate clean and begin again. He now saw that his calling was to be an acolyte for death. It was a calling he fervently embraced, and wholeheartedly pursued with all his energy.

It was getting late. A sliver of a moon rose behind the house as the family slept soundly. Jed knew that with these old houses, it wouldn't take long, so he had to start the fire and flee, but not too far because he knew he would want to watch.

He truly loved fire. Every time he lit one, his mind went back to the best memory of his childhood; his dad teaching him in Cub Scouts how to start a fire with one match. It was a triumph of planning: dig a little trench; lay small sticks across it with paper underneath; then the teepee of small sticks over that. In no time, you'd have a blazing fire for cooking breakfast or to warm yourself at night.

That seemed another lifetime ago. When his dad left him, he was lost. Jed remembered having given up all hope of a normal life, a meaningful life, a life with purpose and joy. In fact, he had increasingly serious run-ins with the law, having served several months here and there for various infractions, and none of it seemed to matter.

That is until he received a visitor from the Salvation Army. He was a tall red-head with an open face and straight teeth. Jed had not seen his like in his crooked world, which is why he immediately did not trust him.

His name was Hal. The air in the jail was heavy, smelling of sweat, wine and urine. As much as they tried, the smell of urine was especially clinging. Hal had tried several things to get Jed to talk and nothing worked. Then one day, he repeated the news he'd heard.

"Another house burned down last night," he said. Jed came to attention, and put his hands around the bars that kept him a prisoner.

Hal told him all he had remembered: that it happened in the middle of the night; that it had claimed a young mother and her son; that they got to it so that other row houses were spared, which was quite unusual for the nature of the fire.

"Was it arson, or was it natural?" asked Jed.

Hal looked at him, cocking his head to the side. "They don't know yet. They're still trying to figure out what happened."

"I'll bet it's arson then. If it's a natural fire, they're pretty quick to say so."

"You seem to know a lot about fire." Hal leaned his arms on the bars next to Jed. "What do you know about another fire?"

Jed sat back, the two moving as in a dance, his eyes wide. "There was another fire?"

"No, no, not another fire. This is the fire within."

"You mean heartburn?" Jed laughed.

Hal's head dropped. "No, not heartburn. This is the fire within. It's passion, not for a woman, but for life. When Jesus died, they called it 'the Passion,' meaning through his sacrifice, he gave those who believe life."

"Stop right there, Pal. I've been a churchgoer all my life, and look where it's gotten me."

"I'm not talking about going to church. I'm talking about giving your life to something bigger, more important than you are. Our founder, William Booth, always talked about a 'fire in the blood,' meaning that without passion, without a burning desire to do good for God, all life is lost."

Jed sank within the darkness of the cell. Hal saw him shut down, like a balloon with the air let out.

"I can see I've upset you...I'll come back later."

Jed leaned forward slightly. "No, Pal, don't bother, I think we're done here."

JED SAT THERE waiting. Jed became exhausted with the waiting, and the remembering. He brought to mind Hal's visits, his identifying with the Salvation Army, and his seeking to understand how he too could have "Fire in the Blood" was—not to put too fine a point on it—grueling.

What began as an exercise in sweet revenge was ending up as a chore. It wasn't supposed to be this way. He was supposed to feel exhilaration. That's what happened every other time he had started a fire and witnessed it destroying what had been in order to make room for something new and pure and meaningful. It was all this waiting. He had waited long enough. It was time for action!

A renewed sense of purpose surged through his veins. He chuckled to himself, *"Fire in the blood" at last. Hal would be proud of me.*

He got down on all fours, too afraid to stand because he possibly would be spotted, and crawled through the damp grass. His senses were at extreme alert. He'd imagined this is how a big cat felt when stalking his prey. He reached the house, keeping a constant watch for anyone who might spot him. The dogs barked once or twice but then went back to sleep. He located the fuse, lit it and ran from the house, unsure of what to do when he reached the tree line. He stopped and looked back.

CHAPTER 32: Smoke Cat

THE SMOKE SNAKED THROUGH the halls, lazily seeking the best place to lie. Angus and Angelica were asleep in their room with Michael and Jessica in the guest room, both upstairs. At this rate, it would take some time for the smoke to reach them.

The two dogs were downstairs sleeping soundly, but Adam, the cat, sensed that something was wrong. He was upstairs, lying on the headboard over Angus and Angelica's head. He lifted his gray head and sniffed the air. He sensed something different, something foreign, alien, and malicious in the air.

Adam rose, arched his back, and stretched his legs before sniffing again. There was only one thing he knew to do; he would jump on the chest of the guest who fed him. That would surely awaken the unsuspecting human.

When he jumped, I jumped. "Ouch," I screeched. "What are you doing? What? Why did you do that, Adam? That hurt!" I said, and stood up. Adam walked slowly out of the bedroom, looking back at me every few feet.

I decided my best move would be to follow him, though I didn't know why. When I got into the hall, I saw why. The smoke slowly slithered up the stairs like a snake heading for our bedroom.

As I turned to wake the house, I tripped over Adam, who had turned back as well. I started yelling as I made it to my feet. I rousted Angie, then Michael and Jessica. We got the dogs and cats and made it outside in the damp night air. We called 911 and then I called Hector. I told him what was happening, and he said he'd be there as soon as he could.

In the meantime, Angie started to cry angry tears. Then Michael said, "What are we standing here for? Let's see what we can do!"

I shook the shock out of my system and immediately agreed. We got the hose and started spraying into the flames and smoke. Michael even went inside with a wet sheet to see if he could stop the fire at its source.

Now the dogs decided to start barking. The fire grew in intensity, but the four of us worked as hard as humanly possible to stem the tide of this disaster. And all the while, I couldn't stop thinking about Jed. Even though he was wounded and under guard, he would find a way to get his revenge.

Michael came out of the house, coughing. "Come on, Dad, get another sheet. It seems to be working. I'm making headway."

It is providential that Angie's dryer wasn't working, and we had sheets drying on the clothesline. I grabbed one, wetted it, and joined my son.

About that time, I heard sirens of the fire trucks rounding the corner and heading toward the house.

I had joined Michael in what seemed like an increasingly hopeful enterprise. Then I heard someone else coming through the smoke. I had expected to see the fire chief, Ralph Crenshaw, but it was Jed instead.

"You weren't supposed to survive this fire," said Jed,

and he lifted a piece of smoldering lumber and swung at my head. He missed and stumbled under uncertain footing.

I flung my sheet at him and fell on him. He pushed me away and I went sprawling. I rolled over just as he was about to jump on me. I recognized that my opponent was stronger than I was, but I wasn't going to let that defeat me. Leverage; that was what was called for. We traded punches several times. It was amazing to me how well I took a punch.

I punched him again, and he lost his balance. I dove at him, and he fell down. I stood up to assess my next move. The wall behind us exploded with a crash, as fire fighters broke through the wall, seeking to subdue the flames. The debris, timbers, floor joists, and the huge battering ram broke through all at once. I was so surprised by the spectacle before me, I forgot about Jed.

When the smoke cleared, I began to think about what had become of him. I started digging, and implored those around me to help. We dug for several minutes, and finally we found him. Jed lay there, lifeless and lost. Jed was killed by his own treachery.

They took me to the EMT truck and administered oxygen to me. I heard ringing in my ears, like I was in a well and couldn't get out. I saw Michael and the EMT talking, but couldn't hear anything. I was exhausted. I couldn't stand it anymore; I could barely lift my head. Finally I saw Angie and stood with a weak smile. We embraced and she held me up, and then placed me back down on the EMT truck's tailgate.

"I can't hear anything!" I finally shouted.

The EMT smiled and said what appeared to be reassuring words. He talked to Angie, who looked back at me with concern.

"I'm not going back to the hospital," I shouted. "I've spent entirely too much time there already. I'm not going back."

The next thing I knew, I'm being taken by ambulance back to the hospital where they ran a battery of tests, and then Angie would write for me what the doctors said. I would be fine in a few days, the note said, which I could have told them if they would only listen to me.

The next few days were difficult, but a week after all that, my hearing did come back. I had been sleeping better than I had in weeks, and could rest easy.

Of course, we had to stay at Hector's house until we could find a place of our own, while our house was getting repaired. Thankfully, the damage was fixable. Hector and Silvia took great care of us.

Not being able to go home was difficult and painful, but it was a small price to pay for leaving all this behind us.

We found a place, not in Austin, but up the street from where we live. We felt it was an easier transition than trying to adjust to the pace of big city life. It was a small, white frame house with a red roof and a sycamore tree in the back. The tree reminded me of the story of Zachaeus in Luke's gospel—the small man who climbed the tree to see Jesus, and Jesus showed him hospitality in the man's own home.

We had a house warming party, inviting Hector and his family, and a few other friends. We had burgers and beer on the back porch. After many of the guests had left, I was able to sit down with Hector and Angie.

"I've heard from the FBI," said Hector. Angie frowned. I saw it and I put my hand on hers.

"I really need to hear this, Sweetie," I said to Angie.

"Oh, I know, but we had such a nice party. Why spoil it with talk of the end of the world?"

"Because there's good news!" Hector almost shouted. "The end of the end is near!"

They all looked at him with puzzled faces.

"I've been waiting to say that all day."

"What on earth do you mean?" I asked.

"We took what Angie and Silvia found on Paul's computer, and we gave it to the FBI. They're going down the list, and shutting them down one by one. Some of the fires and the sterile bugs have been released. But they've shut down about 60 percent of the operation. So while we'll lose a significant portion of the insect population, the FBI's entomologist says the insect population will be back to normal within the year."

"That is good news."

THAT WEEKEND, THE Catholic Church held a mass for Father Paul and Deacon Jed. It was proof that no matter how evil the intent, we all shared a common humanity. The local Bishop with whom I was good friends presided, and he did an admirable job, using the text from the Prodigal Father.

The Father cared for both of his sons, and wanted the best for both. The Prodigal Son came to himself, and the elder brother was only angry. The Father loved them both equally. And as hard as it is sometimes, that's our job as well. All in all, very well handled.

After that I received an invitation to worship at Shoestring. They knew that I wasn't strong enough to lead worship, but they had hoped I would be in attendance at their Christmas Eve Service. I was of course honored and accepted the invitation. Hector and Silvia had decided to go with us, which made it very special

The Christmas Eve service is one of my favorites. Its mystery and grace are unmatched during the year. The mystery of God with us and the grace of a joy made complete make the season so meaningful.

The reason for the invitation was made clear before the service started when the clerk of session, Tom Branch, got up and called me forward.

"We wanted to say thank you," he said smiling, "for all you did for us in the past, and especially how steady you were through this recent unpleasantness. As a sign of our affection, we want to provide you with the funds to fix your house, not covered by insurance." And they pulled out from behind the pulpit a large check with the amount blank.

"I'm shocked and stunned," I said.

"Look at him—a preacher at a loss for words," said Tom. The assembled crowd roared with laughter and good cheer.

"I'm honored and humbled by this gift, and I'll let you know how much it is."

Everyone laughed again.

AFTER THE SERVICE, we went back to Hector and Silvia's. Their family tradition was to open one gift on Christmas Eve, and they included us in their tradition.

We gave Jorge, their young son, a new fishing pole, because that was his passion. We found a nice little story book for Maria, his sister.

Hector, smiling, presented me with a letter. I looked at him and at the letter and opened it. It read, "Please accept our invitation to stay with us whenever you need to come to Shoestring."

We both hugged each of them. We filled our champagne glasses and toasted our growing friendship.

As it happens, I had a present for Hector. It too was in an envelope, which he opened shyly. The letter read, "The recipient of this certificate is entitled to five lessons with the golf pro at the Shoestring Country Club." We all laughed.

"I just thought, since you loved fishing so much, and I joined you in that," I said smiling, "that you wouldn't mind giving golf a try. Just something to expand your horizons!"

"Well...I....I don't know what to say. Yeah, yeah, I'll give it a try." Hector's face was twisted into an unrecognizable expression.

"No pressure, Mate. I just thought...." I patted him on the shoulder.

THAT NIGHT I couldn't sleep. I went downstairs, got a glass of milk, and sat at the kitchen table to drink it. Halfway through the glass, I heard the sound of footsteps on the stairs. It was Hector.

"I can't sleep," I said. "Want a glass of milk?"

"Sure!" said Hector. "I've been thinking about Father Paul and Jed...And....truth be told...I dread learning to play golf!"

We both laughed.

"I could exchange it for a dinner at the country club. I've heard they have a new chef from New Orleans. He's pretty good."

"No, no!" Hector put up his hand. "I'm intrigued. I'm always telling my boy to try new things. I suppose I should be open to that as well."

"Good." We sat together for some time, no words passing between us. "What were you thinking about Father Paul and Jed?"

"I heard from the FBI. They're shutting down some of the people on that printout..." Hector looked like his favorite puppy had just died.

"That's not what's keeping you from sleep." I placed a hand on his shoulder.

"We got Father Paul and Jed. We got to the people on the list."

"And..."

"And we're still too late. What if the ones we miss went on with their plans and extinction carries on from there?"

"Yeah, I've thought of that too. And here's the thing. We did what we could. We did *all* that we could. It would have been great to have gotten to it sooner, but we didn't. At some point we have to accept it. And here's where faith comes in—relying on God to do the rest. I'm fairly confident that we've done enough to make sure this awful experiment never gets off the ground."

If that's true then there's nothing more to say, or to do. We should be able to relax and enjoy the relief of being able to tie up what lose ends we can. But I still felt uneasy, like there was another shoe about to drop. When you've been attacked and beaten as many times as I have in the past weeks, I guess you get a little restless. Is this what they call PTSD?

"But that's not what's got you up in the middle of the night, drinking milk with your fishing buddy," I said, finally.

Hector's face brightened, his smile as genuine and warm as it was the last time his son caught a small-mouth bass.

"It's the faith thing. I had a real connection with Father Paul. He helped me through all that murder business in Shoestring the last time around, and he helped me get back on speaking terms with God. So, now what? I know all that wasn't a lie, but what do I do with that stuff now?"

"I think you can go back to bed now," I said, standing and extending my hand.

"What do you mean? I need your help. You're just going to leave me here?"

"Questions about faith are ultimately about trust. You trust your wife and son to be there with you because you love and care for them. Questions about where God is in your life and the disappointment about the demise of a trusted adviser are all stages on the journey. Soon, your Bishop will assign a new priest, and you may have to start all over again, but you'll be okay.

"And the thing about Paul—he's not God. He's human. That's how he can be so much help to you one minute, and go off the deep end the next. But then, I think you already knew that."

What kept me up this night was thinking about having to face an angry treasurer next week, but somehow I didn't think I needed to share that with Hector at this moment. Besides, I remembered thinking about him during this ordeal as a pleasant alternative to what I was facing now, and I knew that my journey would not be complete until I had made some kind of connection with him.

Hector stood up and we hugged. I followed him up the stairs When I came to bed, Angelica was still awake. I started to get into bed, and then changed my mind. I went to the closet and pulled out a beautifully wrapped present.

"What's this?" she said. As I handed her the package, a look of surprise and wonder lit up her face.

"I figured tomorrow would be crazy, what with our strange surroundings and all the people, so I thought I'd give you your present now." She paused, still stunned by the gesture. "Go ahead, open it."

When she did open it, the look of surprise turned to puzzlement. It was a pair of yellow and blue sneakers.

"I suppose I should shower you with jewels, but in light of recent events, I thought this was more appropriate. Every time you wear them, I want you to remember what you did for me, never giving up on finding me, how dangerous it all was, and how much I love you for it."

She hugged me fiercely. Then she sprang out of bed and went to her dresser, pulled open a drawer, and pulled out a small box. "And here's your Christmas present," she said, as she handed the box to me.

I opened it slowly, like a strip tease. Angelica said, "Oh, open it already," which I promptly did.

It was a wristwatch.

"What?" is all I said.

"Well, as you can see, it's a wristwatch, but so much more. It has a GPS chip in it, so you'll never get lost. But more importantly, I bought myself one, so that I'll know where you are, and won't ever lose you again, like I thought I had."

We hugged, and so much more that night. And as I drifted off to sleep, I thought how lucky I was to be where I am right now. And also, I know it sounds strange after all we've been through these past months, but I can't help feeling, this was the best Christmas we've had in a long time.

About the Author

Born in the Chicago suburbs, Mark W. Stoub, like his protagonist, Angus McPherson, has been a Texas transplant for several years. He received his B.A. from Maryville College in Tennessee, an M.Div. from Louisville Seminary and his D.Min. from McCormick Seminary in Chicago. A Presbyterian minister for over 40 years, he has retired to Kyle, TX, gateway to the Texas hill country, where he lives with his wife, Jane, and their dog, Goldie, and cat, Calvin.

81706062R00176

Made in the USA
Columbia, SC
07 December 2017